ANNIE

Luanne Armstrong

ANNIE

LUANNE ARMSTRONG

POLESTAR
BOOK PUBLISHERS

Published by:
Polestar Press Ltd.
1011 Commercial Drive, Second Floor
Vancouver, BC
Canada V5L 3X1

The publisher would like to thank the Canada Council, the
British Columbia Ministry of Small Business, Tourism and
Culture, and the Department of Canadian Heritage for their
ongoing financial assistance.

Cover art and design, and interior artwork by Jim Brennan.
Author photograph by Joanna Wilson.
Printed in Canada by Best Book Manufacturers.

Canadian Cataloguing in Publication Data

Armstrong, Luanne, 1949-
  Annie
ISBN 1-896095-00-3
  I. Title.
PS8551.R7638A73 1995   C813'.54   C95-910191-8
PR9199.3.A75A73 1995

This book is for my mother and father.
One bought me the outfit, one got me a horse.
What more could any wild cowgirl want?

ONE

A WORLD WITHOUT BORDERS, only wind, grass, hills and silence.

Her horse is small, a buckskin, almost pony size, with a thick rough mane and tail; her saddle is old—falling apart. She mended the stirrup this morning during a brief, hurried stop, tearing a piece of leather from the fringe on her divided skirt, tying the stirrup iron back on. It's not going to hold long. She wears a man's shirt, an old oiled canvas coat, a wide-brimmed hat with a thong tied under her chin, and heavy black boots. Her name is Annie; she left her whole name somewhere behind her, along with the rest of her life.

The old, black dog patiently stalks at the heels of the

horse, head down and tongue hanging, panting in the late summer heat. He watches both her and the horizon with steady yellow eyes, pointed ears shifting. The horse is also patiently calm. The three of them have been with each other all their lives. She got the horse as a colt; her father gave it to her when she was six. The dog was one of many puppies that came and went on the farm. He picked her to follow, or she picked him as a follower. It didn't matter then. It doesn't matter now, when she is sixteen, and they are all that is left of her old life.

She doesn't know where she is. By now, the settlement must be forty miles behind her. She has been riding all day since before dawn; the horse is dark with sweat and his head bobs with effort. They have come into a hollow beside a stream, and her legs shake when she slides off the horse. For a minute, they are all still. The dog collapses into the shallow water, tongue lapping. The horse lowers his head to sniff the grass and begins to graze.

She's done it. All day her heart has whispered that what she's doing is right. All day she's ridden the sharp edge of fear, every step breaking another boundary, snapping the bonds of what had been known and familiar. All day, scenes from the past week flashed and snapped behind her eyes.

"A girl your age should marry. It's the only way you'll be safe. With no husband to look out for you, you're fair game, girl." She didn't know what they meant. She found out one night when she went to the low log barn where she was keeping Duster. Black Dog, as always, was at her heels.

The barn was sagging and dark. She pulled down last year's dusty hay from the loft and put it in Duster's box. He nosed at it, and then at her, plainly wanting better food. She scratched his ears and neck. His body was solid and warm.

As she stepped out of the stall, a voice spoke from the doorway. "Hey girl, what are you doing in there?" She looked up. It was one of the men from the settlement; his face was familiar but she had never spoken to him.

"Looking after my horse," she said, and tried to slip past him. He planted himself in front of her.

"Aw, come on," he said. "How about coming for a little walk with me? Just to talk. Thought it might cheer you up a bit. Things being a bit rough on you and all."

"No, thank you," she said. "I have to get back. They'll be worried about me." He grabbed her arm and, terrified, she wrenched and twisted like a hooked fish, until she scrabbled free. He let her go and stood, watching her, as she walked across the yard. Over the next few days she began to feel them everywhere, men's eyes, watching. She received several more invitations to go walking, riding, fishing. She turned them all down. Men started showing up in the house where she was staying. Trying to be polite, she made excuses about working or looking after her brothers. The men didn't seem to notice. They would sit in the house where she was staying until late, talking, or just sitting silent in the corners. One night when she was walking to the barn she realized there were clumps of men, gathered in corners, beside the houses, outside the barn, watching. Watching her. Once she made it to the barn it took all her resolve to steel herself, make her face shut, and walk back across the yard, holding her body stiff.

The family she and her brothers were staying with, the Gravelys, calmly discussed their futures as though they had no part and no say in it—where they might stay and what they might do. She'd have to earn her keep, they said, as a housekeeper or cook, or maybe by doing laundry. Everybody out here had to work; no one could afford to live, or be kept, without working. But then, it would only be a matter of time before she'd be getting married. After all, there were so many likely candidates around. And the boys would have to work as well. They could go to farm families who'd take them in and give them room and board for their work.

The boys and Annie snuck terrified looks at one another. Nothing in the world made sense now that their parents weren't there. But the two boys, Ben and George, looked at Annie as if she, at least, were some kind of safety in a new and terrible world.

Ben was nine and George was eleven. Ben cried himself to sleep every night while Annie patted his back and made soothing noises, trying not to cry herself. George turned away, pulled the blankets over his head, curled himself into a dark huddled ball of misery and slept.

Annie had been thinking that perhaps she and her brothers could go back to her grandparents, from where they

ANNIE

had hopefully and eagerly started. But it turned out there were no wagons or people travelling in that direction. When she suggested they could go by themselves, the people around her laughed. She'd just have to wait awhile, they said. In the meantime, there were the dishes and the pile of laundry out back to help pay for her keep.

Even she could see that they meant it all more or less kindly. They were just plain folk, trying to survive. But she sat among them on the edge of her chair, in the dress they had made her wear, and tried to find a way to say what she needed to say. "But I can ride and hunt," she said. "I was a scout…in the wagon train coming here." The whole family turned and looked at her and then went back to their discussion as if she hadn't spoken. She sat in the corner as the conversation meandered onwards. Neighbours arrived for coffee, and the talk turned to weather and crops, wood and hay, horses and cows. Finally one of the neighbours said casually, "That there girl get settled?" and Mr. Gravely assented. "Yep, figger we'll send her on over to that family that was wanting housekeeping and then she says she figgers on gettin' married." There was a solemn silence, an acknowledgement that this was a difficult, sad time, but then coughing, a soft joke or two, and general agreement that it was good to get it settled. The conversation continued as before.

Mr. Gravely caught her eye and frowned, nodding towards the stairs. Upstairs, Annie lay in the narrow wooden bed, her brothers on pallets on the floor beside her. They were all that was left of her family, her home. She was all that was left to them.

But how could she manage? Even with her working as a housekeeper, the boys would still have to be boarded out somewhere. She would hardly see them. Both of her parents had been dead for less than two weeks. She couldn't believe how quickly everything had changed. A place and a whole life that had been hers lay in shattered pieces. She wanted to be anywhere else but here. There was no air in this place. She lay suffocating, sweating and furious in the low hot attic, trying to think.

Why had they come here? Her father had dragged them away from the old farm, her grandparents' farm. "Land," he'd said. "We'll have land, all our own and as much as we want. Land to settle and build a home on. Land to never move away from again." He had dreamed it all for them— the meadows with horses and cattle, the new house, the new barn, the mountains behind, a creek running through. This would be their home.

And now he was dead and they would never have the home he had wanted for them. Unless she found it.

And why not? It was true, what she had said. She *could* ride and shoot. She could maybe find another wagon train or join with some other people looking for land. She'd know their land when she saw it, the same as her father would have. It would be their salvation, they'd be a family again, some kind of family, anyway, even if it was just the three of them.

The instant she decided to leave, she felt better. She contemplated this new idea. There was nothing to hold her here; the boys would be taken care of, boarded out somewhere to work for their keep. She could come back for them as soon she got settled somewhere. They would understand once they saw the land. They'd know what it was for, what the dream was about. It was a rotten thing to do, leave them alone when they had already lost so much, but they'd understand and forgive her when she came back, when she had something to offer them that was more than an occasional visit away from working.

She figured no one else would miss her. She was just one more problem for them. She had what she needed: she'd managed to hang on to Duster and her rifle, her clothes, her skirt and heavy oilcloth coat, and even her saddlebags. She could do it. Even if no one else like her ever had. Even if girls weren't supposed to. Supposed to! Do what? Starve. Marry someone just so she could eat? She'd make her own life and find a place of her own. That was what she wanted, a place where she belonged—a place that welcomed her in, where she fitted, not this stifling existence on the bare edge of people's politeness.

And even more, she knew, she wanted to be away from a place where her mother and father had been and were no longer. She had to be somewhere where she no longer saw her father's broad shoulders disappearing around every corner, no longer thought she heard her mother's voice, her mother's laugh, joining in with the rest of the women.

She lay, dozing and catching herself, until the neighbours had left, the family had all gone to bed and the house was still. She dressed in the dark, trying not to move. Her clothing crackled in the dead middle of the night silence. She crept downstairs and pushed the creaky slab door open. Once outside, she headed for the barn where Duster and Black Dog were subsisting on an equally meager diet of charity and occasional meals. Duster nickered and nudged her shoulder. She got his saddle and bridle on and tied him to the outside barn rail. Then she crept guiltily back to the house. The heavy door scraped on the ground; dishes clanked together as she rummaged in the kitchen for a frying pan and some food. She heard a snort as someone turned over in bed. Better to cope without food. She had her rifle and a knife. She'd manage somehow.

TWO

DUSTER'S HOOVES WERE ALMOST SILENT on the white dust-coated road. No one heard or saw them go.

And now, at last, she is alone, away from watching eyes, from people planning her life, from her brothers' stricken eyes. No one will listen to them cry themselves to sleep tonight. A slick thin knife twists in her gut. She wonders if they'll be able to understand what she's doing out here alone, and why she didn't bring them with her.

The sun is low on the horizon, red and swollen in the heat haze, smoking the western sky into an orange blaze. She pulls the rifle from its boot under the stirrup leather. Like the horse and dog, it has been with her most of her life, since she was strong enough to hold it and her father taught her to shoot. The weight of the gun is reassuring. She tucks it under her arm and turns slowly, making a circle. Nothing moves on the bronzed yellow and amber hills which roll away from her in every direction. She doesn't want to move, get wood, make a fire, make camp, or put the gun down.

She notes sandy ground underfoot and a thin dark trickle of water, almost hidden beneath grass-clumped banks. The grass here grows in bunches, intermingled with flowers, tangled willows, alders and cottonwoods. The wind lifts tendrils of damp hair off her forehead. Blue-fingered shadows under the trees shift and dance.

"Evening down-draft," her father had told her. "Wind always shifts at evening." But she doesn't want to think about her father.

On the way out west in the wagon train, she rode and hunted with the scouts. At first they ignored her when she followed them around. When they saw her ride and shoot, they still ignored her, but this ignoring had a different quality. It was the way they ignored each other, the weather, the settlers, concentrating on the task in front of them. They spoke little enough, even to each other. One morning, Nathan, the lead scout, simply included her in the day's orders. She watched what they did and made herself useful. She hated killing things; what she loved best was tracking and riding, always out ahead, into new country.

This morning, which now seems days ago, as soon as it

grew light, she tried to look for familiar landmarks. By then she was several miles from the settlement. She thought vaguely that perhaps she would need to know this country. Perhaps she might have to go back. But the earth rolled by under her, like riding on a giant ball, one hill ascending into another. She checked carefully from the top of each hill, looking for pursuit, not really expecting any, but wary.

Black Dog lapped circles around her, sniffing out the new scents and then returning to the horse's heels. Duster tended to veer steadily to the right; if she left him to it, he would go in a circle and head back the way they had come.

But now it's evening and she is here, wherever that is, and she knows it's important to keep a cool head. That's what her father would have said…used to say. "No use getting upset," he'd say. "No use crying over spilt milk. You see, you do," he would grunt at her when she asked questions.

Fear is creeping in like fog, making it difficult to move. Black trees, the creek, the wind—they want nothing to do with her. She feels like an intruder, a stranger to everything, even herself. She has to change it somehow, make it welcoming, a place to stay at least for a night.

She moves finally, uncramps her stiff frozen muscles, each movement an effort against fear. She decides where to build the fire and then lights it, then unsaddles and tethers Duster. Fear, guilt and a sense that she has come too far— crossed some kind of forbidden barrier—comes and goes in her belly. She has camped, ridden, hunted, scouted, played at being wild Indians with her brothers. But she realizes she has never stayed out all night alone before. It was easy enough to imagine. The reality of what she's done looms over her, asking nasty questions with no answers.

The dog lies down beside the fire, watching her, and she stops to pat his head. The fear grows. It blots out why she is here, what she has come for, her excitement and sense of destiny. It tells her, instead, she is a fool. Forty miles from the nearest settlement, heading into unknown country with a horse and a dog and a rifle, is no place for anyone, let alone a sixteen-year-old girl, however good a shot she thinks she is.

She hasn't brought much with her either, only a blanket, the gun, a few matches, a frying pan, a bit of food, dried beans, flour but no shortening. Useless food. She's left the eyes, the noise and the dark, smelly closed-in world of the settlement, and she's left the memory of her mother and her father, and her brothers' crying for them. Maybe what she is running towards—the dream of land, home—is just a convenient excuse, not as important as the running it-self, the need to get away and breathe free air. The guilt knife twists in her gut again.

The only familiar things here are the horse and dog, as patient as the land and the trees. The dry sandy ground she has ridden over all day holds sharp lumpy cactus, clumped canary grass, junipers, silver poplars; all day, grouse scuttled away from her, under the sage, clucking; ground squirrels and marmots whistled at her from the rocks. She envied them. Everything else belongs here and is familiar with it, except her. She is the intruder, someone on her way to somewhere else.

But not at the moment.

"Oh, bloody hell," she thinks, still patting the dog. "C'mon, Annie, get moving." Her mother used to nag her about swearing, but she did it anyway. She has to feed them all. That comes first. She can figure the rest out later. There might be fish in the creek; she's kept a line and hook in her saddlebag along with her knife, flint and steel. She catches some grasshoppers and uses them to catch three trout. She tries to cook and eat two but with no salt or grease to fry them in, they burn into a stinking mess. They grit in her mouth like a handful of dry sand. She gives them to Black Dog who chokes them down.

By now, except for a red glow along the horizon, it's dark. She puts the sweaty saddle pad on the ground, and lays the blanket and coat over it to fashion a bed. The ground is cold and lumpy; she makes herself lie down, then she sits up again. She can't decide whether to let the fire die in case someone—Indians, outlaws, men from the settlement—might see it. Or should she build it up again to shut out the night sounds and the possibility of wild animals? She realizes she has forgotten to bring in enough wood to last the night.

She shucks off her coat, then stands and steps from the soft ring of firelight into the darkness. The creek clucks and chuckles at her feet. Dead dry willow cracks in her hand; the noise snaps the velvet silence. She retreats back to the fire. The dog and the horse are unmoved, unmovable. Duster tears grass and chomps steadily; Black Dog watches her, the edge of light, and the darkness beyond.

She lies down again. It's getting cold. Her breath puffs into the air above her. She figures they have been climbing all day through the low rounded hills. They must be up high for it to be so cold. What had the scouts talked about before they all got to the settlement? What had they said about this country and the people who live here already, Indian people, about which very little seems to be known? Maybe she'll see them—Indians, wild people. She hopes maybe, she hopes not.

Lying down makes the fear worse. Preoccupied, she stares away from the fire into the dark. She's in a fix, no doubt about that. She'll need food. True, she has the rifle and a good supply of shells, but she's never actually butchered anything. With the wagon train, she mostly rode out front and the other scouts hunted.

Once she shot a deer, a young doe. It was a lucky shot. She saw the deer and brought her rifle up quickly, shot without thinking. The second the deer jumped and fell, she was horrified. She desperately wanted to call the bullet back, say that she was sorry, she hadn't meant it, but by then the other scouts, hearing the shot, had come up. She had to pretend nonchalance, offhand pride. She hated watching while the men, quick and efficient, bled and skinned the carcass; she hadn't had to actually touch it.

There are more deer. There's bound to be lots of game. This is unsettled country, empty except for her, the animals and these strange unknown people. There are rabbits and fish, but she remembers Nathan saying that someone would starve to death on rabbits and fish. "No fat in them," he said. "Gotta have fat. Good deer fat. Off the liver. That's the best stuff right there," he'd said, showing her, peeling the dark shiny liver out of its thin skin sheath, beaded with lumps of white fat.

Here there's no Nathan, no scouts, no family, no neighbours, no ready-to-eat food, no help.

She always had her father and mother to worry about things. Her father, grim and gloomy as he was most of the time, still made sure that she could ride and shoot. On the small farm where she'd grown up, there was no question about working or doing her share.

"Work or starve," her Dad snarled at her one day, as she whined at some task. Duster and Black Dog were her escapes; her father didn't seem to mind the hours she spent riding around the countryside. Her mother fussed, but was too busy with babies and chores to even notice much of what she was doing. Her father would send her in to help her mother, and her mother would send her back out to help her father. With both of them thinking she was somewhere else, she would slip onto Duster's back with a halter and a lead rope and disappear.

Only her grandmother openly disapproved, said girls shouldn't be allowed to behave that way. It would never happen in the old country, she said. Girls were taught manners there. Her mother's parents lived with them; it was their farm. She knew her father hated working with her grandfather, hated deferring to the old man's ideas. At night, unable to sleep, knotted and tense, she listened to her mother and father in the next room, arguing. Sometimes, something her father had thrown would shatter against the wall.

Now they have disappeared. It happened bewilderingly fast. Her mother died in childbirth, and a few days later, the Gravelys told her that her father had been shot in a hunting accident. It was all very mysterious and no one explained anything. No one explained how her father, who was so smart about guns and hunting, and had taught Annie everything she knew, could be killed in a hunting accident. Annie asked a couple of questions and then stopped when it was obvious no one wanted to talk about it. She stored the mystery of her father's death away in a hidden corner of her mind. It made her too sick to even think about. She'd think about it later when she had less to deal with, when something was settled in their lives.

No one in the settlement even seemed very interested in them. She and her brothers were suddenly left to the assistance of strangers, most of whom had only been neighbours for a couple of weeks. It was these people who had so casually decided that her brothers would have to work for their keep and that she, Annie, was easily disposed of because of the plethora of single, hungry men.

She shakes her head. She's sick of remembering. It's worn a hole in her brain. It's worn a hole in the space just under her heart that aches and whines and won't be still, that wants them back, wants them all back.

Now she's worn out but too hungry and cold to sleep. The fish was pretty disgusting. She'll have to find more food. Somehow, she'll have to find everything she needs by herself.

She has stepped off the edge of the known world. Now she has to create a new one. She has left behind anything that gave her substance. She feels invisible. She feels like she is dissolving, bit by bit, leaking out like water into this empty land until she is as light and immaterial as dust. She has to stop it, patch up the holes, fill up the emptiness again.

Out of what she learns, out of what this land will tell her, out of what she sees and knows, out of the steps she travels each day, out of the story she makes for herself day by day, she will write herself into the story of her own life.

THREE

SHE WAKES THE NEXT MORNING hollow with hunger and loneliness. Back at the settlement, they'll be frying eggs, bacon and potatoes, drinking coffee out of tin mugs with fresh cream from the settlement cow. They'll probably be discussing her absence and what to do about it. She could still go back. Probably she should. Then again, they might assume she has run off with some man; they might ignore her absence altogether; or they might think it their duty to come after her. Hard to tell. She thinks of riding back into the settlement, embarrassed, trying to think of some reason for her craziness that they might understand.

But here she is, alive. The sun is warming the ground where she shivered most of the night. She sits up and looks around. She is actually camped on a small flat set between grassy hills, the flat humped and dotted with grass and pools from the creek which twists and winds its way past her camp. Duster is lying down, Black Dog lies curled warm beside her.

She knows so little of this country. She might be in some far-off foreign place; even when she rode ahead of the wagon train, she was looking past the land itself, a traveller passing by. She had looked at the landscape rolling by like she might watch a parade, secure inside the claims of family and friends. Civilized. That's what the women talked about, getting somewhere civilized. They looked back wistfully at the place they'd left, and talked about how they would have to civilize whatever place they were going to. Schools, they said. A church. Laws.

The wagon train never stayed anywhere longer than overnight until they got to the settlement. The only place real to her was the wagon, with her mother and father, her brothers fighting, the familiar scent of food and blankets and things from back home. The land was something to pass through, to pass over, to look at briefly and move on.

But now, she thinks, her life will depend on knowing about the place she's in, really knowing it, as a place to live, a place to depend on. She doesn't even know the names of things, she thinks with disgust. She doesn't know what they're good for, or if they're good for anything. She is disgusted and afraid of being so ignorant. It's a shock. Back on the farm, she thought of herself as utterly tough and capable. She knew what her father had taught her and what she'd figured out on her own. She knew about farming, about hay, fruit trees, gardens, animals, what to feed them and when. She knew about planting and working and the pain in her back from weeding. She knew her father stomping towards her and his thunderous complaints when something went wrong. She knew the names of things back home, what to eat and what was safe and what time of year the berries and mushrooms were ready and where to find mint and clover and sage for tea.

She listened closely while her mother and grandmother talked about plants and herbs and healing. When the neighbouring men came over, she sat quietly in the corner and listened to them tell stories about their younger days, about hunting and camping-out and trapping and Indians. She soaked it in like plant roots taking up moisture.

When she was outside, she learned from everything: the ways the creek ran in different seasons, the time in spring when the frogs came out of the mud, the bitter taste of the small green buds of skunk cabbage, the places where berries ripened early, the alarm call of chickens frightened by a hawk, the flattened round beds in the grass where deer slept, the places in the woods which felt safe and comfortable, the places which were dark and forbidden.

It was everything to her, a whole universe, her home. Then, before she could even get used to the idea that it might not be permanent, it was gone. She hadn't known what it was going to feel like until after they left. The sense of loss was so acute she was sick and feverish. Her mother made her drink sage tea. The fever went away, but whenever she remembered the farm, it was with a clutch of nauseating sadness in her belly.

Her mother had made her the divided skirt for the trip, and a leather braided quirt to go with it; she'd lost the quirt somewhere and still felt bad about it.

When they left, the boys sat in the back of the wagon, watching. She turned around on Duster, and they all waved and their grandparents waved back, watching them out of sight from the front stoop. Her youngest brother cried until his father shamed him into silence. The fat draft horses plodded on, pulling the wagon up and then over a hill, and they were all lost to each other's sight.

Somewhere out there to the west was new land, land her father had dreamed and talked about endlessly. "A new place," he said. "Our dream," he called it, or sometimes, "the frontier." It was like a mad fever in him. He described it, what it would look like, what they would do there, the new life they would make, the crops they'd grow. She had asked him what frontier meant; he only laughed and said they'd probably find out when they got there. He told them they would all have a lot to learn, and as fast as they could, and then he laughed and said, "You'd better teach that there nag of yours to chase cows," and she laughed too. It was as close as he ever came to saying she and Duster might mean something more to him than a nuisance.

Now she is lost in her own dream—another new beginning, hopes and dreams flapping around her like flags in a high wind, fear eating at her, an endless distance to cover to wherever it is she might be going.

She saddles Duster, gathers her few things together, packs them neatly, mounts and rides on up the next hill. It feels better to be moving, and the hills make endless possibilities of seeing and discovery. Her backside is sore from riding so far yesterday. She has never ridden that far and hard in one day. She worries about Duster. But she's a light load and he's used to travelling. She stops at the top of the first hill to look around. Hunger drums inside of her—for food, for her old familiar surroundings, hunger to discover something new. She feels stupid and confused, like a small child who has wandered into adult territory and doesn't know what to do.

"Have to get a deer," she says out loud, too loud, to Black Dog. "I'll have to shoot a damn deer." But no deer presents itself, only rank upon rank of green hills, fading into blue haze. The sun is already hot on her shoulders. She isn't sure of the date, but she knows it's late summer. It was spring when they left the farm, but the trouble with her mother's pregnancy interrupted the trip. They were supposed to be settled in on the new homestead by now, getting ready for winter. "West," she thinks. "Just head west." That's what her Dad said. "Head west and there it is, land free for the taking."

"So, maybe we're lost," she says to the dog. Not quite lost. They could still turn around and go back. But she isn't ready, doesn't want to do that and she's not sure she could find her way back anyway. This land is so immense. It rolls away from her, full of secrets among the blue folded hills. Anything, anyone, could be concealed in the thickets of brush, could be over the next hill.

"I don't care," she says out loud to Black Dog. "I don't give a damn if we're lost." She looks again at the land before her. No borders, no fences, no people, no rules, no restrictions, just blue haze and free singing birds. And no deer anywhere.

"Free," she says out loud. "I did it. I'm free and I ain't going back. I don't care if I die here," which sounds foolish, she thinks; she does care. Dying is not part of her plan and seems a pretty remote possibility anyway, on this hot, bird-singing morning, even if she is hungry and scared.

She gets the rifle out, loads it and rides on, resting the rifle over the front of the saddle.

By mid-morning, they haven't seen anything except grouse and rabbits and by now she is really hungry and more than anything, she wants a cup of coffee with cream in it. She can almost smell the scent of coffee boiling. On the farm they had a milk cow which they brought with them. Now the cow is living at the settlement, providing the Graveleys and the others with milk and cream. She has a bit of loose tea in her bags, but no coffee. She regrets bitterly now the haste with which she left the settlement. She should have planned better. But even if she had waited to get food, she would have had to steal it, and that wasn't right. The wagon, the team, the cow, and their household goods had all been sold and the money had been set aside for them. That's what they told her, anyway. Food! Maybe she should have just taken it. They had lots. She's been crazy to do this, foolish, young and stupid, to head into the wilderness with just a gun and no food or supplies. What was the matter with her?

"You panicked," she thinks. "You ran like a rabbit, and you didn't plan and you didn't think. That won't get you far out here; you've got to plan…you acted like a kid, an idiot kid." But it doesn't help to call herself names, either.

By the end of the day, she has given up on shooting a deer or an antelope. When a grouse bobbles piteously into the brush in front of them, pretending to drag a wing, she sends Black Dog after it, but it merely flies far enough away to frustrate them both. It seems ridiculous to use a rifle shell on a grouse. What else? Surely there were other ways of hunting. Snares, maybe. But she'd have to stop and wait until something managed to get itself caught.

She rides on. Duster plods with his head down. Occasionally she pushes him into a trot but that's her own nervousness and she pulls him back down to a walk. The country seems drier, the hills less rolling, flattening out. By dusk, they haven't found a place she wants to camp; there is no stream in sight. Black Dog is panting with heat and dryness. She hasn't bothered to carry water, because she had no container. She will have to find water. There isn't much point in stopping without it, except to rest.

By dark there is nothing but the endless dry hills. She can't see to look for trees or other indications of water. They stop and she makes a fire, tethers the horse, makes her bed and lies down, watching the stars, shivering and worrying. Tomorrow they will find water, shoot a deer, make a plan. Tomorrow.

FOUR

THE DAWN SUN BLOSSOMS into a huge orange rose, and she rises immediately, muscles still aching from the cold and unyielding ground. There's nothing to wait for. She saddles quickly and they leave. Carefully, she watches the hills for signs of deeper green, for a clump of poplars or other signs of water. She does it. She finds a ravine, follows it and comes to water, sweet flowing water. They all drink and drink. Black Dog plunges in, panting, lies down and looks up at her. She flips water at him, laughing as he ducks and scrambles up the bank. She decides to follow the stream down, since it flows west and might possibly lead to a river. There will be game along a river, fish, fresh water, good grass.

She is riding easily, daydreaming about food, about the future, wondering how the boys are doing, if they miss her, what the land will be like that she finds, that she wants to find. What will she do then? Maybe raise cows, have a big ranch, a lot of horses, get rich; after she goes back for the boys, they'll all live there, they'll be a power in the country, a strong family. "There they go," people will say, "toughest, roughest bunch there is, best shots in the country." They'll have a special breed of horses, fast buckskins, and they'll ride side by side, the three of them, united by bravery, daring, their long lonely struggles and the memory of their father's dream.

The dog stops, growling, one paw lifted, nose hunting the wind. She stops Duster and sits very still, listening. The wind ruffles the grass, tugs at her hair; there is nothing else, no sound on the wind, no smells of smoke, but the dog is still growling. She slips off the horse and leads him, her hands shaking, into a gully. Even the gully seems like no shelter at all. She's not sure what she's afraid of. The dog follows and they wait. Nothing stirs. High above them a hawk circles, slips sideways, drifting on the wind. Wind shakes the silver willows. It's blowing towards them. Black Dog is quiet now.

Tying the horse, she climbs quietly back out of the gully, and over the next ridge. The dog growls and growls, low in his throat. There is a line of crumbling granite slabs on the next ridge, and though they are lousy cover, they are some cover, and she crouches behind them. The rifle barrel grates on the rocks and she slings the gun behind her on her back, shushes the dog by holding his nose.

An Indian camp is almost directly below her, huge conical white tents in a circle. The stream she has been following loops in lazy meanders through a huge flat meadow. Clumps of poplar and willow line the stream and edge the meadow. Horses wander and play, grazing on bright emerald grass. The hill drops away steeply below her and the camp crouches in a hollow between the hills and the stream. She wiggles deeper into a crevice in the rocks and drags the dog in with her. "Now what the hell are you going to do, Annie," she thinks.

There are too many voices talking in her mind. Wild people, savages, killers. Wasn't that what the scouts had said? Suddenly, more than anything, she wants her father to be here to tell her what to do. She misses him so much her eyes and throat ache with the hurt. He would know. He would take charge, and she could just do what he said. She doesn't know enough. She doesn't know why she is here, all by herself, away from anyone who might tell her what to do and how to handle this, lying here on gritty, crumbled granite, staring down at a place full of people who probably want to kill her. She thinks she should, very sensibly and quietly, back away, get to Duster, and lead him around in a huge circle to get past without being seen.

For three days the country has been empty of anyone but her, and she was free to dream into it anything she wanted to be there. But this is like coming out of one dream into another. Her stomach cramps, like it did when they left the farm, only then it was both excitement and fear. So is this. Her father was never afraid. She never saw him afraid. She wraps both arms around her stomach and holds on. The dog crowds in beside her.

The camp is quiet. It is still early morning. Someone, a woman, comes out of a tipi and stretches, calls back into the tipi then goes over to the fire, crouching, stirs the ashes and again calls out towards the tipi. Someone else emerges, a boy about eight or nine, and the woman touches his face, smiling, and then speaks. As he moves past her, she pretends to smack at him, but she doesn't, and he runs off, laughing, towards the edge of the poplar trees. The woman heads into the trees, gathering wood, comes back with her arms full. The boy also carries in wood, and the woman places bits of wood on the fire and sets a pot over it. The pot is steel, Annie notes. So they must go somewhere to trade. Perhaps they are friendly. But how can she tell? What does she know here that's useful?

Other people emerge from other tipis; people wander off to the woods and come back with firewood. A lot of the men come straight from the tents and trot to the creek, step in, lie down flat, ducking their heads under, before coming back to the fires, laughing and calling to each other and wringing out their wet hair.

Women go back and forth between the fires. Not all the tipis have fires in front. Some women are carrying food to the other tipis, stopping to talk along the way. Children slip out from the hide doors, run off, come back, grab food, run off again. It's hard to watch it all. Too much is happening now. The woman who first emerged from the tent below her has another child in her lap and a young girl sitting in front of her. She is braiding the girl's hair, combing and braiding it, pulling it tight and carefully wrapping the ends, while the baby in her lap squirms to get off, pulls its mother's hair, reaches out towards the fire, and finally wriggles free and crawls off. The young girl runs after it, laughing and swoops it up, and she can hear them all, the mother, the daughter and the baby laughing and laughing. The whole camp shines in the morning light.

She smells meat cooking. She is hollow and light with hunger and loneliness. It's not fair. She wants to be able to go down the hill, waving and coming home after such a long absence and dig greedily into the pots of food and have that woman comb and braid her hair; it's not fair. No, what she wants is to quit this whole business, and go back to her grandparents; her parents are probably there, wondering where she is and why she is taking so long to get home. Her mother will say gently, "Sit down, you must be starving," and she'll bring her a big plate of stew and biscuits and fresh vegetables from the garden, and pie after, and then she'll get up and go find her father, working outside, and for once he won't yell at her, but will be glad to see her. The boys will be out back playing in the tree house, and her grandmother will be knitting. Yes, that's it, this whole thing is a mistake. They must be there. She should get up and get away from here, but she doesn't. The rich warm smell of food and fires, the children's laughter, ties her to the ground.

She puts her head down, closes her eyes. "C'mon," she thinks. "Get yourself out of this." Beside her, the dog snarls a warning and turns his head. Startled, she looks around.

Two young women stand behind her, calmly watching her; they look like they are about her age. Their hair is carefully braided, unlike hers, which is a mess, loose and flapping and dirty. They are wearing blankets over their shoulders, and staring at her. She stares back. There is nothing, nothing in her head, to tell her what to do. Without any conscious thought she leaps like a startled deer, on her feet and running, right past the young women, fast and light as air, only faintly conscious of voices behind her, leaping over hills and logs and ledges in her flight back to Duster, pulling his reins free, into the saddle, and slapping him viciously in her haste to run, to get out of there, to get going and get away.

He is willing to run, full of running after a time standing tied and anxious by himself. He puts his head down and digs in with his powerful hindquarters and bolts. Once she won a race on him at the local fair back home, but that was on flat ground. She leans forward, grabs his mane and hangs on as he swoops over the rises, drops out from under her into dips and hollows, rockets furiously on flat places and up and over the hills. Eventually, he slows by himself, puffing hard, and she pulls him down to a canter, and a trot, and finally a slow walk. She stops on a hill and looks back.

"You idiot," she says out loud. "You stupid, blithering idiot. You almost got yourself killed." Duster slants his ears towards her voice. He thinks she's mad at him. Black Dog lies down, panting hard from the run.

Annie is still shaking. The picture of those two girls resonates in front of her... glossy hair, braided with beads, white buckskin dresses, blankets. Annie's own hair straggles in front of her face. She can smell her sweat and dirt from sleeping in her clothes for three days.

What would they have done to her? Raised an alarm, probably. Called the men to come and deal with her. Her mind shudders away from what could have happened. Annie sighs wearily. Next time, she thinks, next time, she'll be more careful. She turns Duster and rides on, her hands shaking on the reins, trying to control it, thinking about food.

There is a grove of trees, and another stream. And there are antelope on the other side of the stream. Heads up. They've seen or heard something. Black Dog stops, points, ears alert. He's even hungrier than she is. She's supposed to feed him. It's her job. But she hasn't done anything smart lately. Her mind is dull. Her body feels slow. Those girls were probably laughing at her. She eases the rifle off the saddle and wonders what to do next. It's too far. She's never made a shot that was anything like this. She's all by herself. The antelope put their heads down again. Eating.

They're at home, eating. She's the stranger with no food; the sound of the shot will be too loud, will serve notice to everything within miles that she's here, a stranger who doesn't know what she's doing.

Killing things. Her father killed everything. Once he killed a cat that annoyed him. Swung it against a tree until its head broke and blood came from its nose. They watched, she and her brothers. He killed Black Dog's mother because she was too old and useless, he said. He killed cows and pigs and she helped him with that. When they killed a pig, they had to dip it in hot water and scrape and scrape to get the hair off the hide, and then her father cut it open, and it was her job to run back and forth from the house to the pig and back again, with basins to carry the liver and heart and the head, which her mother would cook, and then the lungs and other guts, to be cooked up for the dogs. It was fascinating, to see the pig opened up and the insides there, perfectly packed away, nestled and steaming. Her father would hang the rest of the now empty pig, which no longer looked like pig, on a pole between two trees. And there it would dangle until they were finished cutting it all up and putting various parts of it away. Bones from their various meals would litter the yard all winter; the dogs would gnaw at them or bury them and in spring, her mother would gather them up and burn them, until nothing at all remained of the pig.

After the butchering, she would have to help her mother cut up some of the meat to eat right away, and some to hang for smoking. Then she would have to turn the grinder to make sausage until she was exhausted and her arms ached.

She creeps forward. The rifle weighs her down, drags behind her, catches on things. The sun is hot on her back. It's late afternoon. Mauve shadows pattern the dull yellow grass. Grasshoppers smack the sandy cracked reddish ground beneath her and spring away again. Except for the grasshoppers, the hot bowl of ground she lies in is quiet.

It's so silent she can hear the antelope as they pull grass, as their feet thud on the dry ground, as they shake and twitch away flies.

Their coats are red, the same colour as the ground.

It is ridiculously easy. An antelope looks up, shakes its head, and goes back to eating. There are four of them. She aims carefully, fires and one falls. The others run away. The shot echoes and bounces off the hills, and then everything is silent again.

She plods forward to where the antelope is lying still in the grass. There is a hole, just behind the shoulder. She hit exactly where she aimed. She knows what to do now, she thinks, and so she does it, cuts the throat so the blood spills out in a ripe red pool, and Black Dog comes and licks it. Then she opens the belly, remembering how her father did it, cutting carefully from the anus. The guts spill out on the ground. She leaves them for the coyotes; overhead, a vulture circles, then another,.

Skinning takes a long time, far too long. She ties the

hind feet together with her rope, throws the rope over a tree branch, and gets Duster to help her hoist it up. She works as quickly as she can, looking up and nervously scanning around her. Her knife is too dull and she doesn't really know what she's doing. She keeps cutting through the hide; her father would yell at her about that. She thinks that she isn't so far away from that Indian camp. They could have heard the shot.

She cuts the meat up. Her knife feels dull as a piece of rock but she doesn't stop to sharpen it. There's far too much meat to carry on Duster, and it won't keep. She could ride back, close to the Indian camp and leave it there as a gift. But she knows she isn't brave enough to do that. Finally, she leaves it wrapped in the hide and tied in the tree with a bit of rope. She hopes they'll find it, hopes they'll know, they'll understand it's from her. She leaves without looking back, rides on to find another camp.

FIVE

SHE THINKS IT MUST BE THE SEVENTH NIGHT since she left. A week. But it could be any amount of time. There are two sets of time in her head. One is just time, and the other is all the distance she has travelled, all the places she's seen, some she remembers clearly and some were just places to get through.

The country is changing. She's coming down out of the hills and it's getting flatter, easier to travel, easier to see, easier on Duster and Black Dog. She and Black Dog ate all the meat they could, but it wasn't long before it started to taste rotten. The weather is too hot and she feels sick from stuffing herself with all that meat. It was pretty tough and she had no good way to cook it and no salt.

The sky has been clear the whole week; she's been lucky. But now it's clouding over into an irritating, dull yellow haze. The light hurts her eyes and makes her feel sleepy. She's sleepy anyway, tired, bone-tired. Her stomach hurts from the knots that fear and terror have tied there. Her hair is greasy and slicked back against her head, her scalp itches furiously. Her whole body hurts from riding so much and the insides of her legs are chapped and sore.

That night, as she slides off Duster, knives twist in her muscles, her legs aren't where they should be and she falls over backwards. Concerned, Black Dog comes to see and she slams his head away. She gets up, undoes the cinch and heaves the saddle off Duster, yanks the bridle off over his head, not waiting for him to open his mouth and drop the bit, as he's been taught, banging his teeth. In surprise at the pain, instead of standing and waiting for her to put his hobbles on, he skitters away backwards. In a sudden fury, she swings the bridle, slashing his shoulder. "You stand," she orders, but he jumps away, and she knows better but does it anyway, furious and stupid, lunges for his mane, catches part of it, and when he panics at dragging her weight, she can't hang on. She's spooked him. Head and tail up, bucking, running back the way they've come, he's gone. She stares after him, unbelieving.

"Any horse'll spook at anything, you give him a chance," says her Dad's voice, just over her shoulder. "Gotta remember to stay quiet. Not their fault if you're riled over something."

Black Dog comes back, seeking comfort. "Why don't you go too," she screams at him. "Go away, go home, get the hell out of here, leave me alone," and he slinks away behind her and lies down, watching.

There is no time to plan, no time to think. She's got to get around and in front of Duster, calm him down, talk to him, so she can walk up to him, slip on a rope and bring him back. Otherwise, he'll simply set out for home, or wherever he thinks is home, and without another horse, she won't be able to catch up with him. Now that he's spooked, horse fashion, he'll just keep moving away from what's frightened him. He'll slow down eventually, look around, graze or sleep, but she can't take any chance on being left afoot in this kind of country. She looks around. The sky is steadily darkening. It will probably storm soon. She figures she has an hour of light, but the storm will bring the dark faster. Her legs are stiff and twisted, like rope with old knots in it.

She looks around, checking. She can't afford not to re-member exactly where she is. She tries to memorize it, all the things she hadn't noticed…the shape of black cut-out crazily shaped firs against that yellowing sky, an old mon-ster rock with its teeth grinning at her. In the bottom of the hollow is a small shining pond of water with reeds at the edge and a few ducks freckling the middle.

She grabs a rope and trots off at a slight angle to Duster's direction. Black Dog follows. She jogs to the top of the hill they had just crossed, she and Duster and Dog, tired and wanting to stop, and now this. No time to pay attention to the jeering voice in her head that says, "This is your fault, you deserve this." No time except to look quickly, see no sign of Duster, jog down and around the next hill, and the next and the next, still trying to cut a larger circle than him, stumbling in her boots and heavy skirt. After a while, she can't run anymore, and slows to a walk, panting, panic pushing her legs to go faster, walk faster, to slide down gravelly banks, and jam her boot edges into the side of the next hill. She tries to push the fear back because there's no room for it and no choices anyway. She needs Duster—she has to find him, will keep going until she does. She needs him to be there, just over that next lumpy, yellow rock, or there, beside that twisted clump of junipers. But nothing is there. She has been trying to follow their back-trail but this place doesn't even look familiar. She's come too far around, and she changes the angle of her swift, hard walking; she starts to run again, and notices just in time that Black Dog is sniffing, staring off to her left, behind where she has just come. She slows, turns, pauses. Listens and waits.

When she stops she realizes how tired she is, but there's not time to think about it. It's almost dark now and the down-draft out of the hills lifts the sweaty, greasy strands of hair off her face, ruffles Black Dog's hair. Bats jerk and zip through the air; a nighthawk swoops over her head and she jumps. She waits. She hears it again—the soft thud, the click of hoof on stone—and she walks calmly, very calmly, towards Duster, who is standing under a tree and watching. He snorts softly at her outstretched hand and grabs the side of her skirt as always, looking for treats. She turns the rope into a rough halter, swings on his back, and heads for camp.

"All right, Annie," she thinks. "All right. You were stupid and you got lucky. Don't ever do that again." She feels like she used to feel in school, when the teacher would lecture and she would squirm in her seat, trying to make herself small and wishing herself anywhere else.

Finally they make it back to the clearing. The rock and the ducks and the tiny pond are still there. She makes camp and lies down on the filthy blanket. Lightning decorates the horizon and she sits up again with her back against a tree, watching the silver shimmer of the water, the flickering light shaking the banked clouds, the black horizon. She hates lightning, always has. It's so huge, mysterious, powerful. Bigger than her. She's tiny, lying here under a tree, the earth spreading out all around her.

Finally she slides down onto the ground and curls up tight, knees pulled up to her chest, holding herself together. Pictures unreel in her head, too many—too fast. Bright tents against a jade meadow, thick threads of blood pooling on the ground, the men's faces at the settlement, her mother's still white face, calm in death, and the tiny body of her dead sister lying beside her.

Her throat clenches and she grinds her teeth against her hand and bites the blanket, again and again, holding on against the arrow-sharp splinters weaving pain through her head and heart and belly, holding on against the wishing, against time rolling backwards in her head, against all the might-have-beens and what-ifs; against her mother, who should be waiting for her back at the farm, waiting for Annie to come in so she can hug her and sit her down and braid her clean soft hair; against her father's gruff voice; against her brothers, waiting—lost and bewildered—for her to come and explain that soon, soon they will be a family again. Her throat clenches against the pain that wants to come rolling up from her belly and break in wails and waves, shattering the night's uneasy calm. She holds it in, holds on though her body shakes and shivers with the effort.

Lightning cracks and crunches the air into shattered noise somewhere close behind her. She pulls Black Dog in close on one side and cradles the rifle her father gave her on the other. Duster comes and stands near her with his head down. A small circle against the prairie wilderness, they wait out the night together.

SIX

ANNIE AND DUSTER PAUSE ON A CLIFF EDGE over a steep slope, both of them trying to figure the easiest way down. She figures they must have climbed over one range of hills and now they're coming down into a different sort of country. She wishes she had a map or some indicator of which way to go. Ahead of her is a lumpy, confusing quilt of blue hills. She's been trying to keep some kind of map in her head. "Next time you do this, Annie," she thinks, "bring along some paper." And then laughs at herself. Next time!

The descent gets steeper and more difficult. The trees are thicker with more large pine and fir, and tangled cedar thickets in the gullies. There are thorny clumps of white-berried, red-leaved brush and crumbling fallen trees to clamber through and over. She halts Duster at an edge of sloped, worn granite and looks out. Duster heaves in great bellows of air. He shakes his head and foam flies back onto Annie's face. The slope below is gullied, pitted with fallen trees and boulders. But Duster is determined and picks his way over the rocks, sliding and stumbling. He seems to have an idea that they might finally be getting somewhere. She gets off and tries to lead him. Finally she ties the reins around his neck and walks ahead, picking a route for all of them. He follows her, hopping over the deadfalls, sliding on the talus slopes, stopping to rest when it all gets too much for him. Sometimes he makes the decisions for her, goes down rock faces she would have tried to bypass, jumps gullies that seem too wide. But he makes it.

She shivers, feels hollow inside, weighted with fear for all of them. Duster has lost weight, his flanks look gaunt, his muscles stand out, bunched under his golden skin. He doesn't get enough time to graze. She and Black Dog have been subsisting on berries, fish, roots and rabbits. But her body is demanding more—she wants meat, fat, sugar and coffee, cakes and pie and fruit. She dreams of food when she's riding. Sometimes she thinks she can smell bacon frying or bread baking.

It takes them most of a day to work down the slope. Worried, Annie keeps checking Duster's feet and legs. His feet are tough but this going would wear down any hooves. When they left the farm, he had shoes on, but they were thin and worn. She had gotten someone at the settlement to pull them off. But now his feet are chipping and cracking. He needs a rest and some good grass.

By late afternoon, there's a glint of water far below. She can see the light reflecting through the trees. Where there's water, there'll be more sources of food. Or at least grass.

Or, she thinks with a shiver, there might be another Indian camp. This time maybe she'll just take her chances, march in and ask them for food. What kind of threat can she be, a girl and a horse? But maybe they won't believe she's alone.

Finally, the slope levels off, and surprisingly, there they are, near the bottom of a narrow valley, full of mounded, grass-covered hills and hollows. Ahead of them is a glistening blue gap, a space, no, a lake. They come out at the edge of a grassy flat and work their way through grass that's taller than Annie's head. There is white sand curled around the edge of a small bay. Ducks rise in clouds at their approach. Duster snatches mouthfuls of grass. As they come onto the sand, trout flick away under the dark water. A stream comes through the brush and fans out at the edge of the beach. There are berries in the mass of thick bramble bushes edging the sand and freshwater clams in the water. Deer tracks on the beach. Driftwood for fires. Its hers. She's found it.

"We could stay here for a while, I guess," she says out loud to Duster and Black Dog. She unsaddles Duster, hobbles him, lets him graze. She takes off her sweaty clothes, looking around when she's finally naked, feeling silly, still self-conscious. There probably isn't another human being for fifty miles around. The air washes her skin; the sun is warm with just a hint of coolness behind it.

"Fall's coming," she thinks. She tries the water—it's silky soft and cool. She slides into it, rolls and dives and swims a bit, floats on her back, watching her toes, yellowish brown under the water, white in the sun. For the moment, her stomach unknots and she feels a brief, stray happiness, fragile as a new flower. She comes out of the water, throws a stick for Black Dog so he'll go swimming too, trots up and down the beach, loving the feel of the white-sugar sand under her feet. She stuffs herself with berries, lets juice run down her face and goes back for another swim.

Then she climbs back up the bank and surveys as much of the valley as she can see. The lake is set in a bowl of hills, sits there like a small blue drum. The hills are burnished brass, outlined by burgundy and gold willows. She wishes her parents could have seen this place.

Maybe they could have all settled here. They would have been so happy planning a house, over there back from the lake, near that grove of cottonwoods, by the stream for water. That space could become the garden, that would make a good place for the barn, the corral. This tall marsh grass would make good hay until they could get some fields plowed and seeded. There wouldn't even be much clearing to do, just dig some ditches for drainage. And until they got a garden and some cattle they could live off fishing and hunting.

It's almost dark by the time she finishes exploring and finally lights a fire. She's still hungry despite having stuffed herself with berries and some trout which she caught and filleted and skewered on twigs. If anything, this bit of food makes her hungrier. She is sitting dreaming and playing with the dog when she notices, at the northern end of the lake, another dim and tiny point of light. Another fire. Has to be.

And if she can see their fire, they can see hers.

She scrambles for water, puts the fire out, moves her stuff back in the shadow of the bushes, and runs to get Duster. She holds the rifle in the crook of her arm. The thing to do is get the hell out of here, and fast. It's probably Indians. She's heard they don't like to go out at night; she wonders if it's true.

She's holding Duster when he throws his head and tries to whinny. She catches him in time, pinching his nose shut, leads him back into the tall grass, behind a clump of willow. He's excited, smelling other horses, but she clamps him in a terrified grip, willing him to keep still. Black Dog growls softly at her feet. They wait. The grass rustles at their least movement.

Enough reflected light from the water and sky allow her to just barely see the silhouettes of the three men who come riding down onto the beach. They dismount, look around, feel the ashes of her campfire.

"Still hot," one grunts. "Fire's just been put out. Probably still around here somewheres. Could be watchin' us."

The men are uneasy, peering into the dark. "We'd better skedaddle," says one. "T'ain't Indians, that's for sure, and t'ain't ol' Link. Thought it might be him. Well, maybe we can come back in the morning and pick up a trail. Don't know who in the hell'd be this far out, this time of year, lessen it's one of us. But t'ain't right, t'ain't the right sort of camp. Can't figure it." They stand silent, puzzled.

The other men don't speak. Finally, they all ride back into the night. Annie lets out her breath and lowers the rifle. They're men, white men. They probably aren't any safer than Indians, she thinks, remembering the men at the settlement. But she needs to know who and what they are. If they're settlers, they might have women with them and then she'd be safe. In any case, they'll have food and supplies and she needs a lot more than she's got. She can't go on much farther, subsisting on fish and venison. She needs flour, sugar, lard, lots of things. Soap! Maybe they'll even have some of that. They might ask questions about where she's come from, but that's a chance she'll take. She's come a long way from the settlement. She doesn't sleep that night, sits holding Duster, watching the light at the end of the lake wink and blur and finally go out.

In the morning, bleary-eyed and tense, she rides towards the north end of the lake. After a while, she can smell the smoke from their fire, and food cooking. She ties Duster and circles around to where she can view the camp. It's small. She can only see the three men. Trappers or traders, probably. They're cooking. She can smell bacon frying, coffee. They have a string of packhorses which they're in the process of catching and saddling.

Good. That probably means they're getting ready to leave and she can stay in the valley for a while, undisturbed. She keeps watching. Her stomach rumbles and aches. She goes back to Duster, takes the rifle from its sheath, checks to make sure it's loaded, mounts, and rides with one hand on the reins and one carrying the gun.

She comes through the trees and across a small meadow, crosses a gully. They're alert now, watching her coming. She halts Duster at the edge of the camp, near their picketed horses.

The three men look her over carefully. "Howdy," says one, coming forward. He's huge, with a bushy black beard. The other two only dip their heads.

"Howdy," she says, and then, after a pause. "I saw your fire...last night. I'm well, I'm a bit low on supplies." She keeps her voice tight and low. The gun is tucked under her arm, the barrel pointing just slightly down.

"Well, come and set yourself," says the tall one, after a pause. "I guess we still got a bit of coffee in the pot."

She slides off Duster and warily approaches the fire, standing where she can see them all, still cradling the rifle. The coffee comes in a tin mug encrusted with soot, but it's black and strong and heavily sweetened.

One of the men kneels to put wood on the fire and the other goes back to the packhorses. Annie tries not to breathe too deeply. The camp is rank with their smell.

"Come in over the hills, did you?" says the bearded one. "There's a bit of trail, down 'tother end there. Musta missed it. Otherwise, we'da seen you coming in."

"Came down there," Annie says, indicating the range of hills behind them. Slid, mostly."

"Didja now?" says the man. "Steep was it? Tough little horse you got there."

"Yeah," says Annie, "but he's needing shoes. Feet are starting to crack. Too dry."

"Ahh, shoes ain't much good in this country. Wear out too quick. Got to have a horse with tough feet, that's what you need." After a pause, he adds, not looking at her, "Nearest settlement's pret'near a week's hard ride due east. Could get shoes there."

"I'm headed west," she says.

"Best give him a trim then. About all you can do. Al, there, he's pretty fair with horses. Could trim up the feet. Had you some breakfast yet?"

She shakes her head.

"Well, guess we could probably rustle you up a bit of grub. Joe," he says to the man squatting morosely by the fire. "We got any of them killer mean biscuits of yours left?"

Joe, who hasn't yet looked at Annie, gets up without a word, scuttles to one of the loaded packhorses and begins pulling out supplies. Gingerly, Annie squats beside the fire. When the food comes, she has to juggle carefully to keep her rifle in her arm, coffee in one hand and the plate of biscuits, leftover beans and venison steaks which has miraculously appeared in front of her, in the other hand. Finally, she puts the coffee on the ground, stands the rifle beside her, and tries to eat politely, without gulping the food.

"Joe here, he's well, he's kinda scared of women," says the black bearded man. He seems to be smiling but it's hard to tell behind the beard. "Guess he tried to talk to one once, and didn't get much past howdoyedo."

There's a long pause while Annie finishes her food. The men watch her eat.

"Use that there rifle much?" asks the man with the black beard, very casually.

Annie looks at him. "I can use it," she says, deliberately pitching her voice low and level.

"Yep. Good little gun, that. I had me a Henry rifle once. Good little gun. Mind if I have a look?"

She hesitates. Finally, reluctantly, she hands the rifle over. He looks, breaks it, notes the shells and looks down the barrel, puts it back together and hands it back.

"You're needing supplies, you say? Lots of game around this lake."

Annie shrugs. "No salt," she says. "No sugar, no coffee, flour, meal, stuff like that."

He sits back, considering. Then he drawls, "Well, little lady, I'll make you a deal. You show me how you can shoot that there gun. If you're as good as you seem to think you are, maybe we'll see what we can do about them supplies.

Otherwise, you see, I gotta figure this is no place for a girl to be hanging out all by her lonesome."

He looks at the other men. They nod soberly.

"Which means we gotta make some kind of decision here. Now we're heading into the mountains to do a winter's trapping, and we sure cain't take no girl with us. We're waiting for one other feller to show, but looks like he ain't gonna make it so now we're fixing to move on. It'd delay us some to get you somewhere's safe, but if it's got to be done, it's got to be done."

"C'mere," he says, getting to his feet. Together, they walk to the edge of the camp and look out over one of the marshy meadows, towards the lakewater. "See that black stump out there, kinda looks like a big old bear. See that little round spot, sort of a circle? We was all trying to hit that the other day, kind of a contest, just for fun. Think you can make that?"

She doesn't reply, only hoists the heavy gun to her shoulder and looks through the sight. The round circle dances and beckons. She waits until her heart stills, calms, and then almost absent-mindedly, she fires three shots, one after another, into its heart.

She and the tall man walk through the high, wet grass to the stump. The other two watch them.

"Well, I'll be goddamned," says the man. "Three in a row. Girl, that is something, that is really something. Guess maybe you can shoot. But can you look after yourself? You ride in here with nothin' but a wore-out nag and a skinny dog, doesn't look like you're doing so good."

"We been getting by just fine," Annie flashes, with real anger. "I shot deer and rabbits, and caught fish. We don't need your help. I was just asking for a few supplies, is all. But if you can't spare them, we'll be on our way and sorry for bothering you."

"Naw, we got lots of stuff," drawls the tall man, shrugging in resignation. "Come on and we'll make you up a pack."

They walk back to camp. "By the way," says Blackbeard. "My name's Tim, and this here's Joe and Al. Joe does the cooking and Al chases them useless packhorses around, and me, well, God only knows what I'm good for. But you can bet we'll go find some good fur this winter. We gotta get moving, get over the passes before it snows. Be winter up this high before you know it."

"I'm…Annie," she says after a pause. She doesn't like this new friendliness. She wishes they'd just give her the supplies and let her get going. Her head is aching from watching all three of them at once.

"Well, let's see about them supplies," says Tim. Al goes to take a look at Duster's feet. Joe scurries and bustles, making up sacks with lard, meal, sugar, salt, bacon and beans. He still won't look at her. Tim asks her careful questions about the country she's been through, about the weather and game and she gives him equally careful answers. He wants to know where she saw the Indians, but she doesn't tell him about the camp. It sits in her memory like a dream, and she lets it stay that way.

She takes the supplies they give her and packs them into Duster's saddlebags. She can tell Tim is still worried, but he doesn't ask any more questions. She pauses, awkward. She wishes there were some easy way to say thanks and just ride off. She slides up on Duster, but Tim stops her with one hand on the reins.

"Just where you say you were headed?" he asks, a bit belligerently.

She looks down at him. "I'm headed west," she says very deliberately. "My family figures to find land there. We figure to go ranching." It's the closest thing to truth she can give him.

He struggles with himself. Annie remembers her father telling her never to ask anyone's business. "Don't pry into anyone's business, and they won't pry into yours," he'd snapped. "That's the way it is out there."

Tim looks off into the blue distance. "Seems like your folks could take a little more care of you, letting you ride around out here by yourself."

"They're waiting for me," says Annie. "They ain't worried. They know I can ride and shoot and take care of myself."

"Looky here, girl," says Tim, with some exasperation. "You know what you're headed for, don'cha? Up ahead, they's mountains and after them they's bigger mountains, and they sure as hell ain't friendly if you don't know your way about. Now it's near some time coming towards the middle of fall, and up on top of them mountains, its already coming winter. Who the hell's going to look out for you if you get caught up in a storm? Whyn't you just go on back to that there settlement, and wait for some people coming through and head west with them?"

Annie doesn't say anything, just stares ahead, waiting for him to let go of the reins so she can get out of here.

Tim sighs. "Well, just hang on to that nag for a few minutes longer…least we can do is give you some kind of map, show you where you're headed."

He draws the map with charcoal from the fire on a piece of thin bleached hide, rolls and ties it with a piece of sinew.

"There," he says, finally, handing her the map with the air of a man who has done his duty.

"Thanks," says Annie, taking it, "but really, I'll be fine." She stiffens in the saddle, Duster jumps sideways at the pressure from her knees and she lurches to one side, undignified, snaps the reins tight, grabs at the rifle.

"I know what I'm doing. I'd better get going. Thanks for the supplies and stuff." She tenses, tightens the reins further, and feels all of Duster's strength coil beneath her; his muscles tense and his neck curves, ready to run. Sometimes she thinks Duster knows what she's feeling as well as she does.

"Well little girl, it's your funeral. Guess you've been warned." Still he hesitates, then finally waves her off with a shrug. Al and Joe also wave, shyly, and she rides away, back across the mud-holed and stump-littered swampy meadow, through the coulees and along the lakeside to the beach.

She's glad to get back there. She waits for a couple of hours and then rides back again to check that they're really gone. Their camp is deserted. Joyfully, she goes back to her own beach and makes a proper camp, fussing over it. She finds a flattened slab of silver driftwood for a table, piles up rocks for her fire, and then catches some fish. She fries them with bacon, eats meal cakes and drinks coffee; she has some berries and sugar for after. As night sifts shadows into the valley she goes for another swim in the clear water, turns on her back to look at the stars, luxuriating in the sheer pleasure of being fed and clean, and the triumph of having survived so far.

SEVEN

THE NEXT DAY WHEN SHE WAKES, there's blood between her legs and on her blanket. "Damn," she mutters, and scrubs the sweaty horse-hair laden blanket in the lake and hangs it to dry. After that, she washes everything, even her leather skirt. The sun is hot on her skin. That night, she sleeps on a bed of fir tips and a pad of moss. Blood runs down onto the moss. In the morning, she washes in the lake, but still the blood runs down her legs. Finally, she simply goes naked and ignores it, washing in the lake whenever it gets too messy. At night, she makes another pad of moss, and in the morning she burns it in the fire.

The next day, she lashes two logs together with a rope and she and Black Dog play pirate, poling along the brushy edges of the lake, slipping in and out of reed-choked shallow marshes where clouds of ducks startle to flight in front of them. There are huge beaver houses but few beavers, and untidy mounds of muskrat houses. She finds evidence that trappers have been here, a bloated dead beaver floating, one foot still caught in an iron trap, forgotten or overlooked. Once an otter growls and chitters at them from the bank. Eagles and ospreys loop lazy circles overhead, fishing, and she and Black Dog fish too, wrestling trout after trout onto the raft. She takes the fish back to the camp and cuts them in strips, salts and dries them on poles stuck in the sand over the smoldering fire. She thinks about living here forever.

That night, Black Dog wakes her, growling at her side. Then he takes off, barking and something huge crashes through the brush. Duster whinnies in fear and lunges awkwardly in his hobbles. The next day, she finds bear tracks along the beach and a broken smashed trail through the brush. She hoists her pack of food into a tree and checks over her shoulder all day. But the bear doesn't return.

One day she wakes early, shivering. She lies still, wondering what has awakened her. Then she looks around. The sky is sullen grey; drifting curtains of mist hang in the hollows between the mountains. She remembers that she dreamed about the boys and being home, back at the farm. Loneliness clutches her with shining sharp talons. Here she has been playing and being nothing but a silly child when she has work to do, when she is supposed to be finding them all somewhere to live, a home of their own. She shivers. The wind coming down off the peaks has tiny teeth in it, snapping at her skin. The lake shivers too, under the beating of the wind. She remembers what Tim said about storms coming, and winter.

"You've been stupid again, Annie," she scolds herself out loud. "You're not a goddamn baby anymore. Got to get going, get moving!"

While she packs and saddles Duster, it begins to rain. The lake smoothes out, pockmarked with rain, and her footprints on the sand soften and erode under its impact. In the cold rain, she and Duster and Black Dog ride away, past the cottonwoods whose leaves hang forlornly yellow and dripping. She stops and looks back at the beach.

"I'll come back." she says out loud, promising herself, trying to mean it. "I'll come back."

Time to get out of here. She figures she'll try to find whatever trail Tim put on the map that will lead her down out of these mountains. She should have asked more questions about the country, but she didn't because she didn't want them to think she really was lost. But now it would sure make things easier. She frowns. If she goes north, along the line of the mountains, she'll maybe run into easier going. Her Dad had talked about cattle ranching, somewhere north. She tries to connect the scattered bits and pieces of information in her mind. She has heard a lot of stories about the mountains, fearful stories of grizzly bears, blizzards, impassable cliffs. People said without a guide such places were damn near impossible to get through.

Winter's coming. She's going to have to find a place to stay for the winter. "You're stupid, stupid, stupid, Annie," she thinks. But another part of her says, "we're okay, we're in good shape, the three of us." The two weeks on the beach weren't all lazy. She shot another deer and dried the meat. She's packed it along with the dried trout and berries; they'll have enough food to get by for a while.

North of the valley, the going isn't too difficult. She picks up a trail of sorts, leading north. There's horse sign along it, so she follows it.

Over the next few days they make their way up hills and through bogs and over dead falls, until the whole journey is compressed down to the next obstacle, the next rockfall or jungly thicket, or steep ravine or slick-bouldered creek.

One morning she wakes in snow—snow on the ground, snow etching the black-trunked trees, trailing fingers of snow cancelling the landscape. She decides they'll have to drop down into the valleys below, out of these foothills, before they get caught by a real blizzard. Duster is losing the weight he put on in the valley, looking gaunt again. Annie has renewed her practice of swearing whenever they get in a rough spot, "bloody hell" is her favourite.

By her rough calculation, it's got to be sometime in October. They've been travelling most of a month. Winter's frowning at their heels. Gradually they work their way towards the grey and gold plain rolling away to the East.

Black Dog is the first to hear it. He stands alert, nose

pointing, ears lifted. Annie looks, but she can't see any-thing. Then she hears a noise like wind rumbling through cedar, cows bellowing. They're being driven somewhere, she figures, judging by the noise. Where there's a cattle drive, there's cowboys and, most likely, a ranch of some kind—buildings, food, maybe a place to hole up for a bit.

She heads east, towards the noise. It swells in volume as she gets closer. Finally, she tops a boulder-strewn rise, and in the canyon below them is a jostling, muttering, com-plaining mass of cows, jogging downhill, being whistled and yelled at by four cowboys.

Dust smokes the air. At the heels of the herd, a couple of small black dogs streak and scuttle back and forth. Black Dog growls, lifting his lip over his teeth. Annie shushes him, pulls back in the shadow of the hill. These men look young, almost her own age. Tim and his crew had been okay. They were slow and quiet. But suddenly, she doesn't want to deal with these men at all, doesn't want them look-ing at her, doesn't want their questions, their voices, their smell. They look too much like the men at the settlement.

After they pass, she follows them down the hill. Duster snatches at the reins and throws his head back, dancing sideways, excited, wanting to run. Exasperated, she sits braced, holding him back; she grits her teeth. He's almost impossible to manage, the damn fool. That would be a terrific introduction, a runaway horse coming down the canyon into their midst, scattering the cows.

The canyon widens into a small brush-choked valley,

which slopes down into another valley. A creek bounces
and jumps down its middle. A roughly rutted path full of
round rocks and cow patties parallels the creek. Annie stays
back, just in earshot of the cows, far enough behind that
she doesn't think she'll be seen.

She can't decide. She thinks about pulling Duster's head
around and going back up the hill, going on again by themselves. After all, they have been doing just fine on their
own. Mixing with people again will mean talking and explaining who she is and what she's doing out here all by
herself and answering all kinds of dumb questions.

And these are just boys from the look of things, boys her
age. Stupid boys, cowboys. What will they think of her?
And what the hell does she care what they think and why
the hell should she? She touches her hair, matted with dirt
and sleep. There are twigs in it, and bits of moss from the
beds she makes at nights. Her hair is a mess and her clothes
are dirty and she's survived a month on her own in the
wilderness. These boys must work for some kind of a ranch,
though what kind of outfit it would be this far out in the
wilderness, she can't imagine. A ranch will probably have
women on it, but that won't help much, in fact, it'll make
things even worse. They'll be like her mother and grandmother, expecting her to cook and knit and stay in the
kitchen talking. To hell with that.

And of course they'll worry about her. They'll ask questions like "where's your parents?" and "don't you want to
get married?" No, she bloody doesn't. What she wants right

now is a bath and food and a roof over her head for one night, and no questions at all. Maybe this is what her father was talking about when he said "don't ask questions." "It's my goddamn business what I'm doing," she says to no one in particular. She sticks her chin out and follows along.

After a couple of hours, the steep slope they've been sliding, mincing, and stumbling down suddenly ends, and the cows fan out onto a huge, flat meadow. Annie watches in astonishment as the cowboys ahead of her forget about the cows and take off, running their tired horses and yelling at each other. Cowboys—yeah, sure. Idiots is more like it. Probably a bunch of green kids come out west. Thinking themselves so great and then running tired horses like that. If she was the boss here, she'd fire the bunch of them. Or better yet, make them run a mile carrying a heavy load on their backs after they'd worked a full day.

She thinks about what her Dad would have said about such stupidity, and she smiles. At least he taught her a few things about horses. When he got Duster for her she was just a kid, six years old. Duster was a colt, a three-year-old just brought in off a range somewhere and hastily saddled and ridden, a terrified kid himself, snorting at everything, throwing his head, trying to kick or bite his way out of this new life.

One summer day, her Dad brought Duster home, got him in a trade of some kind, she never knew quite what. The next morning he called her out of bed and down to the corral with him. She watched as he caught Duster, handling him as casually as he did the old workhorses, while Duster snorted and trembled and kicked. "Watch now," said her Dad, as he slipped an old bridle and saddle on the shiny gold and black head. Then he took them off again, told her if he ever caught her whipping the horse, or running him unnecessarily, he'd sell him. Then he left her alone with him.

She and Duster regarded each other. Annie with disbelief and terror, and Duster with equal terror and general dislike. He crowded into one corner of the corral and turned his rump to her. She sat on the fence and watched him in silent worship.

For the next few weeks she spent every spare moment at the corral. She brought him hay and filched bits of grain and occasional apples. When he would finally let her, she scratched and brushed his itchy places. When he laid down to sleep, she laid down with him, curled between his legs, scraping a place in the dust and manure for herself.

One day when she went to see him with the usual gifts of apples and carrots, he rested his heavy head on her shoulder and sighed, long and deeply. With shaky legs, she went to the barn and got the halter and came back and put it on him. He didn't seem to mind, even when she had trouble with the heavy buckle. She led him to the fence and slipped on and sat there, with all of his sun-warmed satiny power under her. He looked at her and nosed her leg and chewed on her shoe and kept standing. She slipped off and led

him, towering over her, into the barn. She was afraid he
might step on her and had to walk forward and sideways
at the same time, skipping ahead to keep up with his long
stride. She tied him in a stall and stood on the side of it
and, after some turning the bridle up and down and sideways, figured out how it would have to go and managed
by some miracle to get the bit in through his clenched
teeth and the head stall over his ears. He flicked his ears
and chewed on the bit, tossed his head while she scratched
him in all his favourite places. She tried to lift the saddle
but couldn't manage it. Finally, she left it, climbed back
up on the side of the stall and slipped on Duster's back.
He turned his head, blew warm breath on her leg, turned
on his own and went outside. At the gate, she slid down
again, holding the reins awkwardly over one arm and
scrunching open the heavy gate poles with the other.

Outside the gate, she had to maneuver Duster close to
the fence, so she could balance on the top rail and make a
huge flying leap for the solid platform of his back. Then
she was on.

They went down the barnyard lane towards the house.
Everything looked different, she noticed. Her body rocked
to Duster's easy walk. She was above everything, high, high
up on top of the world, higher than she'd ever been, queen
of it all, empress, general, triumphant. She couldn't believe how huge Duster was.

Together, they rode into the yard where her mother was
bent over weeding the kitchen garden.

"Oh," said her mother. "Oh, well now, look at you. Be careful now. Don't let him walk on my garden," and then she went back to her weeding. Annie and Duster went down the long driveway to the rough road that led to their nearest neighbours. They plodded along under the overarching oaks and beech trees. Duster put his nose down and sniffed the road dust for signs of other horses. He looked at the brush and snorted and curved sideways at a grouse chuck-chucking her way through the leaves and Annie patted his neck and said, low in her throat, "Hey, you be good," like her father would say it.

After a while, they turned and came home, and she put Duster back in the corral and brushed him and rubbed her hair against his warm, sweaty neck so that she would be able to smell him all night.

At supper, she started to say, "Duster and I are getting along pretty good. He lets me ride him now," but her father snorted an interruption. "Damn horse eats more than three cows. Horse'll starve a cow, and a sheep'll starve them both. Don't know why I let that Jack Smith talk me into it. Don't need him. Too small to do any goddamn work. Should sell him I guess, if I could ever find anyone wanted a horse that useless."

She didn't know what he meant. She put away the proud story she had been going to tell. Instead, she told it to herself that night in bed, how Duster had come to her and decided to be her horse, how it felt to sit so tall and straight and strong, passing swiftly over the earth like a story, a prince, a song of glory, a leader heading somewhere new. Somehow, her Dad never did sell Duster, though he threatened to often enough. She wonders now if he ever really meant it.

EIGHT

THE RANCH IS AN UGLY BLOT in the tall prairie grass—
two sod and log huts, a corral and larger pasture, fenced
with poles. The boys have already turned their horses loose
and disappeared into one of the buildings.

She can smell food cooking. Duster tosses his head and
starts to dance, anxious to be with other horses. She rides
to the front of the long low cabin, ties Duster and goes to
the door. She knocks but no one comes. Finally, she opens
the door.

The combined stench of bacon, sweat, tobacco, musty
dirt, horses and cows, hits her first. The men look at the
open door. Light from outside shines into the gloom, which
is lit with one smoky lantern. No one moves.

She has time, before fear grabs her, before she realizes she's made a mistake, to notice details, the chipped and scratched gouges on the door frame beside her hand, her grubby fingers creased with dirt, her chipped nails. She realizes suddenly that she probably smells as bad as the men in the room.

One by one, the chairs scrape back. The men stand up. She stays in the doorway, paralyzed. Two huge hounds lie under the table, chewing bones.

"Well, come and set if you're goin' to. Get some grub," the man at the head of the table growls at her. One of the boys hastens, tripping and stumbling, to bring another chair. Hesitantly she sits while another boy brings her a plate and still another brings a huge pot and ladles stew in a brown fragrant puddle onto its chipped tin surface. One boy leaves the room and she hears the thud of Duster's feet as he's led away to be unsaddled. She hopes he takes time to at least brush him down. Maybe they've got some grain he can have. She hopes Black Dog is waiting, thinks that these dogs might want to fight.

"Eat," the man growls again, gesturing with his spoon like she's an idiot.

The food smells better than it tastes. She digs into the stew, which is thick with different kinds of meat and a lot of chili peppers.

One by one, the young men finish, get up and hastily leave the room, except for the one at the head of the table, who glowers as he rolls himself a smoke. She sits over her plate, paralyzed by the silence. What the hell has she done now, broken some kind of range law? Are they just going to leave her here while they flee for the friendly outdoors? Maybe she's supposed to curl up on the floor under the table with the dogs. Finally, only the one older man is left, the one who growled at her. He looks uneasy and none too friendly. He looks anywhere but at her. He checks out the ceiling, the tabletop, the dogs snoring on the floor, blows smoke towards the ceiling.

He's not such a pretty sight himself. A scraggly reddish-grey beard decorates his chin. He has a full sandy mustache and reddish hair. His face is round and red, to match his hair, and his eyes are bright blue. He wears a torn and greasy grey flannel shirt.

"So," he begins. "Kind of surprised us, you walking in like that. You can get yourself shot, someplaces, doing stuff like that."

"Sorry," Annie mutters. "I didn't think…"

"Well," he continues. "You're here now. Guess we don't get too many visitors around here. Them boys," and he stops to snort, "them boys was like to swallow their cuds, they was so surprised. So what do you want, lady. If you're lost, guess we could put you on your way. You got folks? Where the hell are they?"

The question is more direct and intrusive than she's prepared for. She stares at her plate, trying to get some words out. What the hell should she say? It's none of his damn business, she thinks. She should have made up a bunch of lies before coming in here, would have, if she'd known she was going to get questioned like this.

The man rolls another cigarette. His hands are small, fine, pitted and crossed with nicks and scratches and old scars. A rolled cigarette appears almost by magic from one hand. He puts it in his shirt pocket.

"I'm going west," she says finally. "Going out to join my folks. They're homesteading. I just need a place to rest my horse, maybe throw a bit of grain in him, if you've got any. He's kind of worn out. I can work to pay my way."

The man finally looks directly at her. His eyes are hooded by creased and frowning eyebrows.

"Yeah? What kinda work ? You cook?"

"No," says Annie. "Riding. I was a scout."

The man's only reply to this is another snort.

"Kinda young to be travellin' by yourself, ain't you?" he says after a pause.

She doesn't like this man, and she really doesn't like the feeling in the room. Coming in here was a waste of time. She stands up.

"Thanks for the food." she says. "I'd best go check on my horse."

"Just hold it," he says. "You ain't going no place until I figure out what you're doing here. I got a dozen boys out there, most of them still wet behind the ears. They ain't got much more than a dime apiece amongst them. Now, I don't know what kind of trouble you figure to be causing, but if you do, you've come to the wrong place. You can sleep in here tonight, and I'll lock the door on you. And in the morning, I'll take you on down the road apiece. There's some crazy woman trying to run cows all by herself, over in the next valley. She's run off anyone else who's tried to help her. But maybe she'll let you stick. But you sure as hell ain't coming in here and upsetting the goddammed applecart. We got too much work to get through."

And with that, he stands up and eases his way along the table towards her. She measures the distance between them.

"Easy now," he says. "This is for your own protection. I ain't gonna hurt you none." The cigarette still smokes, dangling, glued to his lip. The spurs on his boots chink softly on the beaten mud floor.

She figures if she lunges for the door, he'll still have time to grab her. She left the rifle in its sheath on her saddle but she still has her knife in her belt. Maybe she can hit him over the head with a chair. She tenses, but he eases past her, jumps out the door before she can get there, and she hears it thunk behind him. She slams against it. It's locked, or barred somehow.

She hears footsteps coming back and steps back, tenses. The door opens again. Her saddle, with the blanket, the rifle and saddlebags, flies through and lands on the floor. The door thunks shut again.

She grabs the rifle and holds it pointing at the door. Perhaps she could just shoot the door to pieces. The shack is made of sod packed between small unpeeled poles. She could probably bash her way out. She pokes experimentally at the walls. They feel pretty solid. The spaces between the poles are too small to crawl through. She looks around. They've left her the lantern, and there's a tin stove in the corner with a fire still burning and firewood. Dirty plates still litter the table. There's a galvanized copper kettle of water simmering on the stove. Shelves line the walls, filled with wooden boxes and burlap bags. She looks in some. Beans, chilies, flour, cornmeal. There are mouse turds all over the shelves.

Yuck. She wants out of here; she has to stop herself from crashing again against the door. She gets up on a chair and then on the table and looks along the roof line, between the logs and the sod-covered rafters. There's a space there, but only about two inches. She can see stars, and her breath frosts away into the night. Black Dog must be out there, waiting for her.

What the hell was that man talking about anyway? Something about money and her causing trouble. What kind of trouble? Her stomach twists. She should have run while she had a chance. She goes and stands with her back to the stove until some warmth starts to seep into her bones. She realizes she's still shaking. "You idiot, Annie," she says. "Now look at the bloody mess you're in." She stands there a long time, trying to think.

Finally, she takes the plates off the grease-stained table and stacks them in the corner. Let the mice clean them. She finds some loose tea and a half-clean cup, makes herself tea with the hot water, puts sugar in it, carefully sifting out the mouse dirt, then paces the circumference of the cabin, around and around.

When exhaustion overtakes her, she washes the table, makes up a rough bed on the top of it, propping the rifle beside her. The table smells of wet wood. She thinks she won't sleep but she does, dozing off periodically and opening her eyes again at the small creakings and scratching from the mice running races up and down the rafters.

It's dawn when she wakes and sits up abruptly. She remembers what that bastard did and she's still mad. She should have shot him. She could have shot up the whole stupid cabin and gone outside and run off their horses and terrified that batch of Eastern fake cowboys and then ridden away, instead of lying here like a dumb scared girl. The cabin is murky, but thin shafts of grey light slant from holes in the walls, down through the dust motes onto the table. She looks around. In the dim light, the cabin looks depressing and filthy. It smells even more strongly than last night of smoke, with an underlay of dirt and mold and mice and sweaty unwashed men.

A shadow creaks onto the step. The door swings open. It's the same man. He beckons her outside. His face is cold and hard and he still doesn't look at her. Mud flecks his face. Annie thinks it looks like ashes. "Pig face," she mutters.

Duster is outside, beside another saddled horse and Black Dog. Black Dog noses her knee. His tail makes frantic circles in the air.

"Get your stuff," the man says. She grabs her saddle and gear and silently lugs it outside. She saddles Duster and, still fuming, swings into the saddle.

The man mounts the other horse, nods his chin to show a direction, and rides away. She follows. Bastard. She'd like to shoot him, right now, right there in that spot of dirt on his faded torn shirt. Bet he'd love to be locked in a stinking hole of a cabin with thousands of mice, treated like some kind of criminal. If she ever gets a chance, she thinks, she'll show him, she'll get her own back. He's like all those other men, those idiots at the settlement. But she's not the same dumb scared girl that she was when she set out. After all, she's faced down hunger, Indians, a grizzly bear, a whole lot of wilderness and maybe a few other things inside herself she didn't even know about.

With something akin to pleasure, she notes these new furious reactions in herself; she's almost too busy thinking to notice where they're going. The man just keeps riding ahead of her and she keeps following. She thinks of turning and riding off but curiosity holds her in place, rocking to the familiar rhythm of Duster's haunches, sliding along underneath her. She wants to know more about this woman. After all, she can still leave anytime she wants to. But a woman, living alone away out here, and with kids, running a ranch and from the sounds of it, a woman of an independent nature—that's someone she'd like to meet.

The morning is still cold but the poplar trees blaze in iridescent clumps from the blue hills. Scarlet weeds spark the yellowing grass. They ride through a wide valley, rounded like the bottom half of a tunnel. A river plays tag with them through the trees. They climb over sandy benches, with thin grass clinging to the sandy soil, and clumps of spiky black juniper lining the deep eroded breaks that run down to the river. In the distance, a line of mountains marches away from them. They ride for an hour before they see a cluster of straggly corrals, three or four grey sagging buildings. A line of blue smoke disappears from one of them into the sky.

At the top of a hill the man stops and turns to her. "Well, there it is, best bet you've got. See if she'll take you. If not, best you keep riding. Ma'am." He tips his hat, turns his horse and kicks it into a lope.

Annie looks after him. Crazy. Men are just crazy. Her Mom used to say that. "Men are all fools," she'd say, glaring furiously after Annie's father, stomping out of the house after yet another argument. "Children. Just grown-up children. Your father would starve to death if he was left on his own. How any of them ever survive without a woman to manage them is beyond me." Then she'd slam wood into the stove, clang the stove lids and pump water for dishes with furious energy.

Annie never really thought about what went on between her mother and father. She knew that she hated them fighting—and they fought a lot. Annie would lie upstairs late at night in her little gabled room over the kitchen, and listen. No words came through, just the sound of their raised voices. The walls of the old farmhouse would tighten around her and she'd try to think of ways to get them to stop. Maybe if she pretended she was sick and went downstairs they'd stop, but she didn't and they didn't. Sometimes she'd creep out and sit on the stairs, shivering, but they never found her there.

It was her father who was strong, so strong he was terrifying. It was her father she walked behind, trying to match his long strides, her father she listened to, her father she worshipped despite her fear. She felt sorry for her mother, trapped in the house, in an endless round of cooking and cleaning and babies. When her parents fought she went back and forth, trying to decide whose side she was on. Because her mother was weaker, she defended her. Because her father was stronger, she secretly thought he must be right. Helpless and dizzy, she zinged between them like a demented spinning toy.

"Little girl," her father would grunt. "Go tell your mother…" and she'd trot away with a message. This always infuriated her mother, who seemed more angry at her than at her father. "That's right," she'd say. "Take his side. You're just like him."

"I'm not," Annie would say, "No I'm not," knowing all along it was true. But how relieved they all were when her father would go to town for the day with the team and wagon. Her Mom would sing and sometimes tell them stories. Chores would get done late and the farm would vibrate with lightness and ease.

The ranch sits below the curving ochre and red bluffs.
Annie looks around and understands why someone might
build a house here. Below her, the river glitters, shimmering steel in the October sun. The cottonwood leaves have
turned bright yellow, the willows growing beneath them
are bright burgundy. The corrals and the building are on a
flat at the top of a long slope. Beyond them, by the river, is
another flat, still green with benches of land stepping above
it. She can see cows moving by the river; a good place to
winter them, she thinks. Protection from snow, and lots of
grass on the benches.

Annie sits on Duster and looks over the brow of the hill
down to the flat below. The corrals scraggle over the slope.
The buildings are made of thin poles, with sod roofs. No
one appears to be moving. There are no horses in the corrals, no dog in the yard. She rides down the slope, scrambling through a small creek and up the other side. Someone, kids maybe, has built a crude dam across the creek so
it widens into a small pool.

NINE

AS SHE RIDES UP, A DOOR OPENS in one of the shacks and
a woman steps out. They look at each other. Annie feels a
rush of glad relief. She hasn't seen a woman for so long.
This one is wearing heavy breeches, a crumpled hat with a
wide brim, a man's shirt, and boots. Her hair hangs in a
heavy braid down her back. Her face is thin and lined,
browned by sun. She's not smiling.

"Howdy," says Annie.

"Howdy," says the woman, still without expression, not
giving anything away, not even surprise. Finally, she adds,
almost reluctantly, "Something I can do for you?"

Completely unexpectedly, tears start up in Annie's eyes
and she blinks them away in shame and anger. She stiffens

her face and shoulders. What the hell's the matter with people in this country? Haven't they ever heard of simple friendliness?

"Sorry," she says, with her chin up, looking away. "I didn't mean to bother you. Man over that other place said you might be needing some help. But if you're busy or something, I'll just be riding on," and she starts to turn Duster to leave.

"Hey, wait a minute," says the woman. "No, come on, it's just that I seen that lousy Joe Littlefoot coming over the hill, and wondered what nasty trick he was up to now. He's about to drive me crazy, that bastard." She stares furiously up the hill, as if she could still see him through the distance, then turns back to Annie.

"So...What can you do? Kinda young, ain't ya? But if you can ride, maybe you could be of some help, just for a while, though...Hey, what's the matter? You look a mite peaked to me. That lousy Joe. What's he done now? And you just riding through. Where in hell's your folks?" The words come out all in a rush, like the woman wasn't quite used to talking and had forgotten the order of things.

Annie turns back and slips off Duster and stands very straight and stiff, holding the reins. "I'm on my way to do some homesteading," she says, wondering just how much she can lie to this woman, "but I figured to find a place I could stop for a while, maybe spend the winter. I can ride and shoot and track and whatever else you got to do. But I'm kind of tired, and I could sure use a bath and my horse is near worn out." Despite her desperate effort to keep her voice level and flat, it trembles ever so slightly.

The woman smiles, finally, and the smile lights up her whole worn, tired face. "Well, Jeezus, lordy," she says, "why didn't you say so in the first place? Well, if you ain't just a girl, riding around on your own and figuring things out as you go. If you've got a story to tell, it'll probably keep. For now, I think we just might be able to come up with something to keep you busy. Gawd, it's been so long since I seen another woman, I cain't even remember how to talk. Gerald," she bawls, looking back inside the house. "Honey, come here. Momma needs you."

A sleepy-looking boy of six or seven appears and stares at both of them.

"Honey, looky here. We got company. Take the lady's horse down to the barn and come back and I'll make us some biscuits or something. Okay?"

But the boy just keeps staring. Another face appears in the doorway, this one even younger, a boy with red hair and freckles and pointy ears. He looks like an imp, a mean imp.

"Boys, one of you, the horse," but the boys appear deaf and dumb, staring at Annie. Finally, the woman leans over, shakes the oldest and yells, "I said, take the bloody horse to the barn, okay?" and the boy, barefoot, wearing only a pair of tattered pants, trots over to Duster, pats him and takes the reins.

"He ain't deaf. Just acts like it. Shy though. No school

here. Don't get to see strangers much. Growin' up kind of wild, I guess. C'mon in."

Inside is one room with a loft, a fireplace in the corner, shelves, a round tin stove. It looks a lot like the room she spent last night in; Annie's eyes narrow at the memory. A rough plank table is set with tin plates and mugs, a tin jug with milk in it, a chipped enamel bowl heaped with cold boiled beans, a lot of flies, crawling all over everything.

Two more children, girls this time, climb down the ladder from the loft. More staring. The girls are older, probably nine or ten. Annie looks at the woman.

"Yep, four kids. Would have been more if their Pa hadn't gone and got himself lost in a blizzard. C'mon girls, hurry up. Get your breakfast. I have to get out and find some more of them wild-eyed cows."

Annie watches as the woman mixes flour and lard together, pats the dough into biscuits, sets them in a Dutch oven on top of the stove. All the woman's movements are quick and sharp. Annie sits, self-conscious under the stares of the two girls. They don't move or smile, just stare. Finally, the oldest comes forward and wonderingly touches her leather skirt, her shirt. The other joins her. Their hands move over her clothes and hair in swift gentle pats and then they retreat to a corner to stare some more.

The woman slaps the food onto the table, along with tin plates and mugs. Coffee, cold beans and biscuits, and a jar of homemade jam to help it along.

"We eat okay here. Got a cow but she's dried up right

now. Got a bit of garden. Get supplies when Joe feels like sending a wagon in to the nearest settlement. By the way, name's Lucille, Lucille Claire Randall. These here are Alice and Carrie, boys are Gerald and Nathaniel—Gerry and Nat." The woman is still talking all in a rush. The girls rush forward and grab at the food before even sitting down.

"Name's Annie," she says, and leaves it at that. The door opens and the boys explode in, hit the table, grab two biscuits each, fight over the jam jar, and sit down, still talking about who got to unsaddle the horse, and who dropped the saddle in the mud. The girls, meanwhile, have finally gotten over their staring and begin to ask questions she isn't sure how to answer. Lucille ignores it all, not seeming to notice the noise. The jam jar goes flying off the table and someone spills a glass of milk and Annie thinks desperately of how quiet it was riding through the mountains. She tries to eat, waves her hand to keep off the flies.

"Well, c'mon," snaps Lucille. "If you're gonna be earning your keep, we'd better get a move on. You kids clean up now and mind each other."

She leads the way back outside, into the sun, and down to the barn, where two horses are standing in stalls beside Duster, exchanging snorts and little squeals.

"Take the grey mare," says Lucille, and saddles a tall lanky bay gelding. Annie is still trying to get used to how fast Lucille moves. Lucille is out the door while Annie is still doing up the cinch on the grey. Outside, her head feels numb. Her eyes water in the bright sun. The grey feels strange under her, and the landscape tilts away, spilling down the raw hills. They ride down the slope through a scattering of cattle, splattered like bright multicoloured seeds over the golden grass, into the next draw and over that and on. Annie follows the woman.

Maybe Lucille is crazy too, she thinks. Maybe she's somehow ridden into a valley of crazy people, something in the air and water. She should leave now, head for the jagged blue line on the horizon and take her chances. Maybe she should have just stayed in the tranquil mountain valley, anywhere but here, with an aching head and sleepy eyes, following this crazy woman around.

For the rest of the day, they ride up and down the hills and draws, their horses puffing and dark with sweat and foam, finding small bunches of cows and herding them together in a bigger and bigger clump. The grey knows her job, and Annie remembers what she learned on the farm about herding cattle. But these cows are different than farm cows. They come in many colours, brindled and patched in white and red and black. They have long sharp horns and a ridge of bone along their backs from which their bony ribs swell into prominence. They run like racehorses and bellow to the sky their anguish at being caught. They spook and startle when she least expects it. Her Dad always said cows were the stupidest bloody animals on earth except for sheep; these cows are not only stupid but jumpy, taking offense at the slightest wrong move on her part.

Dust seams the lines of Lucille's face, dust coats Annie's

already sweat-soaked shirt, and blackens the lines of foam on the horses. Annie tries to find chances to rest the mare, who pants and heaves but is still willing. Lucille's face is set and grim. She hasn't said a word to Annie all day except to grunt or nod to show her which direction to take.

"Okay, push'em on, eh?" Lucille says finally, and rides to the front of the small herd they've collected, leaving Annie to puzzle out that Lucille means her to take up the rear and collect any stragglers trying to sneak away into the brush. Finally, they leave the cattle grazing on the flats below the house with the others.

It's dark by the time they get back to the house. The kids are in the loft asleep. The house is a chaos of food and unwashed dishes. Lucille slices bacon and bread and heats the beans and coffee from the morning, while Annie sags onto the nearest chair.

"Here, take the lantern and get on down to the creek." Lucille snarls, and hands her a piece of soap and a torn cloth rag. "Wash yourself. You smell as bad as them cowboys. Here's a clean shirt and an old pair of pants."

The water in the creek is so cold it burns Annie's face and hair. She strips completely in the dark and washes herself all over, and puts on the clean dry clothes. Then she takes her shirt and soaps and rinses it and hangs it on a tree branch. When she gets back to the house, Lucille is asleep in a chair, snoring slightly. An empty plate sits in front of her and a full one sits in front of the chair Annie was sitting on.

In the lamplight, Lucille's face is cadaverous, sunken, and etched with lines and craters full of darkness. The corners of her mouth stretch down into bitterness. The world outside is silent. Annie sits on and on in the silence. A mouse scratches in the corner and the fire pops and murmurs to itself. She falls asleep there, stretched out in the chair, beside Lucille, then wakes in the night and makes herself a bed of sorts in the corner. She wakes in the morning to Nat's chubby dirty face, six inches from hers, peering into her face to see if she's awake.

TEN

IT'S SNOWING, SNOWING, SNOWING, dreary flakes from a splintered grey sky. Annie stares out the open door of the small shed she's moved into. Lucille has built a rough pole bed in the corner, and sewed together an old blanket stuffed with grass for a mattress. She also made a sort of stove out of sheets of tin hammered together. It works if Annie sits close enough and stuffs it with splintered chips of dry wood, but it smokes, and she spends half her time sitting over the stove shivering and the other half hanging out the door, breathing the freezing air.

She watches the snow fall in monotonous melancholy patterns. Occasionally the wind swirls it sideways in little dancing coils, but mostly it streams by in long ribbons, driven by a wind that feels as if it could slice flesh like a razor blade.

There's nothing for her to do. Duster is out there, somewhere in the snow with Lucille's other horses, sheltering in the willow breaks, grazing on the long slough grass along with the cattle they rounded up. Black Dog lies at her feet. He seems determined to sleep the winter away. Annie wishes she could do the same. While it's snowing, she has too much time on her hands, too much time to think and dream and fret. Once the snow quits, Lucille will think of something for her to do. Lucille can always think of something to do.

Annie hunches over, squatting on her heels, with her arms around her legs, rocking back and forth, shivering and dreaming.

She could go over to the house and visit with Lucille and the kids. They'd be glad to see her. At least, the kids are always glad to see her. It's taken her time to sort out how to treat them. At first, they immediately adopted her as some kind of long lost big sister, not letting her out of their collective sight. Annie tried to be nice, but the more attention she gave them, the more they went after her. They were like little starving hungry animals, and she was their prey. Desperately, she began to try and avoid them but that didn't work either. There weren't enough places to hide around the homestead. Finally, she began treating them as Lucille did, which meant mostly ignoring them and that helped. Either that, or the novelty wore off and she became simply part of the background with which they lived.

They were impressed by Black Dog and adopted him too until he took to snarling under his breath and hiding under the house. Nat kept calling him "my black dog," and dragging him around by the fur when he could catch him or sliding his leg over Black Dog's back, squealing, "go horse, go horse," as Black Dog slunk away, and tried to hide again under the house.

But even so, if she goes over there now, it'll be a circus. The boys will pull her hair and climb on her shoulders and slide down her legs. The girls are always after her to tell them stories, draw them pictures, sing them songs, or take them for walks even in the freezing cold. Now that it's snowing the kids are even more restless than usual, stuck in the house. Despite its tiny size, each of them has managed to stake out a corner of the house where they keep what few possessions they have, regarded as precious, fanatically guarded, the cause of major wars. The girls have two homemade dolls with fantastic clothing braided and knotted out of scraps of torn cloth, and strange, wonderful histories. The boys have an assortment of what seem like mostly sticks, but which serve as horses, guns, cows, cowboys, or Indians, depending on what game they are playing.

The children puzzle and amaze Annie. She remembers her mother's lectures about washing before dinner and manners for company. Lucille doesn't seem to have any rules for her kids. Sometimes they don't seem like kids at all, more like wild deer or goats, running and screaming and fighting, falling in the river or climbing the cliffs behind the house. Weather never bothers them. Annie has seen the boys outside, barefoot, wrestling with each other, red-faced and yelling in the snow. The girls take their dolls everywhere and hold long conversations with them. Sometimes they look puzzled, waking up from these conversations, as if uncertain about which world they are actually living in.

Sometimes, Annie's afraid of them, like a pack of small wild animals who could turn on her at any second and eat her alive just by pulling and pushing and pinching at her until there's nothing left. Often she thinks that Lucille isn't doing them any service, letting them drag themselves up on their own in such isolation.

At least she has the cabin to escape to. But right now, she knows they're sitting in the house, waiting for her, waiting to pounce.

It's a strange outfit. Annie hasn't wanted to ask questions and Lucille has ventured very little information, other than that her husband's dead and the rest of her family is back East somewhere. She doesn't talk much. And she doesn't ask Annie questions either. The other thing she doesn't understand is Lucille's feud, or whatever it is, with Joe Littlefoot.

She and Annie have spent the past several weeks mostly on horseback, riding out daily to bring any strayed or drifted cows they can find down from the hills to pasture on the flats for the winter. Lucille seems determined to find every last head. She complains that if she doesn't, Joe will add them to his herd in the spring, branding the new calves as his own.

When they come home, Annie falls off her exhausted horse, barely able to find strength to feed and water it, but Lucille finds time to feed the cow, make supper, haul water, even work in the garden, bringing in the last bits of produce to store for the winter.

Lucille works like a driven person, Annie thinks. But she also seems to have a bit of money stashed away. The wagon from the outfit to the north, Joe Littlefoot's outfit, just stopped on its month-long journey to and from the settlement, bringing in supplies, grain, newspapers, and tools. Annie hasn't seen Joe Littlefoot again. The boy who drove the wagon was shy, but had a few sticks of peppermint tucked away for the kids. He stayed for dinner, but didn't talk, just ate an astounding and annoying amount of food then scuttled out of the house and left. After he was gone, Lucille cursed how much money it cost, how Joe was determined to squeeze her out, take her cattle, take her land. She ranted while Annie stared. Finally Lucille seemed to calm down and forget about it.

Annie figures they have close to three hundred head of cattle gathered in. Lucille has two other horses as well, a mare in foal, and a two-year-old stud. Duster's happy to be with other horses again. In the brief moments when they haven't been on round-up, Lucille has found lots of other work for her, sending her to drag in downed trees and cut them up with a Swede saw for firewood, or for poles to patch the corrals, or out with a scythe to cut grass for hay against the time when the milk cow decides to calve. Not a word has been mentioned about pay, but Lucille feeds them all well. They supplement the supplies with fish the kids catch from the river, with potatoes, onions, beets and carrots from the garden, and with occasional fresh beef or venison.

Maybe this afternoon she should go and visit. They'll be wondering what has happened to her. They'll think she's mad at them or stuck up if she stays out here too long. The snow is coming down with finality. It's going to stick hard this time and stay, cover the ground, layer upon layer of it. The day is half dark although it's only afternoon. Annie doesn't know about the winter here, what it might bring. The snow makes her feel suffocated, closed in. She pictures it mounding, growing, shutting them away here together until spring. This was probably why Lucille was in such a big panic about grass for the cattle and wood for the house, even though it didn't seem such a big deal to Annie.

There's a sharp bang on the door of the other cabin; the door to Annie's cabin springs open and Lucille marches in, bringing swirls of snow with her, carrying a stack of old newspapers and the chipped enamel bowl which does duty for everything from washing kids to holding potato peels.

"Meant to do this earlier," she announces. "Here," and she hands Annie the bowl. "This here's paste. Put these papers over the wall. It ain't much but it'll help. You warm enough? C'mon over to the house later," and she vanishes out the door.

Annie stares after her, her mouth twisted. The woman could be just a little more civil. Resignedly, Annie slaps the paste on the wall and smoothes the paper over it. She stops to read now and again so it takes her a while. The end result looks pretty much like newspaper glued on four rough board walls. Maybe she can hang some old blankets over it for extra warmth. Maybe some pictures or something would help. She doesn't know much about fixing up houses. Her Mom could probably have done something, somehow, to make it feel more like a place to live in. Her saddle hangs over the rafters and her rifle hangs in a scabbard beside it. Her saddle blanket is on the bed and Lucille has slung an old cowhide on the floor.

It's getting colder. Annie can feel the chill creep up through her feet. It's dark outside. She opens the door and trudges through the falling snow to the other house. The snow is already getting deep. She stands outside and looks down to where the river should be, and beyond, into the blackness where flecks of snow flicker, catching bits of lamplight and throwing them back.

Somewhere out there is her valley, the lake, the flickering trout, the sandy beach, the bramble bushes bending under their own weight. The beach will be white now, without tracks. The cottonwood trees will lean out over the black water. The lake is probably frozen solid. Her and Black Dog's raft will still be there, stuck in the reeds or frozen into the sand. She could go back there sometime, maybe in the spring. They had a time of it, the three of them, playing, swimming. Being lazy. She'd just as soon be there, she thinks, instead of stuck here with this surly woman and her too-friendly kids.

She sighs and opens the door. The minute she's inside they grab her and pull her towards the table. "Look," they all holler at once. "Look what we made," and she sees they've been carving a few scraggly, half-ripe pumpkins into odd shapes, cutting faces in them. Lucille is cutting up another pumpkin and slicing it into a pot.

"Want tea?" she yells over the din, and doesn't wait for Annie's reply, but pours the tea, and then more tea for the boys, who put too much sugar in it and then promptly spill it on the floor, where it runs through the cracks between the planks and disappears.

Annie moves to a corner, where she can watch the door and the room. She tucks her feet under her on the chair and curls her arms around her legs.

"Soon as it stops snowing, we'll ride out. Check them critters for drifting…shouldn't go far. Lots of feed in them flats for a month or so, anyway," says Lucille.

"Might be hard to find the horses…" Annie ventures.

"Nah," snorts Lucille. "Be holed up below here…river stays open, warm springs probably, lots of grass."

Lucille stirs onions and beef into the boiling stew, slaps flour and lard together, mixes and rolls it out, sticks the biscuits in the oven, stoops to break up another fight between the boys, smacks them both and sends them howling into Annie's corner, fills the kettle, and ducks out the door for wood. Annie huddles in the corner, feeling useless and slow. The boys play catch-me around and around her chair, poking their fingers into her ribs and pulling her braids.

When Lucille comes back in, she says, "Got anything you need me to do?"

Lucille looks at her. "Jeezus," she says. "Ain't you a bear for work. Figured you'd be glad for the rest." She pauses, says awkwardly, "You know, that was okay, what you did, helping me out like that with all them stupid, ornery, spooky cows. Lotta work. Didn't think you'd be able to keep up, but you did okay."

Outside, the wind rolls down the hill and smacks at the little house, which crouches and shudders under the impact. Lucille stops, stares at the door, listening.

"Goddamn," she says, and her voice twangs like a string pulled tight. "I hate that bloody wind."

"Yeah, sometimes it sounds like there's voices in it," says Annie. "My Mom used to tell us ghost stories on nights like this. We'd be scared to go to bed, but she'd come and tuck us in, then we'd feel okay."

"To hell with ghosts. No ghosts around here," says Lucille roughly. "Not enough people to make ghosts. Takes people to make ghosts or be scared of them…might be animal ghosts, Indian ghosts…listen, I been thinking, come spring we might build ourselves a corral down there on them flats, for branding and such. Might come in handy. And I been figuring on putting in a bigger garden, maybe a corn patch or something. But I'd need a plow and team. Your horse pull a plow?"

"Well, he ain't yet," says Annie, "but…"

"And you know what else?" Lucille goes on. "I got to get some kind of school going for these damn kids…you know anything about teaching school?"

"Well no," says Annie, "I mean, I can read and write and do figures…"

"That Joe Littlefoot…that little cock-eyed pip-squeak runt, that two-bit sawed-off excuse for a cowhand, had the nerve to ask me last time I saw him, which is when he was riding over my damn place looking at my damn cows, what the hell I thought I was doing out here on the edge of no place in particular with a bunch of kids and a few lousy wild cows." Lucille sails on, words tumbling out like water with no particular direction to take.

"What the hell did he think I was doing…not my fault my man up and gets himself lost…could be starving back home, living with relatives, living on charity." She laughs and her laugh is like glass breaking.

"What do you think? Do you think they're all right, I mean, like other regular kids and all? I ain't seen other kids for a while, so it's hard to tell. We could have us a real school here, maybe a few hours a week, what do you think, get some books or something. Maybe they got some back at that settlement where we get supplies. What else do they need, slates maybe, paper?"

"But when will the wagon go in again?" Annie interjects. "Can't hardly drive it in the snow."

"Oh yeah, you're right," says Lucille, looking surprised. "Damn, we'll have to wait… should have started this last fall, maybe, next shipment in the spring, I should send the kids back East, see their grandparents, go to school. What do you think?"

Annie thinks about school. Mostly what she remembers are long hours spent looking out the window, the grey curtains of boredom that cobwebbed the hours until she could get home to Duster. She thinks about Lucille's wild curly-headed ragged whirling children in such a place.

"Be a long way from home," she says cautiously. "They might not fit in too good. They seem to like it here."

"Yeah, I guess it's home now, such as it is. It ain't much, but it's mine. Mine. Imagine that. My place. My house. My cows. My table. My kids. Now why the hell would I give that up to get married again."

"Married?" Annie asks. This is a word that somehow doesn't fit much with Lucille.

"Yeah, Joe asked me one time should I marry him. Says we could build a cattle empire together. An empire. You see me as a goddammed empress? I don't want no empire, just what's mine, a place to set down in and put my feet up once in a while. See, we wandered a while, Mike and I. He was always looking for something. He missed the old country, Ireland. That was home to him. Not here. But here he landed and here he stayed. Now that damn Joe want it, wants what's mine. Well, he ain't getting it." Lucille gets up, goes to the door, opens it and looks out, bangs it shut again.

"Goddamn," she says. "I hate nights like this. I feel shut in. I get edgy. Girls!" she hollers suddenly. "Come here and help clean up this mess. Let's have some supper and after supper, we'll find a deck of cards, eh? Teach you all a little poker."

She winks at Annie. "You play poker?" she says. "No? Then it's about time you learned. Next time you come across a bunch of cowboys, at least you'll know what to do."

"He locked me in," says Annie.

"What?" Lucille turns and looks at her, suddenly paying attention.

"Joe. He locked me in that stinking cabin all night. I slept on the table. Only reason I didn't suffocate was all the holes in the roof. Said something about not disturbing his boys, or interfering with the work or some damn thing. I don't know what he was on about."

"His boys. Ah, the man's a jackass. A bunch of jackasses, the whole pack of them. Joe's got this twisted kind of religion. Don't worry about it. You can ride and herd cows, same as them. That's what counts."

"I'd like to shoot his goddamned head off," says Annie fiercely, suddenly, the words bursting out of her as if they've been contained too long.

"I couldn't stand that, being locked up, walls....I wanted to crash through them. No air. I'll get him back someday. Somehow."

"Yeah, well, stand in line, girl, stand in line. Look, forget it, let's eat and play cards and shut out the wind. But hey, don't shoot him, just in case I decide to marry and get to be empress of this whole shebang. Now wouldn't that be a laugh and a half. Guess I'd have to get me a gold-plated saddle to chase those ornery cows in. Then just my luck, I'd get caught in a blizzard like the old man. C'mon, supper, enough of this horse-hooey."

"Kids," Lucille bawls, "food." The four of them slide down the ladder from the loft and attack the food while Lucille is trying to get it on the table.

"Hey, slow down, we got company, remember. You kids are like damn bear cubs or something," and she cuffs at the boys, who duck, with the ease of long practice and shove each other. Alice, blond and taller than Carrie, who is dark and short, slides in beside Annie.

"I'm sitting beside her," she announces. Carrie's face turns crimson and her lip comes out.

"You always get to sit with her," she wails. "It's my turn, Ma said, and I'm sitting there!" With a wild scream, she launches herself sideways at Alice, who has already filled her plate and continues eating, immovable.

Annie grabs Carrie and swings her over to the empty chair on the other side of her. "Now, see, you're both beside me," but Carrie simply sits and weeps and glares at her sister, until hunger takes over and she too begins to eat. Lucille has prepared a feast, enough for a small army. They eat white beans boiled with onions, fried potatoes and biscuits, and the pumpkin stew. Annie is always astonished at how much food Lucille cooks and how quickly it disappears. Black Dog lies contentedly under the table, licking up the hail of food scraps dropped from the kids' plates.

After supper, they all help with the dishes, and then play cards. It gets later and icy rivers of cold creep in around their ankles. Lucille stokes the stove until it glows red but still the ones sitting on the far side of the table by the wall shiver and find excuses to go warm up by the stove. The wind toys viciously with the house, slamming at it from different directions. Snow sifts under the crack by the front door.

"You'd better sleep in here tonight," says Lucille. "You'll freeze in that shack. Got a norther coming. It'll last a while. You can curl up with the girls or crawl in with me."

Annie says nothing. Her cheeks burn. She has nothing to sleep in, no nightgown, not even underwear. Mostly she sleeps naked or in the clothes she has. Lucille has given her a couple of old shirts and a pair of canvas pants.

"Well, don't make me no never mind what you do. Suit yourself if you'd rather be alone. I know it gets kinda wild

and crazy in here. You got something warm to sleep in?"
Annie shakes her head.

"Well, there's an old shift of mine I'll find you. Guess
you'll be okay but if you get cold, you come back over
here."

Annie thanks her, takes the shift, shrugs on her coat,
and hugs the kids goodnight. As she ducks out the door,
she gasps for breath, sinking into the cold like sinking into
freezing water. The snow has piled up and her earlier footsteps have already disappeared. She makes it back to the
cabin, lights the lantern, re-lights her fire, crawls out of
her clothes, into the nightgown, and into her freezing bed.

When she closes her eyes, she can still see Lucille, tall
and thin, her forearms corded with muscle, her brown hair
pulled back in a knot from her tanned lined face. How old
is she? She said once she had her first baby at 16, same age
as Annie is now. And Alice is nine or ten. So she is 25 or
26. She isn't much like any other woman Annie has known.
Lucille seems to expect her, Annie, to be as tough and strong
and capable as she is. She doesn't lecture or preach. She
just accepts that Annie is like her, running her own life.
And Joe Littlefoot wanted to marry her. What a joke.
Lucille would never marry anyone. There probably isn't
much she can't do by herself. And those kids. They're kind
of fun sometimes. They had a good time tonight. Annie
smiles. Maybe in the spring they will start a school. She
and Lucille could make good partners.

Lucille. She's survived out here, on her own. She manages. She doesn't ask for help and she's managed to make a home for them all. So it can be done. Annie feels safer, somehow, and reassured, thinking about Lucille. At least, if Lucille is crazy, it's a worthwhile craziness, one Annie can learn from, even share.

She sighs and curls her feet up under her and shivers until her teeth clatter. Finally, she gets up, pulls her clothes on over the shift, pulls the blankets off the bed, wraps them around her and sits on a wooden box, hunched over, as close to the stove as she can. She warms up enough to sleep, but every hour or so the cold wakes her and she stuffs the stove with more wood and then goes back to sleep. In the morning, her back aches. Snow has sifted in through cracks in the walls and lies in little heaps and drifts on the floor.

ELEVEN

COLD. ANNIE HAS DECIDED SHE HATES COLD. And she hates this goddamn ranch and these crazy kids and their crazy mother. She never seems to get warm anymore. Her hands ache and burn, are sore and cracked and bleed when she chops wood.

After the first blizzard ended, Lucille established an iron regime of work for them. Ride out and check the cows for drifting. Cut more wood. Cut more fence poles. When she can't think of anything else for Annie to do, she sets her to playing teacher with the kids, using charcoal and newspaper to write on. Lucille tried to teach Annie to cook and sew, but without much success.

And now, suddenly, with nothing but a muttered explanation, Lucille has taken off and left Annie with the kids, the chores, the fire, and the responsibility for keeping it all intact.

Annie growls in her throat. Lucille's been gone two damn days now. She had decided, she said, that they needed some more supplies, or tools, or something. She wasn't very clear about where she was going or why. She said she was going to see if Joe Littlefoot's crew was going to try and make another trip out. But Annie can't see that they're all that short of anything. Maybe, Annie thinks, Lucille was just restless. Despite Lucille's efforts to keep them all working, there wasn't really that much to do. Too much snow, too much cold. The cattle seem to find food on their own. Duster, when she tracks him down, snorts and pretends he's a wild horse, a shaggy bundle of hair peering out at her from the gloomy light under the cottonwood trees.

She mutters to herself and goes to the door. It's not snowing at the moment, but the sky is a sleek pale grey, and the country is washed clean of colour. The bluffs behind the house have faded in the pale light to shades of buff and dingy yellow; the cottonwoods are black statues, and beyond them the valley ripples into fingers of pale lavender, blue and black. The mountains are hidden in grey haze.

The kids are sliding on an old steer hide, yelling and screaming, but for once, not fighting. Black Dog bounces and barks beside them. Annie has stayed inside to cook and try and wash out some clothes. By the time she gets them hung outside, they're frozen stiff. By the time she gets back inside from hanging out laundry, the biscuits have burned. She can't get the hang of the Dutch oven on top of the stove. It's either too hot or not hot at all. She's always forgetting to put wood in the stove, and then having to chop wood in splinters to relight it. The stove is small and balky, and either burns red hot or goes out.

The kids whine at her cooking. Her stew is lumpy with clots of flour. Her beans taste burnt. They complain that she doesn't cook anything they like. Little Nat's face seems pale and he's whining more than usual. Last night he went to bed with a stomach ache after refusing to eat. She's run out of stories and games. She feels trapped and desperate with the strain of keeping them all fed and amused and warm.

She stands at the door and strains her eyes. Damn Lucille anyway. She didn't even ask if Annie could manage, or if she wanted to look after four whiny kids, didn't ask anything, just rode away on her big bay horse, while the kids stood silently looking after her.

What if she gets lost, or hurt, or something? Anything could happen. What if Joe kidnaps her? Annie looks at the tiny enclosed space behind her, the messy smoky cabin, the cracks between the floorboards, the piled accumulation of clothes and bedding and dirty dishes and riding gear. Lucille has lived here for four years, one year with her husband and three without. The kids can remember when they lived near other families, other kids. They have talked a bit, wistfully, to Annie about that other life, about friends they miss and relatives they still remember. But they don't remember much. They seem to have patiently accepted their life.

Annie shudders and turns back to the house. The floor is grimy with spilled food, and a new batch of dishes has accumulated from her attempts to cook. There is no water left. She will have to make the long hike down to the river, again. And they need more wood, again. She's beginning to see where Lucille's constant strain and worry comes from.

An ear-piercing scream comes from outside, down the hill. Annie makes it to the door and outside in one jump and is running down the hill before she even thinks about it. She hits the patch of ice where the kids have been sliding and half slides, half runs, stumbling and wind-milling her arms, to the bottom of the hill, where three disconsolate figures stand around a small fourth, sprawled on the snow. She can't see any blood.

She bends over him. Should she pick him up? Look him over first? He opens one small blue eye, shrieks, "He pushed me, Gerald pushed me, you pushed me," and heaves himself to his feet, apparently intent on killing his brother. Annie grabs him.

"That's enough. In the house. Time for supper." But Nat pushes her away. "Mooooommmmmmmy," he screams, all the way home, over and over, as she carries him up the hill, twisting and pushing at her with small frantic hands until she almost drops him. "Moommmy...I want my Mooommmmy, you're not my moommmy..."

She makes it to the house, and then she does drop him on the floor; he scuttles away backwards into the corner and proceeds to howl, in a dull monotone, for his Mommy. The other kids come in, throw their outdoor clothes in the corner, munch dispiritedly on the food, and then the girls retreat to the loft. Only Gerald hangs around, looking at her curiously.

"My mom is better than you," he announces. "She makes pies sometimes. How come you don't make pies? Are you like an Indian? My Mom likes Indians. She says they do what they want. She says they're tough. I'm tough. Nat's just a baby. What is tough, anyway?"

"Well, being able to look after yourself, I guess."

"Ma says we're tough. She says when I grow up, I'll be rich and I can live here and have a thousand cows. My Grandma and Grandpa were rich. I think they were anyway. They had a big house."

"Where do they live?"

"Dunno," says Gerald, losing interest. "Is Duster your horse? Did someone give him to you? How come you have a gun? Can I shoot it? Joe Littlefoot has a gun. He let me hold it once. He shot a deer. I'm hungry. Is there anything else to eat?"

Annie silently hands him the leftover biscuits and a pot of jam. That night, she curls up in Lucille's bed, in one of Lucille's big shirts, and listens to the wind hunt and snuff around the corners of the house. She dozes off, having made a decision that she is definitely never going to get married and have kids. Waking, she hears Black Dog barking and then voices in the yard. Before she can get up, the door opens and Lucille comes in, followed by Joe.

"Shhh," Lucille says, and giggles. Annie sits up, hastily pulling on pants, but neither of them pays much attention to her. She slides down the ladder, to be met by a jovial Lucille and a sullen Joe. Annie can smell whiskey fumes radiating from both of them.

"How're all m'babies?" Lucille whispers loudly. "C'mon smile, don't look so damn crabby. It's Christmas, fer Chrissakes. Didn't you ever have Christmas. Hey! Look what we got. Joe sold some of them ornery four-legged cross-eyed critters of mine way last fall, and looky here, we got stuff 'till hell won't have it."

Annie pokes some wood into the dying fire and puts water on to boil. She tries to smile, but all she can think of is that she still wants to kill Joe Littlefoot and here's Lucille, smiling and laughing like the man was not their mutually agreed upon worst enemy. What is he doing here?

Joe has set a wooden crate on the table and is opening it with a screech of nails and splintering boards. He seems to be taking a long time at it. Both he and Lucille seem clumsy and stupid, stumbling over things and laughing like idiots, but trying to muffle it so as not to wake the kids.

Annie stands, frozen still like an alert hare, by the stove. Joe sees her, finally, and sticks out his hand.

"Howdy, ma'am. How ya'll doing." She touches his hand with the tips of her fingers and nods. He and Lucille look at each other and laugh some more. Joe returns to the box and lifts out slates and chalk, books, two porcelain dolls, two wooden toy guns, candy, socks, heavy boots, long underwear, a toy ball, and a few tiny bags of frozen dried fruit. From another box come extra supplies of food.

"C'mon, let's get them kids up," he whispers. "I wanta see their sweet little faces." But Lucille won't hear of it. She's calming down now, coming back to her more recognizable self, stoking up the fire, making tea, and arranging the kids' presents in a corner by the stove. One of the brown paper parcels has Annie's name on it.

Annie shivers in her bare feet and Lucille notices.

"You, girl, get back into bed before you freeze. Joe, you go sleep out in that shed," she snaps. "I'll call you first thing in the morning, soon as the kids wake up." Joe disappears meekly, and Lucille undresses, slips on a shift. "C'mon girl," she snaps again. "Get into that bed. I ain't going to bite." Awkwardly, Annie undresses again and climbs into bed beside Lucille, who sighs deeply, exhaling a cloud of sour-smelling breath.

"Good to get home," she says. "How was it. You have any trouble?"

"It was fine," says Annie, stiffly. She lies on her edge of the bed, carefully not touching Lucille. "Nat like to had a fit, missing you."

"Yeah, he would," says Lucille. Her voice softens. "How about them others? They give you any trouble?"

"Well, they didn't like my cooking much."

Lucille laughs.

"I'm sorry I didn't tell you," she says shyly. "I wanted things to be a surprise, even for you, seeing as how you don't have your own family to make Christmas with."

Annie sighs. She hates the smell of whiskey. Her parents never drank, and wouldn't have alcohol in the house. When she was little, she thought only wicked people drank. But on the trip west, lots of the men drank whiskey and rum. No one noticed. It was a regular part of life.

"Well, good night," says Lucille, and yawns and sighs deeply and wriggles her body into a more comfortable hollow in the flat hard mattress. She tucks her feet in next to Annie's legs, and wriggles the rest of her body in closer to Annie's warmth.

Annie lies without moving, looking at Lucille's long dark braid of hair on the pillow. Reflections from the fire dance in tiny flickers over the ceiling. She smells the combined smells of Lucille: horses, sweat, soap, and something underneath, something warm and musky which she figures must be Lucille herself. Outside the wind mutters and drones. Maybe if they're lucky, Joe will freeze to death in the shed. She almost feels sorry for him.

Lucille's breath sounds like she's asleep. Shyly, Annie reaches and tucks the covers a little higher over Lucille's broad shoulders. But Lucille reaches and pats her hand.

"Thanks, Annie," she mutters, drowsily. "You're a good kid."

Annie lies back in the dark. It's just too damn hard to

LUANNE ARMSTRONG

stay mad at Lucille, crazy or not. She curls her body next to Lucille's warm breathing and drifts off. Sometime in the night, she turns, so her and Lucille lie cupped together, warm and safe, like two spoons in a drawer, and she wakes and sleeps again, safe.

The next morning is pandemonium, but with a happy edge to it. Even Joe manages to smile a few times through his sullenness. The package for Annie is a set of long underwear, rough and woolen and itchy, but warm, very warm. She thanks them both. Joe nods. Lucille demands she model it for them, but Annie shakes her head.

Joe only stays long enough to drink coffee and watch the kids, who are so excited they fight over everything, burst into tears and screams, but then forget what they're fighting about in their excitement over the next new thing. Finally, abruptly he leaves, rides his big horse up from the barn and past the house without a backward glance. Annie and Lucille watch him leave.

"That man is crazy," Lucille says, staring after. "You know, the whole thing was his damn idea. Because he feels sorry for me. It won't stop him trying to steal my cows or my outfit. As far as he's concerned, I don't belong here and I never will. Bastard!" she flings after him and then marches back in the house to make them all an extra large dinner, even if it is only a gussied-up version of the usual beef stew, biscuits, beans, and a few candies to round out the day.

TWELVE

ANNIE IS SAWING WOOD WITH THE SWEDE SAW. The snow squelches under her feet and the icicles on the roof drip steadily. She straightens up. Her back hurts; her hands hurt. After she saws the wood, she'll have to split it, stack it, carry it in and, after it's burned, carry out the ashes. The saw is dull. Neither she nor Lucille can figure out how to sharpen it properly, and their efforts have only made it worse.

The morning sky has lightened to a faint pale blue, after days, weeks, months of varying shades of grey. She slicks her hair back off her head. Her scalp itches. It's hard to carry enough water for cooking and ordinary activities. Extra water has to be carried for bathing. They manage to heat up enough water once a week to bathe the kids, but laundry and baths for her and Lucille happen less often.

She searches the river flats below her for signs of the horses. Lately, they've been staying close to the house as if something has spooked them. She's been riding out every three or four days, restless, finding excuses to check the cows. Spring has got to come sometime, although all she can see ahead of her right now is more endless days of cutting wood and carrying water and trying to keep warm.

She returns to the wood and the saw screeches and catches its teeth on the wood. Furious, Annie flings it across the yard. "Goddamn," she swears out loud, and then looks around. Her mother always told her not to swear, and even Lucille never swears around the kids. But they're all in the house, driving each other nuts with boredom, picking fights as an excuse to pass the time. Annie's mother isn't here, won't ever be here. There's just her and Lucille and this freezing grey country which doesn't give a goddamn about their puny efforts to wrestle some kind of living from it.

She stoops to pick up a block of wood to put on the stack and it slips, catching her cold, cracked split fingers in a vice of sharp wood. Now her hand hurts even more, not enough to yell about, just enough to add to the dull ache in her shoulders and back. She looks at the length of jackpine she was sawing and the pile of jackpines she dragged with Duster a week ago. She should finish it. If she doesn't, Lucille won't say a word. She'll just do it her-self, faster and quicker than Annie could. Then every block of wood they burn will be a silent reproach. And Lucille will snap at the kids for being lazy and never finishing anything.

Damn, damn, damn. She's not Lucille's hired hand and Lucille isn't her boss, or her mother or anything else to her that matters. She's done enough helping out to pay for whatever she's eaten. This is just a place to survive the winter. She's riding on through, on her way somewhere, and she's leaving here just as soon as there's a single patch of bare ground. This isn't her home. Why is she sweating and breaking her back for Lucille's cows and Lucille's kids and Lucille's future? She won't even be around long enough to watch this spring's batch of calves grow up.

To hell with the wood. Lucille's been staying in the house lately, interminably cooking and sewing and trying to make the kids practice the letters Annie has shown them. When she comes outside, it's to give Annie more orders or to talk about work she's thinking of doing in the spring.

Last fall, when they spent hours riding through the breaks together after cows, they didn't talk much either, but at least they shared something, the same problems, the same sweaty dusty stinking air and sore legs. Then at Christmas, they had a good time with the kids, playing, even made taffy candy. But now Lucille is acting normal, like her mother, like anyone's mother, snappish and crabby and worried. She's even trying to make the kids learn manners, as if anyone could teach that bunch of wild-eyed monsters anything.

Annie goes and picks up the saw, hangs it on the log, and heads for the barn and a halter. She can always say she went riding to check the cows. But right now, all she wants is to get away from this place, from the same dull round of work, these grey sad shacks stuck on this hill, and from going in the house to a crabby Lucille and the bored, pale-faced kids.

It takes her a while, wading through drifts, but once she's found and saddled Duster and they're out of sight of the house, she starts to feel easier. Where the wind has blown the ground bare of snow, she lifts Duster into a trot and they head upwards, away from the cows and into the hills, into the grey blue distance she's been staring at all morning.

They climb steadily. After a couple of hours, she realizes she's into new country, higher than where she and Lucille have ranged looking for cows. These hills lift towards even steeper hills and the trees thicken. They change from jackpine and juniper to low fir and spruce. Duster sweats from the steady climbing in his heavy winter coat, but his pace doesn't slacken. She stops, finally, to let him breath and looks around.

She is at the top of a small steep valley. Ahead of her, the hills gather together around a small jagged peak, like a steep tooth gashing the grey skinned clouds. She stares at it for a long while.

She ties Duster loosely at the foot of the talus slope and begins to climb upwards. The soles of her boots are slick;

she has to watch for patches of ice on the rocks. She moves steadily upwards, sweating and panting, pulling herself up over the rocks, clambering over downed trees and through matted scrub brush. She climbs faster and faster. The top of the mountain recedes into mist. The last part is steep and slippery with drifted snow and she crawls over it on hands and knees. When she comes to the lumpy sharp ridge that slopes sharply to the peak, she stops and looks over.

Below her, the mountain drops away into empty air. Two ravens float, drifting, reflecting light from their obsidian feathers. She holds on to a rock until the mountain stops spinning and then crawls carefully upward, handhold to handhold, until she stands on top. Bits of mist, like torn tissue paper, drift past her. Below, soft waves of grey muffle the hillside. The rising wind hits her face. The cold sneaks inside her sweaty, damp clothes, and claws her skin. She begins to shiver but remains standing there.

Finally, slowly and carefully, she backs away from the edge to the safety of a large boulder. She sits down, her arms around her knees, her head on her arms. When she lifts her head again to stare out at the grey sky, she realizes that behind the white streaks is darkness.

And she's left Duster down there by himself.

She scrambles back down, from rock to rock, handhold to handhold. Her feet are freezing and numb. Her torn hands scrape the frozen granite. She slips and stumbles, and then her feet slide, her knee comes down on one point of rock and her elbow on another. She has to sit for a while. Her head spins and red angry points of pain dance in her vision but anger and fear for Duster forces her to her feet. She comes to a place she doesn't recognize. A cliff drops away below; she can't see bottom. She can't see much of anything. The light is almost completely gone. There's only a faint brightness along the western horizon, which disappears as she looks at it. She tries to find a way along the cliff, but one end is blocked by a wall of rock. The other slopes away. Rotten granite crumbles to sand and slides under her feet. She can't see what she's climbing into.

I could die here, she thinks. It would be easy. She clenches her teeth and tests each hold, moving slowly, but moving, until she's down and into the thick black of the trees. She can see the spaces between and she aims for them. She comes out, finally, onto the snow and grass, which shine for her in the starlight.

She's relieved to be down but cursing herself for a fool. Duster will be frantic and Lucille and the kids will be worried. She's been foolish again. She's always so stupid. Why doesn't she learn to be more careful?

But Duster is not frantic. He's not there, just a broken piece of rope hanging from a tree. The snow is trampled flat, except for one place where's he's lunged and pulled back, broken the rope, and taken off.

Something spooked him. Her scalp tightens and her back feels naked. Carefully, she looks around at what she can see. There are lumpy black shadows under every tree, clumps of shadow on every branch. Her rifle is at Lucille's, hanging on the wall in its scabbard, carefully cleaned and loaded and useless.

She shrugs. Whatever was here is probably gone. She starts walking, her feet numb, the walk home long and cold. After she's gone a couple of miles—checking behind her occasionally, seeing nothing, breathing easier when she's away from the trees—she starts to relax. But her back still crawls. Occasionally, she stands still, listening, her mouth open slightly, her breath whistling in her throat.

She hears the tiniest scrape of something on stone, a claw maybe, a faint snow crunch. She looks around. There are no trees worth climbing, and if it's a big cat, a tree is the last thing she needs. She can't see anything. She starts walking quickly, her feet crunching and squeaking in the frozen snow, her breath puffing white vapour in front of her.

Behind her, the snow crunches again. She whirls around. The moon is coming out from behind the cloud and the light reflects silver and lavender shadows on the snow. Her eyes focus. A wolf is standing looking at her. She looks back at him. He's about thirty feet away, just standing, looking. As she watches, he yawns and sits down, ears pricked, waiting. She almost laughs. He looks a bit like Black Dog, who is back at the house playing with the kids instead of out here, guarding her.

He also looks huge, half the size of Duster. His colour is hard to tell in the light, but he looks mostly grey and black, with a gold silver sheen from the moonlight. He stands, and fear snaps her spine straight. Then he turns around, sits again. She waits, frozen.

She says softly, desperately, "What do you want? Go away, get lost. Leave me alone." Her father always said animals wouldn't attack without a reason. He said what they wanted was food, and since people were usually around food, that's what they were after. He said wolves would follow people, but not to hurt them. "Ah, they're just curious," that's what he said.

But there were no wolves left in that part of the country. People had shot them all. So how did he know? And this is a mountain wolf.

"Go home," she says. "Just go home. Please go home. Find something else to chase. Leave me be." Her voice sounds thin and foolish in her own ears. The wolf, ears pricked, keeps watching. Then he yawns.

The air is luminous between them. The wind whispers past her ears, curling bits of hair around her head. She could just stand here all night. Lucille will come and find her. As long as she watches him, he won't attack. She can hold him away, just with her eyes.

The wolf lies down, curling his tail around him and licking his paws. He looks bored. She feels ridiculous and tired and sleepy. She'd like to lie down too, on the cold ground, and lick her paws and smell the scents coming off the wind, listening for the sounds of her distant kin. She'd like to feel at home here too, where there is nothing to mark a home. She'd like to feel at home in the whole world. Her eyes burn from the wind and the dark. She's tired and it's late and Lucille is waiting. She turns and walks away. When she looks behind her, the wolf isn't there.

After hours of sore-footed trudging, she makes it to the yard. She comes up the hill half asleep, but she goes first to the barn. Duster is tied there, still eating. He's likely only been back for a short while, and Lucille will be really worried, probably thinking about coming to look for her. Annie stands for a moment outside in the yard. A lantern is hung by the front door of the house; it pours yellow lights towards her. She looks back to the moon-drenched mountains and thinks about the wolf. She can see him so clearly, lying in the snow, head up, sniffing the wind, free and alone. She steps quietly in the house.

Lucille is lifting a pot off the stove.

"Well, about goddamned time," she snaps. "We were worried sick, and then Duster come back. I figured something must have spooked him and he run off. I was just fixing to come look for you. Thought I'd have some food waiting." She thumps the pot onto the table, bangs a tin plate down beside it, and ladles out stew.

"You'd better eat. You must be damn near froze through. C'mon, sit down. Don't stand there like a bloody ghost." Lucille is even meaner than usual. She could have been at least a little glad to see her, Annie thinks. The heat from the stove begins to trickle through her clothes and she starts to shiver. At the back of her mind, the wolf is still there, watching.

Annie sits, eats, staring at her plate, not speaking, not looking at Lucille. Lucille slams some dishes into the enamel dishpan, pokes wood into the stove, goes outside, comes back in.

Finally, Annie speaks into the silence. "I went for a ride. Duster run off. He got spooked by a wolf."

Lucille doesn't say anything. Then she plunks her body into a chair across the table from Annie.

"All right," she says. "What the hell's going on? What's got you so riled? Ever since Christmas, you been edgy as hell…and then today, taking off like that, not telling anyone nothing. You got way more sense than that. I know you."

"I just went for a ride," says Annie, coldly. "Sorry I worried you. Guess I'll go to bed now," and she gets up to leave for the freezing cold shed.

"Annie," says Lucille. "I'm sorry, I got a hell of a temper, I guess. I'm just glad you're okay."

"Yeah?" says Annie, and her voice rises and tightens. "Are you now? Well, listen, thanks for the food, but I'm cold and tired and I don't know much of nothing right now, and I'm going to bed."

"Annie," says Lucille. There's a new tone in her voice that pulls Annie around. "You gotta talk to me. You gotta tell me what's going on. 'Cause I sure as hell can't figure it out."

Annie stares at her; a knot, a boil, a surge of heat loosens in her chest. "Me, tell *you* what's going on? Why don't you tell me? You're the one that's so goddamn moody, always yelling orders, never hello, or how are you, or I'm glad you're alive, just did you get the goddamn wood done?"

Annie is almost yelling now. "Maybe it has something to do with Joe. Maybe you're feeling lonely again or something. Maybe you need to go for another ride, or…or something."

"Joe?" Lucille sounds astonished. "How the hell did he get into this? And I ain't moody. I'm just fine…you're the one with all the goddam moods, never talking, just working all the time."

"Me…work? All you ever do is tell me what to do and how much more there is to do and then go and work your tail off so I have to try and keep up."

"I do not," says Lucille indignantly. "I don't do no such thing. Nobody's making you work like a grizzly bear was biting your rear except you. You always go around looking like a damn storm cloud is hanging over your head. I'm scared to say two words to you."

"Look…" says Lucille, her voice like saw teeth being filed. "I'm sorry. I'm no damn good at talking. I been here pretty well alone these past years, trying to keep it together and make a life for me and these kids. I've thought and thought about chucking it all, and going back east…it seems crazy to try and stay here. And sometimes I get so crazy lonely I don't even know if I'm thinking straight anymore. What if something goes wrong…if one of us gets sick or hurt? What if something happens to me? I know it's wrong to take chances with these kids. I feel so damn bad about them. And then I think about what it'd be like going back, cooped up somewhere, taking in washing or sewing to survive, or marrying some man just to put food on the table. It just never seems like I got any choice that makes sense. So I stay."

Annie doesn't say anything. She looks at Lucille's face, the bitter lines curving down from the corners of her mouth, her brown hair swept back from her forehead, her brown eyes, intense and shiny wet, now, staring at a corner where there's nothing to see.

"So when you come along," Lucille continues, hesitantly, "I was scared, see. Scared to get to know you. Scared to like you. Scared to be friends. I never had no friends since grade school. I wasn't even sure I remembered what the word meant. And you were always so serious and never saying much. So how could I know what to do, or what to say?"

Annie looks at Lucille in surprise. "No, I guess I never had no friends either. Just family, brothers, parents, Grandma and Grandpa. Couple of kids from school. But friends. Yeah, guess I don't know much about that either."

They are both silent. Then Lucille starts to laugh and sticks out her hand. "Well, shoot me dead for a dumb cow," she says. "Howdy, friend. Guess that's what we are, if we can fight out loud and not kill each other."

"Friends?" echoes Annie, dubiously. Then she adds, "Yeah...yeah, you're right, I guess." They shake hands, solemnly, and then both quickly look away again.

"Kids get to bed okay?" says Annie. "They must have been worried."

"Them kids," snorts Lucille. "They think the sun rises and sets on you. Worried? I practically had to sit on them. They're probably still awake, listening. Why don't you scoot up and check on them, and I'll make us some tea. Then we'll get to bed and get some rest. You'd better sleep in here from now on. I know you been freezing in that shack. Tomorrow, I figured we could get a start cutting poles for that new corral."

"Yeah, sure," says Annie, climbing the ladder. "Good idea. About time we started on that."

Later, lying in bed, Annie says softly into the darkness. "I saw the wolf, the one spooked Duster."

Lucille doesn't say anything. Maybe she's asleep and doesn't hear. Annie is glad. She doesn't really want to talk about it. She closes her eyes and there is the wolf in front of her. His eyes are shining gold and his coat is mottled grey and black, with a sheen of blue light. He is looking at her. What do you want, she thinks. What do you want from me? The wolf just keeps looking. The picture is so clear and vivid, she thinks if she opens her eyes, he will be standing there, over against the wall.

"Annie," says Lucille, "I don't mean to pry, but if you want to talk about anything at all, I'd be proud to hear. Just if you want to, mind."

"I went way back there, behind the ridge," says Annie

after a pause. "There's a peak there, like a set of shoulders with a pointy head. You know it?"

"Yeah, I know the one," says Lucille.

"I dunno what happened," Annie continues, "or even why I went. I just got to feeling bad. Seemed like everything piled up at once, you, the kids, winter, missing my folks bad, that just never goes away, you know. It just goes on aching inside. So I rode up there and when I saw the mountain, I climbed it. Seemed like something was pulling at me, to get me to go." Lucille says nothing.

"I climbed for a while, made it to the top. It got foggy, going up. I looked down from the peak. I could have just stepped out on that fog, it looked so solid...I was missing them so bad, my Mom and Dad, the boys." She can feel something as solid and thick as an oak plank in her chest begin to splinter and crack; her chest heaves for air. Lucille turns and puts a hand on her shoulder.

"Yeah, I know, I know about that kind of hurting...it's okay," she says softly. Annie chokes, holding it back but it won't go and she turns to Lucille and pushes her face into Lucille's solid shoulder and starts to cry, and her throat closes and chokes it into sobs. Lucille's arms tighten around her and she smoothes Annie's wet hair off her face.

"And I get so scared, and I don't know what the hell I'm doing and I don't know if I'll ever have a home again...just a home, a place of my own, my family..." Annie can't stop it anymore. She opens her mouth and strangled wailing sounds and sobs choke their way out. Lucille makes soothing shushing sounds and strokes her face and hair.

"Sorry," Annie says finally, pulling away. "I'm real sorry. I didn't mean to do that."

Lucille chuckles, says, her voice very soft in the dark, "After Mike died, I did my crying by myself, mostly outside where the kids wouldn't hear me. Took it out on the woodpile a lot, but there never was much time for crying. So it's okay. I'm glad I'm here. You just go ahead and cry anytime you've a mind to."

She gets out of bed and comes back with a clean rag and Annie wipes her face and blows her nose. Then Lucille puts her arms around her again, and Annie pillows her head on her shoulder. Lucille tucks damp strands of hair behind Annie's ears. Then she leans over and kisses her, very shyly on the cheek. Annie curls her cold feet up by Lucille's legs. A friend. So this is what it means to have a friend. They lie in the dark together, not speaking. The wolf comes again, his eyes luminous and beckoning. "Not yet," Annie thinks sleepily at him. "Not yet. For a while, a little while, just let me be."

THIRTEEN

THEY ARE DRINKING COFFEE TOGETHER, much later in the morning than usual. It's a sunny morning, with warmth in the air. They're both feeling lazy for a change, something about the sun—about knowing they've made it through the worst that winter can throw at them—has led to sitting, talking lazily about nothing in particular.

Black Dog's sudden barking startles them both to look out the door.

"Well hell, it sure must be spring," Lucille drawls. "Cowboys are coming out."

Annie raises her eyebrows in a silent question.

"We're the only single women around these parts for about two hundred miles." Lucille laughs. "Must be Sunday. I haven't been keeping track, but Sunday's the only day Joe lets his boys have off. In fact, he fires the boys he catches doing anything that looks like work on a Sunday."

Annie steps out in the yard. Small trickles of water are running off the icicles on the eaves. The packed snow in the yard gives way and squelches under her feet. The yard looks like hell, piles of dog and horse dung, old bones, cowhides, tin cans, litter everywhere.

Two men ride up the hill to the yard. They stop their horses, touch their hats and slide off. They are wearing huge spurs; pistols protrude awkwardly from their hips. Torn, dirty hats slouch over their eyes, but their plaid shirts look clean. Their horses are brushed and cleaned.

"Howdy," says one, and the other nods. The first continues, his voice a little too high-pitched and careful. "We thought we'd uh, come by, make sure you ladies was making out okay and not in need of anything. I'm uh, Fletch, and this here's Charlie. Seems like we've, uh, met before...uh, ma'am."

"We're doing just fine," Annie snaps, but Lucille appears beside her and says in a sweet and syrupy kind of way that Annie has never heard her use before, "Why, that's very kind of you boys. Won't you come in for coffee. And I was just about to make some biscuits for lunch." Annie sidles away, figuring on slipping off to the barn, but Lucille catches her eye. "Let's all go inside," she says, "and have a nice visit."

They troop inside. The kids appear out of nowhere. Black

Dog sneaks in and hides under the table, anticipating hand-outs. Lucille flies around, putting cups on, making biscuits, shooing the kids out from under her feet, finding a last jar of jam.

"Been a purty hard winter," says Fletch, who so far has done the talking for both of them. Charlie just nods and nods. He has a red round face and nervous hands which go to smooth his hair, rub his recently shaved chin, and play with his spur rowels. Fletch looks older. His hair is black and long, tied back with a piece of leather, and his face is thin and crafty. Both look to still be under twenty. The kids circle them, trying to get up the nerve to attack, to pull the guns from the holsters, to examine everything, to ask them questions and pull their hair. Nervously, the cowboys eye them back, trying to protect themselves and their guns, trying to be polite at the same time.

"Been out looking for wolves," Fletch adds. "Wolves and thievin' Indians. Lost some cows due to calve. You ladies having any trouble?"

Annie is about to make some sarcastic remark about their ability to look after cows, but Lucille jumps in first instead, asking questions about cattle prices and wolf hunting and what they think about the weather and prospects for the spring. Annie fidgets. She can think of a lot of work she could be doing instead of sitting here. Charlie keeps staring at her. She thinks his eyes bulge out. He looks bug-eyed and not very smart. She looks at the wall.

She finds excuses to play with the kids. Nat slides onto

her lap and sticks his tongue out at his brother. Gerald whacks him and Nat screams. Annie wrestles them apart then distracts Nat by tickling him. The girls hang over their mother's chair, staring at the strangers.

Annie keeps count. Each of them has five cups of coffee. She makes a few pointed remarks about work she'd planned on doing. Finally they get up to leave, but Lucille hangs in the doorway, asking a few last questions, telling them to come back anytime. Annie rolls her eyes in disgust. Lucille adds that they should give her regards to Joe.

And then, finally, they're gone. Annie breathes a huge sigh of relief, picks up the cups, carries them to the sink, thinks, well, that's that.

"Well, guess we'll have to go over there sometime for a visit," Lucille says cheerfully. "Those thievin' bastards. Picked up some strays, they said…drifted in that last storm. Wonder why they bothered to tell me. They know goddamn well the only strays around here are mine. And we're getting low on stuff, I'm damn near out of flour so that's a good excuse. Can't get more until after mud season, after it thaws and dries out. That could be a while. I'll have to take them over a list. And they say there's Indians around. We'll have to face down Joe. He'll try to say them damn yearlings are his or he can't find them or some stupid excuse. I know that man." Lucille's face is red; she rants and stomps around the cabin. Annie thinks with disgust that she acts like one of her own kids having a tantrum.

"Yeah?" says Annie. "Well, you go. I'll stay here."

Lucille laughs at her. "Hell, they're just little boys, lonely for their mothers. They're harmless enough. What's the matter? You don't like being stared at?"

"I ain't nobody's mother," says Annie, "and no, I don't like being stared at, especially by someone looks like a giant bug," and she leaves for the woodpile.

Lucille shouts her laughter across the muddy yard. "Well, get used to it," Lucille yells after her, still laughing. "With that yellow hair and green eyes, you're gonna get stared at. They'll be back. We gotta go branding with them anyway, whether you like it or not."

Annie is too disgusted to say anything more about it for the rest of the day. But she manages to saw an impressive pile of wood.

The next day, she takes Black Dog and rides a long circle on the flats. She doesn't believe they've lost any cows. It sounds like Lucille wants to pick a fight, and even though Annie hasn't forgiven Joe, she hasn't seen any evidence that he's a thief. She only has Lucille's word for it and it sounds like she's about to be dragged into a fight which doesn't mean a whole hell of a lot to her.

"That stupid Joe again," she mutters. She and Duster make a careful circle around the whole flats, staying clear of any cows that look threatening. The cows have clustered in several scattered groups. Lucille has said they'll be calving soon so she watches them carefully. She's not in the mood to get in a fight with a new mother.

Black Dog runs ahead of her as always, circling in wide

loops and coming back. Suddenly she hears him yip, a frightened unusual sound for him, and then he scuttles back out of the brush towards her, looking over his shoulder and growling.

Three Indians ride up out of a brush-filled gully as if they had all the time in the world, up out of the hollow where Black Dog has just been. Now that Black Dog is with her, he takes a guard position up front and barks and threatens hysterically. She tightens her legs and the reins. Duster half rears and turns, prepared to run, and then Annie thinks of the kids and turns him back. There's nowhere to run that the Indians couldn't follow. There's three of them and one of her.

She waits while they ride towards her. Absurdly, she's suddenly reminded of Charlie and Fletch, something in their faces. Shut up, she thinks. Breathe. Smile. Force it.

One of the men is old; his long grey hair is neatly braided; the other two are young, their hair loose over their shoulders. They look almost the same age as her. They stop in front of her, about twenty feet away and she waits and they wait and Black Dog subsides to growling. She wonders if she's supposed to do something. Abruptly the old man points at the dog, makes motions of clubbing and then eating, rubs his belly, and laughs like a fool. Annie wonders what the hell that's supposed to mean. Is it a joke? Is she supposed to laugh too?

At a nod from the old man, one of the boys slips off his horse, and comes forward, bringing a bag, hands it to her.

The bag is made of soft leather, beaded with quills. She looks inside. Dried meat. Do they think she's hungry? Is this what's left of one of Lucille's cows?

She looks at the old man. He looks away. She has nothing to give in return, she thinks, then remembers when she came away this morning; she brought lunch, intending to be gone all day. She takes the wrapped parcel of sandwiches out of her saddlebags, slips off Duster and carries it to the old man.

He nods. Up close, his face is shiny leather, seamed with a million fine wrinkles. His horse is a sturdy pinto, smaller than Duster. She pats its shoulder. "Nice horse," she says.

For some reason, they all laugh again. The old man points at Duster and then at the pinto and then at her. Then he points at himself and laughs like an idiot. Still laughing, they all turn and ride away; once, they turn and look back at her, and disappear into the brush, sliding away like an early morning dream. Annie stares after them, her eyes full of questions, the sound of their voices and their laughter carrying through the soft spring air, still in her head.

On the way home Black Dog gets over his fear and runs ahead again. He likes to make wide circles, when they're riding, especially on the way home, when he doesn't have to worry about losing track of her. He disappears for a while, but she doesn't worry much. Then she comes up on him, standing beside the carcass of a cow, an old dry cow with twisted mossy horns, not one of Lucille's. It's been shot. There are three dead coyotes lying around it. Annie's belly clenches in fear. No one said anything about leaving out poison. Annie calls Black Dog to her and watches him closely. She makes him stay beside her all the way home.

That night after supper, when she goes out to feed him, he's standing retching, in the yard. He chokes and retches and won't look at his food. She calls Lucille, and together they stand, helplessly watching. He begins to circle the yard, falling and retching and finally lies down, his whole body twitching in spasms. Annie grabs him and they carry him in, put him on a sack in the corner behind the stove. He lies there, eyes closed, his body occasionally convulsing. A thin line of silver drool trails from his mouth.

"Ain't much we can do, Annie," Lucille says softly. "Never heard of a dog that's taken poison coming out of it." Annie ignores her.

Annie tries. She wraps him in a blanket, heats milk and spoons it in through his clenched jaw. It dribbles out again on the blanket. By midnight, Lucille persuades her to go to bed, saying there's nothing they can do. When she comes down in the morning, Black Dog's eyes are open and his teeth are bared, but he's dead. His body is bent into a last stiff pose of fierce defense.

Annie takes him outside. She doesn't want the kids to see him. His body lies on the torn piece of blanket, on the wet snow. She'll have to bury him somehow, but the ground is still frozen. She'll find a hole in the rocks maybe, safe from the coyotes. She looks at him, numb. That goddamn Joe. Those goddamn fools of cowboys. Black Dog never had a chance. What a rotten trick after he followed her all this way. And why, why did he have to leave her now?

He never asked for much, she thinks, food when she had it, the right to sleep beside her. She remembers him laughing on the raft at the lake, playing pirates with her, chasing sticks when she'd a mind to throw them. He's been with her as long as she can remember.

"I never even gave you a real name," she thinks. She ties his body in a scrap of hemp sacking from an old flour bag, hoists it over her shoulder and trudges away from the house. The morning is grey and dreary. A bitter wind whines over the flats from the east. More snow, probably.

"Just a dog," her father's voice says in her ear. Animals didn't count. Animals came and went. She finds a crack in the rocks and lifts Black Dog's body into it and pries some more rocks from the frozen ground to pile on top of him. By the time she's done, her hands are numb and bleeding.

All the way home she feels him behind her. She knows if she turns, she'll catch him in the corner of her eye, his plumy tail waving as he comes up, mouth open and laughing, trying to tell her it's all a mistake, he isn't dead and can they please go home now. She does look, finally, can't stop herself, but there's nothing there, just the persistent feeling that, at any moment, there will be.

When she comes in, Lucille has obviously told the kids. No one says anything. They have a grim silent breakfast, and Annie goes out to work. That night, long after Lucille is asleep, she lies awake, waiting for Black Dog to scratch at the door to be let in. She wishes she could cry. She wishes she'd paid more attention to him while he was alive. He used to come and shove his nose into her hand whenever she was feeling bad. All the way from the settlement, he slept curled beside her. At night, when she'd wake up, she'd feel him there.

Something thumps by the front door and she startles awake, but then it's quiet. Probably snow coming off the roof. Her thoughts drift and clog, like slush-filled runoff in a ditch.

That old Indian man, looking at her. She'd like to know more about that. She doesn't know anything about Indians. He was so different, strange. Everybody she knew was afraid of them. Indians were thieves, they said, savage, crazy, murderers, lived like animals. Wild, her mother had called her. "You're just like a wild Indian," she'd say, but she smiled when she said it, because it was a joke.

She'd like to know where they lived; she could maybe find out, take them some more food or something to trade with. What do traders use? Knives? Blankets? She doesn't know anything; she wishes Black Dog would come home. She's crazy and stupid to be fantasizing about Indians while her dog lies out there among the rocks, in the cold.

Would the Indians feel sorry for her? Would they take her and let her sit with them? How could they talk together? Language would be a problem. Maybe she could teach them English. Maybe that could be her gift to them. But why would they want it? They have each other, their families, that bright circle of tipis against the green grass, the laughter and the children running, a mother's soft hands braiding her daughter's hair.

She has no one. She is alone, thinking about a circle of mystery and togetherness which shuts her out and which she will probably never come to understand.

FOURTEEN

ONE DAY, LATER IN THE SPRING, Lucille decides it's time, and they all ride together to Joe Littlefoot's place. Lucille is riding the stud colt, who is barely broken and thinks this excursion is an excuse to shy and buck at every tiny thing that crosses his path. The boys ride double on Lucille's bay while the two girls ride the grey mare. The sun is shining; the horses' feet squelch and suck in the mud. Gerald and Nat wrestle and hit each other, until Nat climbs on behind Annie and Gerald uses this as an excuse to race the bay ahead of the others. The stud fights the bit, throws his head, wanting to run too. Gerald comes racing back and the bay shies. Gerald falls, rolling over in the mud, and then leaps to his feet, crawls back up onto the saddle while the bay is still dancing sideways, and lashes it back into a run.

Annie has been holding her breath, waiting for disaster. Lucille just laughs. "Tough," she says, "they'd better be tough if they want to survive in this country." Nat wriggles, wanting Annie to run too. But she and Lucille plod on, content in each other's company, in the sun on the yellow hills, the white river with a thin crack of black water showing in the middle, and the grey-fingered trees.

"Gonna be kind of late tonight, time we get done rounding up them strays," says Lucille. "Be near to a full moon. We could trail them back, I guess…"

Sure, Annie thinks. Set it up so we have to stay over and you have time to fight with stupid Joe and drink whiskey.

"Guess we'll just have to stay over then," Annie drawls.

"Stay over," Lucille hoots. "You're the one can't stand them boys looking at you crosswise. What happened? Change your mind? Hoping for a little action? Got your eye on anyone in particular…old Google-Eyes, now he sure fancies you."

Annie looks away. There are some parts to Lucille she doesn't like at all. Lately, Annie's been thinking a lot about when she should be leaving. It's complicated by not knowing the country, or what it might do. There's still deep snow on the hills. When it warms up the rivers will rise. Lucille says when the frost comes out of the ground the whole country turns to mud and nothing moves until it dries out. Lucille has talked a lot about the work they'll do together in the spring, calving, branding, doctoring, building corrals. Lucille talks like they're partners, like Annie will be around forever with nothing more interesting to think about than chasing cows in and out of the bush and riding herd on these wild kids.

She'll have a fit, likely, when she figures out that Annie is serious about leaving. But it's not her place or her future she's building here. Lucille, Annie thinks, takes one hell of a lot for granted.

After all, Annie still has her brothers, her mission to find land and their own future to think about. She should have written them by now. Her stomach hurts whenever she thinks about them so she tries not to, shoves them away into a protected corner of her mind. Right now they seem far away and very hard to think about. But she should have tried to send a letter out by one of the cowboys. It would find them eventually. The people in the settlement wouldn't care, by now, where she's gotten to. But her brothers should know she's out here thinking about them, still hanging onto the dream she created for them. When she does finally return, she'll explain, she'll make it all up to them.

Do they still think about her, she wonders? She wishes right now, just for a moment, she could hold them, tell them to hang on, have faith, that they will all be together again. They'll have a home, a house with real windows and a kitchen with a big cookstove and a porch. Outside will be their cows and horses, and a barn, the kind of barn she's always wanted, a red barn with stalls and a big loft for hay, a room in the back for the chickens, another room for feed and tools. This will be a proper barn with doors that open and close, not like the few ramshackle sheds that Lucille survives with.

They'll have fields. Proper fields, hay fields and pastures and strong stout corrals with proper fence posts, no leaning saggy fences on her place. And chickens. A place never sounds like home without a rooster crowing to the world about his place in it. And food. Food like she used to have at home. A garden with fruit trees. Fruit. She hasn't so much as tasted an apple for months now. There were wild plums and berries at the lake, but she and Lucille have survived on dried beans, lots of meat, onions, potatoes, and carrots stored from the straggly garden, and not much else. What she wants is a whole tree, no, a whole orchard full of apples and pears and plums. And peaches. Best of all, it will all be hers. And then, of course, lots of horses, as many as she's ever wanted. All colours. All sizes. She'll name them…

"Hey," says Lucille. "We should maybe at least take them some fresh meat, though they probably got plenty. Boys, shut up! I just spotted some pronghorns. Annie, you think you can hit one from here?" The question is casual but there's something around the edges Annie doesn't like. But she shrugs.

"Sure," she says.

Annie rarely carries the heavy Henry carbine with her

unless she has to. It's a nuisance on the saddle, heavy, catching the rope and chafing Duster. She's hunted for Lucille before, and helped Lucille shoot cows that were crippled or too sick to survive, but she still doesn't care much for killing things. She thinks that Lucille could just as well kill her own deer or sick cows, but she puts it on Annie because she doesn't much care for it herself.

Annie doesn't say anything, but stores it away in a corner where she has stored a whole series of little grudges against Lucille, building them up like a wall against her affection and admiration, adding them to the little pile of irritations that are growing between them.

She stops Duster, takes quick aim, and drops the pronghorn with one quick shot. Lucille shoots her a look of pure admiration.

"Annie, where in hell's bells you learn to shoot like that? I couldn't hit a barn if I needed to. You've got a talent, girl, a real talent. Them cowboys at Joe's see you shoot like that, it'd scare the bejeezus out of them, that's for sure."

They ride down to the antelope, quickly skin and gut and pack the quarters on behind their saddles. It's not until they're headed back that Lucille says solemnly, "Y'know, I been meaning to talk to you about something. Now, I know you don't think them boys of Joe's are worth a whole hell of a lot, and maybe I don't think so much of them either, but Jeezus Murphy, Annie, you don't have to show it so plain. For one thing, they're my neighbours. They're the only neighbours I got and I need them. I need their help.

I need their company. Even if I got to be sure they ain't
stealing cows from me. That's just part of being neighbourly
too, out here. They ain't no bloody laws out here except
for what you can make up, and what you can back up.
And for another, if you want men to pay any attention to
you, you got to at least try and be nice to them, and look
like you think they're big and smart, and not the dumb
jackasses you think they really are."

"I don't want them to," says Annie. "I don't want no
attention from any of them. I don't need it. I don't need
them for nothing."

"Annie," says Lucille with exasperation. "I know you're
tough and all, but this is the west, the frontier. People die
out here, they get hurt and shot and lost in blizzards and
eaten by grizzlies and bit by rattlers and cut up by Indians.
What I'm trying to say is, you're a girl. You can't just ignore that. Sooner or later you're gonna need a man to help
you get by."

"Sure," says Annie. "Like you do. Like you need a man.
Like you needed one so goddamn bad the past few months.
I'm just part of the goddamn scenery."

"Annie, before you came, I was scraping bottom. You
and everybody else seem to think I'm so damn tough. And
sure, I was getting by. But there were nights I laid awake
and worried and stared at the wall, so damn scared that
something would happen to me or the kids that I just laid
there and shook. I would have kissed Joe and married him
on the spot if he'd shown up then, but he never did, and

when daybreak came, I usually recovered, enough, anyway, to carry on for one more day. Sometimes, me and the
kids would just cry together. Somedays, I'd come home
and they'd been alone all day and I'd be so tired and they'd
need me so much. I just wanted someone else there, some
to talk to, lean on, share stuff with. Anyone. But then you
come along and things brightened up considerable. No,"
she adds softly, "you're gonna need someone, if not a man,
then someone, Annie, sometime, someday." But then she
grins. "But hey, now I got you, and things just keep on
looking a whole lot brighter. They sure do."

"Well, there it is," she adds, and there it is for sure, the
long low shed where that conceited fool Joe locked her up.
She managed to ignore him when he came with Lucille to
bring the Christmas presents. He didn't stay long, but now
she supposes she'll have to be polite, at least until they find
whatever cows they're supposed to get and then head on
their way home.

Annie stiffens in the saddle, pulls her whole day-dream-
ing self back inside, and tightens her face so it's straight
and tough, showing nothing at all. They ride across the
flats to the ranch, the kids racing ahead, whooping across
the intervening space while cowboys are loping in on horseback or stepping outside the bunkhouse to say hello.

As they ride up, Annie inspects the place. There's a pile
of grey hides on the porch and one stretched out on the
wall. Could add Black Dog's to that pile, she thinks bitterly. A couple of huge hounds crawl out from under the

porch to bark and snarl until one of the men calls them off. A few horses stand listlessly in a corral, piles of dog and horse dung everywhere. As they come closer she can smell the place again, the same stink as before.

The cowboys are shuffling and grinning, and teasing the kids and sneaking glances at the two women. They look like they're so damn glad to see someone else for a change, they wouldn't care who it was rode up to their front door. Joe comes out and snarls at them to all get back to work. There is a handwritten list posted up by the front door. RULES it says, in big crude printing. Well, Lucille said Joe was strict.

Joe yells back inside for someone to put on some coffee and maybe rustle up some biscuits and they all get down and go inside. Annie stays right behind Lucille, and once inside, she moves to the corner and sits so she can see them all. She leaves the rifle on the saddle but she's not real easy without it.

She'll have to sit and wait until all this visiting business is done and Lucille and Joe have talked each other around in dizzy circles for a while and they can get on with what they came for and go home. She never has understood why people feel they should spend a lot of time sitting in a room discussing things like the weather when all they have to do is step outside and take a good look at it.

Well, it's Lucille's country and Lucille's life and she can have any friends—or enemies—she wants to. What she, Annie, needs to find out is when the river ice might go out and when things dry out so she can start planning to leave. She also needs to know if there's a trail over the mountains…if anyone here knows, which is doubtful.

Lucille and Joe talk around one another. Annie thinks they act like two strange dogs trying to decide whether to fight or play. The kids leave to find the cowboys, and Annie sits on, partly listening to Joe and Lucille, mostly dreaming and planning about leaving and finding her own place.

They hear yelling and hoofs pounding outside and they all go out. The cowboys have run in a small bunch of horses. The kids are with them, riding ranch horses and looking excited. The horses stream, biting and kicking and looking scared, into one of the smaller corrals.

"Thought we'd put on a little show for y'all," says Joe, grinning. "Thought you girls might like to see some roping and riding." Annie rolls her eyes. As if we don't get enough of it, just working, she thinks.

Two of the cowboys rope a small black horse, which lunges away, gets its feet over the rope and trips itself. They throw themselves on its head, choke it down so it can't move, and two more men come running with a hackamore and saddle. They get it up and saddled; one of them leaps on and spurs the horse while it bucks frantically around the corral. When it stops bucking, head down and sides heaving for air, the cowboy swings himself off and struts to the fence, laughing and waving in mock heroism. He glances at Lucille and Annie as he walks. The men ear down another horse and the same thing happens. Charlie contrives to sit beside Annie, and stutter the odd, awkward question. She answers him to be polite, which seems to be all he wants.

The cowboys compete with each other, yelling cheerful insults about each other's riding ability, but there's a seriousness about it. These are horses that need to be broken, so they're working, but with an audience. Even Joe can approve of this kind of fun.

Dust rises out of the pounded frozen dirt of the corral; the sun dips lower and blue shadows come creeping like thieves out of the cracks between the mountains.

"That's enough, you boys," hollers Joe. He turns to Lucille. "Best you stay over. You can sleep in the cookshack. We'll put some sleeping rolls on the floor for you. We got most of the wolves, but there's still a bunch over to your way we haven't knocked off yet. And one of the boys says he seen Indian sign too. They been pretty quiet but it can't last. Sooner or later they'll bust out and then I guess we'll have to kill them too. Kinda too bad, I guess, but it's us or them. They're just gonna have to learn to move over or get the hell out of the way."

"Wolves don't chase people," says Annie. "I seen wolves before. They never bothered me."

"Then I guess you're just luckier than the rest of us, little lady," snaps Joe. "Guess you've never seen what them bastards can do to a cow and calf. They've followed the boys here lots of times. Maybe they have nice tame wolves back where you come from."

"My Pa saw wolves," she rejoins. "He always said, leave them alone, they'll leave you alone."

"Yeah, well with all due respect to your Pa," says Joe, "he can handle his wolves and I'll handle mine. I got a cattle operation to run, and my owners would just be pleased as hell if I told them it all got eat up by wolves, eh? And I ain't losing none of these boys if I can help it either."

"Yeah, well I lost my dog to one of your stupid poison baits," spat Annie. "I had that dog since I was a kid..." her voice choked. She glared at Joe. "You could have warned us about it."

"My baits?" said Joe. "Hell, Lucille knew about them baits. I told her a long time ago. She figured it was a good idea. Gotta fight to survive out here, wolves, weather, Indians, you name it. We're here to survive, little lady. That's our business."

"Well, then it's a cowardly, sneaky business," says Annie. "You're killing every damn thing, coyotes, ravens, and my dog. Kill your own damn dogs, why don't you? Or learn to shoot straight. You bunch of cowards." She's ranting. She knows it and doesn't care. Lucille just stands there, looking stricken. The cowboys have come up and are standing around them in an uneasy circle. Their boss and a girl, yelling at each other. Not a situation they have any sure answers to.

"Ah, c'mon," Lucille says, too quickly, far too cheerfully. "Let's go get some grub. Them kids'll be starved. C'mon Annie. You ain't had nothing to eat today. Those prong-

horn steaks should be downright tasty. Annie shot a young
buck on the way over," she says to Joe. "Made a great shot.
Just one quick shot, but a long one, uphill too; she's good."

Joe and Annie are still glaring at each other.

"My boys shoot just fine," snarls Joe. "Who the hell do
you think you are? A lot of brag and talk, most likely. It's
easy to shoot your mouth off, when you only been here a
few months, don't know what the hell you're talking about."

"Ahh," Lucille says loudly, "Annie here could outshoot
any of your boys any day of the week and twice on Sun-
days."

There's an uneasy silence at this. None of them want to
take her up on it. They're not easy as it is with Lucille and
Annie's competence at roping and riding but at least they're
getting used to it. Beside, given how unusual these women
are, compared to the women they were used to back East,
they can be dismissed as abnormal, a result of the country,
the weather, the strange and unsettled times they live in.
And unfortunately, given these women's general craziness
and all around competence, this story about shooting the
pronghorn just might be true.

They can't resist answering for long. A woman, shooting?

"Nawwww," drawls someone named Lester, "cain't no
woman shoot. They ain't got the strength for it. Now, to
really learn to shoot, you got to be brought up to it, got to
develop the right muscles and they hain't never had a
chance. Now back home…"

Joe cuts him off. "I saw a woman shoot once." His voice is deadly quiet with a little edge to it like a rusty razor. "In a circus. Kind of a freak of nature, she was. People paid a lot of money to see it, like watching a monkey do tricks. So then," he says to Annie, "care to show us?"

Annie sits still, feeling sick and empty. A cold wind whistles down the hollows of her heart. Damn Lucille for getting her into this. She's done it just to be mean, just to save her own hide and try to take Annie's mind off her, Lucille's, betrayal.

But something else is wrong here and she's not sure what it is. Why are they looking at her? She's not the one trying to show off. It's Lucille who has set this up, lied to her, and is now riding her, goading her, setting her up. What has she done so wrong to deserve this? She glares back at them.

"Sure," she says finally. "Why not," and gets up, walks stiff-legged to her saddle and rifle, hanging together on the corral fence. Her legs are shaking a bit. It's just shooting, she thinks. It doesn't matter. It doesn't matter a bit. She's leaving anyway. She'll never see any of them again.

She gets the rifle, loads it, goes back to the circle of men. They're quiet, none of the jostling and laughing and goofing off she's gotten used to in the last few hours. Joe is leaning back on the fence, picking his teeth with a stalk of grass. She goes and leans against it as well. Maybe they'll forget about it.

Joe says, "So, see anything you want to aim at?" The other men snigger uneasily.

Annie looks around. It's almost dusk. There's a shining salmon band of light along the western horizon, against which the cottonwood trees display their new green leaves. Above that, the sky is a sheer joyous blue, deepening into darkness. She can hear the jingle of a horse bell on the lead mare. She can smell the dust and horse dung pounded into the air from the afternoon.

A rock sits humped on the horizon. She picks up an enamel cup sitting on a fence post, walks the long, long way over to the rock and back and still no one says a word.

She shoots. Everyone watches the cup leap into the air and descend, clattering, among the rocks. Then Joe walks over to a wagon, fetches out several empty liniment bottles, moves away from Annie and tosses one into the air. Without her thinking about it, the rifle leaps to her shoulder and the bullet smashes the bottles into a million shining splinters. Joe throws the next and the next and the next and each one shatters. He stops and the echoes come back from the hills behind the camp.

Joe stretches and yawns, shrugs. "Well, you've had your little show. Better get to the house, boys, and get your dinners. We gotta bunch of herding ahead of us tomorrow." He turns back to Lucille. "I'll go see what the cook mixed up for us, and you round up them wild kids of yours," and he marches off to the house.

One by one, the men drift away. Annie is left with Lucille, both of them sitting on the fence, staring at the horizon.

Lucille turns to Annie. "You showed them," she crows,

"you sure showed them, and they ain't men enough to admit it. Ah, to hell with them. C'mon Annie," Lucille says cheerfully. "I guess you get your wish, looks like we're staying over and taking our beef home tomorrow." She marches off after Joe, yelling for the kids.

Annie remains sitting on the fence, watching the horses out on the flats shift and mingle together. The mountains across the valley are blue shadows, layered one against the other in successively darkened hues. Beneath them, the valley floor and the flats are darker blue-green, shading to black. Even the horses shine pearly blue over their shades of black, brown and red. Light shimmers just behind the hill where the moon is due to rise. A first star winks into existence. If she was up there, in the valley with the lake, she would be alone with the quiet and the peace and the silence. Perhaps there the wolves would come to know her and not be afraid. Black Dog would still be alive. The snow on the mountains glows in the ascending moonlight.

Up there, she thinks, I want to be up there, alone and safe.

Time to go, says a voice in her head. Time to get out of here. She starts feeling frantic, her thoughts going round and round in her head; she's trapped in a whirlpool of travelling and planning and where to go and what Lucille will say. Lucille appears beside her and climbs on the fence and puts her hand on Annie's shoulder.

"Hey, kid," she says softly. "C'mon, supper's ready. Can't keep hungry cowboys waiting." Furiously, Annie shakes off the hand, doesn't look at Lucille, climbs down off the fence and walks stiff-legged ahead of her to the smelly cook shack full of men who probably hate her guts.

FIFTEEN

ANNIE DOESN'T TALK TO LUCILLE about leaving. She hardly talks to her about anything, avoids her and the kids as much as she can. Neither of them mention the day at Joe's. When they're forced to talk it's only about work. They speak in clipped tones, avoid each other's eyes.

It gets cold again, really cold; then it warms up and snows just about the time the cows start dropping calves. She and Lucille spend their time riding out, checking on cows and doctoring and helping heifers that are having a hard time. They leave in the morning and come back at night. The kids are left with the responsibility of the fire and the house and chores. Annie worries all the time that they're away that something might happen to the kids, but Lucille never talks about it. Only once, she snaps in exasperation, "Look, I can't afford to worry about them. Once I got started worrying, I'd never stop. I've gotta keep thinking they'll be just fine."

Annie wonders how Lucille managed before she got here. Lucille never talks about that either. One day, Annie ropes a calf with an infected eye and while she's down off her horse, she hears a snort and looks up to see the mother charging towards her. Suddenly Lucille is there. She calmly ropes the cow, flips her in the middle of her charge, and holds her while Annie finishes with the calf.

The next day, Lucille's horse goes through the ice in the river they've been crossing all winter. He panics, starts to plunge and rear, trying to get his feet back out on the ice. Lucille falls off and almost slips under the frantic horse as Annie runs out on the ice, flops down, grabs Lucille's hand and pulls her free. Annie spends an hour getting the exhausted horse out of the freezing water and back onto shore, while Lucille rides back to the house, changes her frozen clothes, and comes back again to help.

Each day as they ride out and the work envelops Annie with its immediate demands, it gets harder and harder to think about leaving. But she knows she's going to have to, and before that she has to talk about it.

Once, she tries.

"When do you think the ice will go out?" she says, one day, when it stops snowing and finally starts to warm up a little.

"Ah, could be any day, could be weeks," says Lucille cheerfully. "You never know in this godforsaken country. Could snow until June. Could thaw tomorrow. How the hell do I know?"

"Well, when do you figure you'll get started on branding?"

"When the boys are done theirs, they'll swing by and help out with ours, next month sometime, or the month after. Depends on the weather, how the calves are shaping, when there's enough grass to turn them up into the hills."

Annie sighs. "But I thought as soon as it warmed up the river flooded, and you and Joe said the country would be impassable then."

"Yeah, well, if it gets hot early, we'll have a little flooding—maybe, maybe not, all depends, y'see."

Annie gives up and goes back to work, riding herd and doctoring calves.

Annie wonders if Lucille is being purposefully vague, or if she's still upset at her for her behaviour at Joe's. She spent that evening in the corner of the cookshack, went early to bed, and didn't bother hiding the fact that she was glad to be going the next morning, ate a silent breakfast, saddled Duster and waited outside while everyone else was saying goodbye.

Not that she thought she was outrageously rude. In fact, all things considered, she thought she had behaved pretty goddamned well, putting up with Charlie Google-Eyes staring at her like a sad calf, and watching the boys show off all afternoon without saying a single sarcastic word, listening to them boasting about all the wolves they'd killed and the Indians they were going to kill if they got a chance, and the deadly rivers they'd swum on the cattle drive north and the blizzards they'd faced. It hadn't seemed worth it to say anything at all, except for letting fly at Joe and Lucille, who damned well deserved it.

"You killed my dog. You bastards killed a poor innocent dog that never did you a damn bit of harm," she thought over and over, but didn't find a good chance to say it.

She's still furious at Lucille for not warning her about the wolf baits. That, she thinks, was unforgiveable. Everytime she misses Black Dog, she flushes with anger all over again. Plus she's also just generally irritated that Lucille put her through the whole idiot show when they were visiting, made her show off, and then had the nerve to gloat over it to the embarrassed cowboys when Annie just wanted to forget the whole thing. Lucille manages to irritate her a lot these days.

One day, they swim the river from which the ice has finally left and head east. It's a sunny day and what's left of the snow is going fast. The country is still bleak and bare, but there's a sense of promise and hints of change. Annie rides ahead of Lucille. They don't talk. Things feel tight and miserable and stretched between them.

They spot some antelope and Annie drops one with a single long shot from a hilltop. Lucille whistles in admiration. "Nope," she says, trying to to be nice. "I ain't never gonna have to worry about Joe or cow thieves or nothing as long as word spreads that you're in the country."

In a tight angry voice Annie says, "But I got to go, come spring. I got to head out. You know that. I can't stay here with you."

Lucille doesn't say anything, not for a long time. Then she sighs. "Yeah, well I should have known it was too good to last. You were like an answer to a prayer, but maybe prayers don't stay answered for long."

They ride on in silence. Finally Lucille says, "Well, I'm sure glad you told me, anyhow. Save me making any more foolish plans about stuff we could do here together."

They don't say another word all the long ride home across the river and up the hill. Annie takes the venison to hang in the barn and Lucille unsaddles and feeds the horses, rounds up the kids and goes to put supper on.

Supper is quiet. The kids look from one silent woman to the other and don't even bother to kick each other under the table. After supper Lucille says coldly, "Guess it's getting warm enough, you could move back out to the bunkhouse. I'll total up your wages tomorrow, see how much you got coming."

Annie feels the heat coming into her face. "Fine," she says, "that'll be just fine. I was thinking about it myself."

But later as they're washing dishes and getting the kids to bed and going through routines which have become familiar and comfortable, the tension is too much. Annie figures she has to either go to the cabin or say something.

"Look," she begins, "I don't know why in hell you're bothered about this. You knew I was gonna go eventually. I guess I should've said something before."

"I'm not upset," says Lucille. "People come, people go, I can maybe get Joe to lend me a couple of hands for branding."

"Yeah, fine," snaps Annie. "That's just great. Thanks for nothing. Sorry about your poor damned dog. Sorry he died but it was just one of those things, just an accident. Life in the west is like that." She hates that her voice is rising and starting to shake.

"So, what do you want me to do?" Lucille says, her face frozen, her hands continuing to dry dishes and put them away. "What's done is done, and cain't be undone. Even if I said I was sorry, you're so damn righteous about everything, it wouldn't make any difference."

"Well, you could at least try. But what the hell. It's your damn place. Anytime you want me to be just a hand, just your cowboy, you can say so. Don't matter about me, or my dog, or my horse. We're just drifters, got no home, got no goddamn land. We don't count for nothing. That seems to be about the size of it."

She turns and starts to march out of the door, then turns back.

"We didn't even mention money before. I never asked for it. Now you're gonna give me wages. I don't want no goddamn wages."

"What the hell do you want then?" snaps Lucille. "You

want me say I'm sorry, okay then, fine, I'm sorry about
your dog. I'm sorry. It's my fault, I should have told you
but I figured you'd be mad and I had to do it, I had to. I
couldn't take a chance on wolves eating up my stock, my
profits, my livelihood. And that's not your damned problem. That's mine," and then she marches around Annie,
disappears out the door for wood.

When she comes back in, she continues, her voice a little
more human. "You didn't ask about money and I didn't
want to bring it up because I figured it didn't matter. I
figured we'd settle up at some point and there wouldn't be
nothing to make a fuss about. What are you looking for,
Annie? What do you want? If you want to go shares in the
place, we can work that out. You need a home so bad.
Hell, if you want, I'll even sign half of it over to you...there
isn't much land anyway, everything is tied up in them cows
out there."

"Lucille..." Annie begins, but Lucille interrupts.

"Annie, goddamnit, I need you here. The kids need you.
I...I want you to stay."

"I can't," Annie says. She looks at the scarred, worn wood
of the table. Her head gets heavy and stones collect in her
stomach. She feels colder than she's ever been. She wonders if she'll ever get warm again. Lucille just keeps staring
into the cold pan of dishwater in the sink.

Finally, Annie says, "I been trying and trying to figure
out what I'm supposed to do, what I'm after. I been asking
myself why I need to go. When I left the settlement, I had

an idea—a dream, I guess—but now I'm not so sure. I guess more than anything, what I want is to be home, somehow, to feel at home, to know that where I am is home. I want to get up in the morning and walk outside and know that I belong in that place. I want to look at a tree and know that tree is going to be there everyday of my life. And I want that returned, I want to go outside and have every damn thing out there know that I'm there and they belong there and so do I and we're all in it together…and if I ever do have kids, I want them to have that too…to get up every morning and to know what they belong to, and where their place is in the world."

Annie pauses in frustration. "It's so hard to talk about. It's just a feeling…there's no real words for it…when we were at my grandparents' farm, I didn't really belong there, but I liked it, and when we were travelling, I didn't belong anywhere, but I didn't care, because it was so exciting and we were going to find out, we were going somewhere. And when I was travelling by myself, there was this one place…but I didn't stay, couldn't have…When I saw that wolf, remember, that I told you about, just standing there looking at me, and that old Indian guy…they knew where they were, it was me that was lost. I'm still lost. And maybe I always will be. So I can't stay. It ain't time yet. I still got some travelling to do, some things I have to figure out. But wherever I'm supposed to be, this isn't it. I don't know. I just don't know. But I figure I'll know it when I find it." She says this very softly and then because she's afraid she might cry, and because Lucille's back is still turned to her, she gets up and gets a couple of blankets off Lucille's warm and welcoming bed and heads outside, into the night.

But not before Lucille looks at her, and Annie sees her white face. There's anger in it, sadness and desolation, like a little kid left alone in a night full of demons.

SIXTEEN

BRANDING TIME IS NEAR. Lucille announces it one morning over the grits and biscuits. Annie wonders how she knows. No one has come by from Joe's, not that she's seen anyway. The kids are excited, hollering, wanting to help. Even Alice, the more prim of the two girls, can ride like a burr when she wants to. Brisk and efficient as usual, Lucille assigns everyone a job, gathering piles of wood down by the flats where she and Annie have a rough corral built, cooking food ahead of time, stretching ropes, mending saddles and bridles. She treats Annie like a hired hand, giving her orders and food, nothing more. Annie wonders what friendship means, if it can come and go so easily. She avoids Lucille when she can, works by herself, but spends even more time than usual playing with the kids.

Nights in the shed, she tries to work it out, plans conversations with Lucille which never take place. It doesn't make sense. She never promised Lucille anything, she argues with herself. And Lucille betrayed her. Nothing has been settled between them. She has to do what she promised herself she's going to do. She promised her brothers. She's doing it for her mother and father. She goes around and around the possibilities until her head is sore. Going over and over the good times she's had with Lucille, her heart stings as if little shards of glass are stuck in it, aching and bleeding and working themselves in deeper. She wants to say she's sorry; instead she spends more and more time by herself. Over dinner she keeps her face and body stiff; they exchange polite comments about the work, nothing more.

Maybe, after all, she could stay at Lucille's, they could make it up, get over the bitterness between them. She could make a home here, get some cattle of her own, start ranching. Lucille has explained that it's pretty easy to get started. Lucille thinks she's going to be rich someday, when the country opens up, when more people come, when there's an easier way to ship beef back East, where the markets are. She's determined about it.

But no, it's not Annie's place, not the place she's looking for. She's learned a lot from Lucille, for which she's grateful. And one thing she's learned is that she's not sure she wants to be a rancher. Every time she has to doctor another impossibly stupid, mean cow, she's sure of it. This is a mean, hard country, she thinks; rivers rise without warning, ice breaks under horses, blizzards trap people. Joe and the boys talk a lot about close calls they've had. She thinks of the forest, fields, lush abundant gardens and fruit trees of her grandparents' place, the sense of peace and order that prevailed there. She likes the wildness here, the emptiness, the sense of possibilities over every hill, but no, it's not her place. And she sure wants to see a lot more before she makes up her mind to settle down.

Deep down, under her sadness about Lucille, she smells a trap waiting, a whole weighted net of needs and wants and desperation. Lucille is too tired, too sad, carrying too much of a load with her kids and her hopes and dreams. It's not a load Annie thinks she's ready for. Even if she did want to share it, it's too big, too hard, and too frightening.

Lately, even the kids, sensing something wrong, demand more and more attention. They pull and tug at her, want her to tell them stories, want her to play, make them dolls, accompany them to do chores. They brag about her shooting, which doesn't make her feel proud, only sad.

It's a relief to be back in the bunkhouse. Sometimes, shivering through the cold nights, she remembers the warmth and comfort of Lucille's bed. She thinks a lot about that night when she cried and put her head on Lucille's shoulder and Lucille held her. No one had ever done that before, as far as she can remember. Her Mom must have held her when she was little, but that was a long time ago, a very long time. She remembers Lucille lying there, warm and solid, night after night, both of them feeling safer because the other was there.

One night, she remembers, the wind hit the house particularly hard. It shrieked and curled, crashing under the eaves, trying to lift the roof to get at them all. She knew Lucille was awake too. They laid together without speaking. Annie could feel Lucille shaking, a fine tremor running through her limbs and body like insects running over her. She calmed down after Annie grasped her hand. Their two hands clutched and clung together. A warm red blossom of caring, love, pride and responsibility had flowered then in Annie's chest. They both went back to sleep like that, holding hands like little kids.

SEVENTEEN

"I HATE COWBOYS," Annie mutters to herself. She's on one end of a calf and Google-Eyes is on the other. The calf is caught by ropes stretched to their individual horses. The calf hoarsely bawls its torture to the sky. Google-Eyes is swearing at his horse to make it back up, but instead it's getting upset, jumping around and jerking the calf.

Annie is beginning to wonder how they're ever going to get through this task, branding and castrating an endless supply of yelling miserable calves. She hates it already. She hates the noise the calves make; she's sick of jokes about prairie oysters, the smell of burning hair and dust clogging her nose and throat.

The mother cows bellow, the calves holler back, and she

thinks about the fact that it's all to make food for rich Easterners; all these sweet sad little calves that she's worked so hard to bring into the world and protect and look after will grow up to be meat.

Not that she loves cows overmuch either. She figures they're about as smart as the cowboys. It's one long war. The cowboys grab the calves, kick them when they're down because they're still struggling as hard as they can. The mommas linger nearby, hollering their own misery, trying to get up the courage to run in and massacre the men who are torturing their offspring. The horses and dogs work furiously, the dogs herding and holding everything together, the horses cutting out calves, holding them on the end of long ropes, still with enough energy to dash to the edge of the herd if it looks like someone might be straying.

Lucille loves it. She's in the middle of everything, roaring around, working hard, showing off her roping skills, even taking a turn at branding and castrating. The kids work hard, everyone works hard. Lucille and Annie and the kids go back to the house at night, but the cowboys have brought a couple of wagons with their gear and they eat around a fire and sleep under the wagon rolled in tarps like so many canvas-coloured slugs.

One night they're finally finished. Lucille and Annie and the kids are all formally invited to dinner at the wagon. The cowboys still don't say much to her.

Annie herself says nothing, just sits, staring into the darkness. Beyond the circle of firelight she thinks she can see a wolf who paces and paces, back and forth, the firelight shining from his green eyes, his mottled black-and-grey coat shining gold on the tips. He's waiting for her to leave, to follow, to go into the soft black night and sleep with her tail curled around herself, safe and at home forever.

After such long intense effort, Lucilles' small shack feels quiet and dirty and neglected. They're all exhausted. The kids whine, wanting something, more excitement, more attention. Lucille makes huge meals. For days, they eat and do chores and fall into bed. Annie lies in her room on the creaking pole bed and broods.

"You're afraid," she says to herself one day. "You're afraid to go. You're afraid to do it." She lies awake at night, staring at the newspapered walls and the fear hits her the minute she lies down at night. It stands around her bed and whispers about blizzards and bears and lonely places. She won't have Black Dog to keep her warm, to warn her about intruders.

"I don't want to go," she thinks over and over. All the things about Lucille that have been irritating her now seem, if not wonderful, at least bearable. The land itself is becoming amazingly beautiful. The grass is still yellow but with a promising emerald underlay. The slow spring evenings glow with promise and sleepy birdsong; the kid's voices, yelling to each other over their games, resound through the golden dusk like bells.

Lucille is going about things with her usual frantic energy. She's planting her garden and trying to get it fenced at the same time. She wants to start another corral, she wants a new barn, she wants to buy some more horses and break them in, she wants to take a trip and is figuring out how to get a wagon, she wants everything at once.

Annie works alongside her. She figures at this point that the easiest and probably the best thing to do for everyone would be to sneak out, leave at dawn, or even at night. She can't face saying good-bye to Lucille, and especially to the kids. She wishes she were already on the trail. Then the preoccupations of travelling would take over and she wouldn't have time to brood or worry.

Lucille's even paid her off, left the money, more money than Annie expected, in the cabin on her pillow. They didn't even discuss it. She wants Lucille to talk to her, wants Lucille to put her arms around her and invite her back, tell her it's all right, she can stay, she can bring her brothers, she can live here forever, and it can be her place after all. Lucille is making plans for a round-up to push the cattle up into the hills for the summer, leaving the grass on the river flats to get tall for winter.

One morning while they're having breakfast, she hears horses and riders in the yard. Charlie and Fletch open the door and step in. Lucille is pleasant, pours them coffee. It's not until they ask where to put their stuff that Annie realizes what's happening. Lucille has hired them to replace her, right under her nose, without asking or telling her or discussing it. And now they're moving into her bunkhouse.

Lucille says, still being pleasant, "You can move back in here with me if you like, Annie. The kids would like that. And I hate sleeping by myself."

Annie nods. Her face is stuck into an idiot half smile, frozen, like glass that's melted and run. Her shoulders ache. She retrieves her stuff from the bunkhouse and takes it to the barn. There are bits and pieces of junk she's accumulated through the winter, presents from the kids, extra clothes, a few old newspapers. She spends time sorting it out, then puts what she needs into her saddlebags.

The kids come to talk to her and she tries to smile, but they figure out what's happening and run hollering and wailing to the house. She finishes her packing and goes up to the house to get supplies. She's not sure what Lucille will let her take, but Lucille has it already figured out. She has a couple of bags of supplies packed, waiting. Annie's face burns when she sees that. So Lucille's been planning this all along. They're polite with each other. The kids stand wide-eyed and silent. Nat hides behind his mother's skirt, scowling. Annie goes back to the barn, packs the supplies, gets Duster and rides up to the house. Lucille is waiting.

"At least come and have a cup of coffee, say good-bye," she snaps. Annie hesitates, then gets down and they go inside. Lucille pours coffee all around but she won't look at Annie. Charlie and Fletch talk about routes west, rumours they've heard, trails through the high passes, they tell her the route they think she should take, then go on about Indians, bears, wolves, rock slides. The talk swirls around and around and then stops. It's clearly time to go. She kneels to hug the boys. Nat starts to scream. Gerald hangs his head. Alice and Carrie sniffle and hold on to her. She has to peel all of them off her neck. They stick like small fierce mosquitoes; no sooner does she brush one off, than another grabs her hand, her leg, her ankle.

They all file outside. Annie wishes desperately to just be done with it, that they would leave her alone, let her go, but Lucille walks beside her, not speaking, as she nudges Duster into a walk. The kids stay behind on the hill in front of the house, faces stricken, silent.

Side by side they go down the hill, down to the little pool in the stream where she went for a wash, that first night after that first long sweaty day at Lucille's.

Lucille stops. Annie pulls Duster to a halt. For a long moment, they are just there, frozen in silence and immobility. Then Annie sighs, slides off Duster, goes over to Lucille. They put their arms around each other, hug and weep, rocking and swaying together.

Lucille says, laughing through her sobs, "I'm so goddamn mad at you, I could kill you, you scrawny little thing, you goddamn rifle-toting cowgirl...how could you think you were just going to ride away and not say a real good-bye, how could you? You're my very best friend, oh hell, you're my only friend." She starts sobbing again. "Oh Annie, I don't want you to go. I know you have to...it's okay. I just don't want you to. I'm going to miss you...what in hell am I going to do without you? I wish you'd never come...no,

I don't mean that. I thought I knew about loneliness before. Oh, goddamn, goddamn, GODDAMN, Annie, why is
it all so hard?"

Annie can only nod. It hurts too much. Lucille is right.
It is too hard. Why did her parents die and Lucille's husband die and why can't she just say that she'll stay forever?
Why is she leaving this woman she loves like she loved her
mother, like a sister, no, just plain loves? They rock and
cry some more until they finally slow down to sobs and
sniffles and long, shuddering sighs.

"Please Annie, please, please, be careful, and eat. You
never eat properly. You can't even cook."

"I'll try," says Annie. "And when I find what I'm looking
for, when I get my place, I'll come back to visit and tell
you all about it."

"Yeah," says Lucille, "sure you will. By then I'll have the
new barn built and the corral, and a new house with a big
soft double bed, and we'll sit on the porch and watch the
cows get fat and make me money."

Annie thinks she's going to start crying again and she
can't stand it. Blind, she turns away, gets on Duster and
rides up the hill, over the grass, through the sage and the
tiny prairie flowers, up through the stand of resiny pines,
all the time feeling this is all wrong. She ought to just turn
around, go back down, fall into Lucille's arms and stay
there, but she can't, she can't.

Duster plods on, and she rides like a sack, bent over and
not caring where they're going or why.

EIGHTEEN

DUSTER'S HOOF SLIPS ON A SLICK, pine-needled edge of
granite, and for a moment, Annie is dizzy with terror.
Adrenaline rakes her spine. She curses out loud, fear es-
caping her control. Nothing has gone right since she left
Lucille's; she doesn't even know where she is. She headed
towards what the cowboys had described as a pass, but
either she missed it or they didn't know what they were
talking about. As usual, she thinks bitterly.

Either way, she's lost in this morass of hills, pine trees,
and talus slopes. Cliffs suddenly open beneath her feet into
sudden, down-swooping vistas of distance and fear; Duster
valiantly struggles over rocks and dead logs with spiked
limbs which stab at his belly while she holds the reins and

tries to help him with sheer willpower. They climb in and out of deep dead ravines holding black icy pools of water and shiny slivers of rapids, following deer trails which wind back on themselves and fade into tangles of brush.

Even more than the knowledge that she's lost is the growing conviction that she's out of place, that this time she's taken on too much, dared too much and this implacable unforgiving place is nowhere a girl and a horse should be, even a girl with a duty to fulfill, and a rifle and a deadly aim, even a girl who's tough. The knowledge that she could die here, die easily with one misstep, one broken leg, or even just go on being lost wandering and circling back on herself with Duster patiently following along, clumps in her stomach like sickness.

There's nowhere flat to camp. The whole country has tilted and settled insanely, slabs of sheer granite sliding into careless lumps of hills and matted brush, long slopes of rolling rocks and at the bottom of each slope a creek, winding and foaming its way downhill. Annie and Duster are either climbing up, puffing and blowing and grunting with exertion, or sliding down, knees shaking, through small avalanches of rocks and boulders sliding down the hill past them.

She doesn't know what to do. She can't even think of what to do. She's too scared too think. She just has to keep moving. She's got to get over these mountains. From a distance it looked easy enough, but now that she's in them, she's in a maze. She's already fought her way up two long heavily treed valleys that ended in unclimbable slopes. Joe had talked offhandedly about a pass, but he hadn't been over it, only heard about it. He said the Indians used it, it was their old trade route to the northwest. He said he'd always wanted to go and someday he would. He said there were two mountains shaped like wolf teeth, unmistakable. Annie had listened carefully, tried not to appear too interested.

But now all the mountains looked like sharp canine fangs. The trick was to find the right valley, the valley with the trail in it, but she'd missed it. She could be too far south, or too far north, heading in the wrong direction. She could be anywhere.

Lucille and the kids, the ranch, cows, and flat land are a million miles away, unimaginable, unreachable, unbearable to think about. The worse thing is the fear that reaches out for her at night. She had gotten used to sleeping out, before she got to Lucille's; she had Black Dog and the rifle and the country was open and somehow friendly, or at least not openly hostile, not like this black rough place. This country doesn't want her here, she thinks, wants to shrug her off, a fly off its back.

At night, after she's made a fire, fed herself and given Duster a tiny bit of grain, the fear is waiting for her, crouching among her blankets and under the surrounding trees. It's familiar, she waits for it, greets it. It takes various shapes—skeleton shapes of death and hunger, Duster's trusting puzzled eyes after he's made it across yet another uncrossable ravine, the image of him lying in agony with a broken leg, a punctured belly, the image of them sliding helpless down a granite slope.

She's taken to sleeping sitting up, her back against a cliff or a tree, the rifle across her knees. She dozes, then wakes at every noise, sticks cracking, branches rubbing together, owls, wood popping in the fire. What is she waiting for, she thinks crossly to herself. All those damn cowboy stories have got her spooked. They've got her waiting for bears, wolves, Indians, rock slides and evil spirits.

One night, around the fire during branding, they got to telling ghost stories. Everyone had a couple of good stories, things they'd heard or had happen to them. Annie had a few herself. Her Mom had always told wonderful ghost stories, but she had to be coaxed and maneuvered into it. After supper, after the dishes were washed and put away, their mother would get out her sewing or knitting, her bags of multicoloured scraps of cloth, a jar full of buttons, all sizes and shapes. Annie and her brothers would start to coax. Her mother would peer over her tiny gold-rimmed glasses, which she wore only for sewing. "Tell us, Mom," they'd say. "Tell us about the time you and Pa saw the ghosts."

"Oh no, you don't want to hear that old thing again," she'd laugh and keep sewing, sorting through the buttons to find just the right size.

"Yes, yes, we do," they'd chorus. "Yes, we do want to hear it again." Then one of them would start, "Remember you said it was when Pa was building the house..." and another would interrupt, "No he wasn't, he was away, wasn't he, Mom? And that's when you saw it, wasn't it?"

And their mother, still frowning over the buttons would say, "No, no, that isn't it, you see, your father and I had just gotten married, and he had to go away to find some work for a bit of cash. See, we needed cash to get a cow and a team and plow. Oh, we were so hungry sometimes. I learned to be a dead shot with that old Henry rifle. Why, I shot a deer right in our front yard one time and then I screamed for your father to come running. The poor little thing, just a doe, maybe with fawns." She'd pause to shiver, shake her head, remembering, the buttons forgotten. "You were just a baby, Annie. Oh, you were the cutest little mite of a thing. So there I was, all alone in that drafty old farm-house. It belonged to your other grandparents, your Dad's parents...you never knew them, they died before you were born, and no one wanted to live in their house because they told such stories about it. Oh your Grandma was a strange woman, tiny and fierce. But fey, they say she had the second sight, and oh my, she was a great cook. She made the best gingerbread...Your Grandad was an old tightwad—Scots and mean—but even he said he'd seen something. Said once he heard the furniture crashing around upstairs, but when he went to look, everything was in its place. He came back down and it all started crashing and banging again. He just shrugged and let it fly. Well, your Dad had grown up in that house and he just laughed, said his parents had gotten foolish in their old age and he didn't believe in ghosts. No one had lived in the house since the old people died. So there I was, all alone with a new baby. I'd bring you into bed with me at night. I even dragged the cat in with me and kept the dog in the house."

"But what did you see?" they'd demand, in an agony of impatience.

"Oh, just a shape—misty, it looked like a little old man. We thought it was the man who built the house…he died building it. Fell off the roof. But it never hurt me. Even your father saw it once. He got up and walked through it. It just sort of shimmered a little. Actually, we got feeling friendly towards it after a while. But I never liked staying alone in that house. And that poor cat, she wouldn't stay there at all. Even the dog would scratch to go out."

They would sigh in satisfaction, no matter how many times they had heard the story before.

"Yes, it's a queer old world," their mother would sigh pensively. "With strange sights in it. I remember once I woke up and the bedroom was filled with a wonderful red, rosy light, like a big clear cloud…it was so warm and soft. I tried to wake your father, so he could see it, but I shook him and called him and he wouldn't wake up."

"But what happened…?"

"Oh, nothing, I went back to sleep. I felt there was nothing there to hurt me, it was a very friendly cloud, quite pretty. It didn't bother me at all…"

Annie sighs. Story-telling nights had been wonderful but they're long gone. There's no one to tell her stories and no one to show her the way. Above all, there's no one to rescue her if she falls off a cliff or if Duster does something stupid like break a leg or if a bear eats both of them. No one will ever know what happened to them and her brothers will grow up thinking she deserted them.

She has to find the pass, even if it means going up every silly valley in these stupid mountains. She'll find it if it's there...if Joe didn't lie, if the cowboys weren't totally confused, if the Indians actually *made* trading trails, like everyone said they did, and then used them enough to keep them open and marked.

She makes camp one night in a steep valley by a creek. In the fading light from higher up on the hill, it looked like there might be a trail by the river. It's damp and dark by the creek. The fir trees here are old, huge, grotesquely twisted by age and wind. They lean together, rubbing their branches in strange squeaks and mutters. Even Duster is jumpy, snorting and spooking at shadows in the brush. But it's too dark to go any further. She's too tired, and tired of being tired, and mad at herself, mad at the mountains looming over her like a self-righteous circle of old women demanding to know what she's doing in their territory, wandering over their old bones and disturbing their sleep.

As always, the warm fire and some food cheers her up. She's trying to be careful with her supplies, though she's always ravenous from the effort of climbing. It's too dark to catch fish, so she has burnt bacon, iron-hard biscuits baked in a pan on the coals, and a lot of hot and very sweet tea.

She's sleeping when the bear comes. At least, she thinks it's a bear. The night is black-dark, with no moon. Duster wakes her, thrashing against his tether. She hasn't hobbled him because of the steep rocky hills. His rope snaps, and he crashes away through the brush. She can hear his hooves clicking, banging and thudding on the rocks, the brush crackling into the distance. Then something solid blots out the light from the coals still glowing red in the fire. She lies still, panicked, unable to think what to do. It paws at the fire, grunting. She hears the dim thud of heavy feet as it moves away. She can almost see a huge shape lift against the tree where the food is tied. It snuffles, snorts, grunts at her saddle hung over a rock. There's a crash in the brush as the saddle goes flying.

It comes over to her. She lies frozen, not breathing, willing herself to be dead, to be still, or gone, out of this place, this life, this overwhelming terror. She can feel its breath on her face, sniffing. The musky smell is all around her, heavy and strange. Something nudges her back, lifts her delicately, rolls her over. She stays limp, pretending. It shakes her, growling and muttering. For an eternity she lies still, not breathing, wishing herself already dead, unconscious, gone somewhere else.

Then it's gone as suddenly as it came. She lies, not moving, still not wanting to breathe, shivering in every muscle and praying, she doesn't care to who or what, to get her out of this, rescue her from this mad vicious place she's wandered into where everything hates her. She lies still for a long, long time, she has no idea how long. Then she remembers that Duster is gone.

She forces herself to get up. It takes all of her will to pull the blanket back off her face, and look around. It's still dark but there's a watery grey look to the eastern sky. She builds up the fire. It's hard to make herself move, agonizing to step next to the dark trees to pull away dead branches. All her muscles ache. As soon as there's a faint light, she gets the food out of the tree, fishes around in the brush and finds her saddle. There's a rip in the seat that looks like it's been cut with a knife. She forces herself to eat, hoists the food and saddle back into the tree, takes her rifle, some matches, some cold biscuits, and goes to look for Duster.

There's a game trail, not much of one, by the creek. Instead of running back down the valley, like she would have expected, he's turned upwards, following the trail. She's relieved. It's likely she'll find him tangled in brush or grazing somewhere. He's still trailing a tether rope.

But the morning wears on without a sign of him. She climbs higher and higher, over steep and slippery talus slopes where the trail is just a faint indentation in the rocks. At this height, there are patches of snow, places where Duster has had to cross hard, crusted snow, where a slip could mean a thousand-foot fall. She follows, carefully wedging her boots into his hoof prints. From his tracks, Duster is traveling at a steady pace, not stopping for food, not running, moving along just fast enough that she's not even close to catching up to him.

By late afternoon, she's realized the trap she's set for herself. She could go back, get the food and saddle, which are too heavy for her to carry far, and try and catch up with Duster tomorrow. Or she can keep following him, sleep out without blankets or food, and leave all her gear farther and farther behind her.

Or, she could be sensible, forget Duster, go back, make up a pack for herself, and try and find her way back to Lucille's.

She goes on. She can't do this without Duster. Losing Black Dog was bad enough. She can't lose Duster, too. He's all she has left. The trail climbs steeply, switching back and forth between house-sized boulders strewn over the hill face, and occasional wind-bent twisted trees. Finally, it climbs out of the trees altogether. There's only rock and wind and clumps of grass and spring flowers. Almost everywhere, trickles of slick water-washed weather-polished granite.

The trail edges along a cliff face. She comes to a place where there's a drop of four feet to the next ledge. There's a sheer drop of a thousand feet if she stumbles or misses her footing. But Duster's tracks are there; she jumps, makes it, and comes to a ridge where the trail starts steadily to descend. Dazed and sweating, she finally understands. She realizes what he's done. He's found the pass, gone over. Something has to be pulling or pushing at him. He would never have done it by himself, never made that insane jump, never gone in this direction at all.

The trail drops sharply over small round talus stones which slide and bounce ahead of her, then continues down through trees and more rocks. But now she can see it's a trail. She's stumbling with weariness but she keeps going, down and down and down. By the time she gets to the next valley bottom, it's dark. She'd keep going if she could see, but she can't. She's hungry and out of food. Despite her boots, her feet are sore and bruised.

She can't figure it out. What has got into Duster? Why does he keep going in such a hurry? She'd bash him one if he was here, stupid, bloody, contrary, goddamn horse. Where in hell does he think he's going? How is she ever going to get back to her saddle? She thinks of the trail she's just come over. It took all the nerve she had to face those heights. She didn't know she was that afraid of heights. She's climbed enough trees, jumped out of barn lofts onto hay piles, and never thought about it. But this is different. Faced with that light-filled immensity of air and space opening under her eyes, she felt she could float away, weightless as a cloud; only her feet kept her anchored, cling-ing, determined as lichens, to the rocks, to the earth.

When night comes, she makes a fire, then crouches over it, shivering. She can't get warm and she's so hungry. Tomorrow, if she can't catch up with him, she'll have to do something else, maybe give up and go back, face the pass even though it makes her wince to think of it, try to get back to the ranch, where they'll all have a good laugh at her expense. She'll have to try to get another horse. At least she knows now where the pass is. She adds more and more wood to the fire, crouching beside it, shivering, staring into the flames. She sits there until dawn.

Once again, she walks, plods, stumbles, shivering, unable to get warm, following Duster's signs: bent grass, faint imprints in the pine needles, occasional dung. She trudges steadily through a forest of thick fir and cedar, which finally opens into a long series of beaver meadows. The bright emerald grass is as tall as she is. It's only when she stumbles, trips over a downed tree and finds herself falling onto matted thick old grass, that she realizes how dizzy and weak she is. It's not just lack of food. She figures she must have some kind of fever. She lies there, cursing with all the curses she can think of. She can't get sick. She never gets sick and this is simply the wrong time. "Get up," she orders herself. "Dammit all to hell, get up get up get up."

But she lays there for a long time. It seems very far to get up. She does, rolling onto her knees and hoisting herself with her arms. She goes on, trudging through tree patches and over grass, past beaver dams in a small brown and blue creek. Part of her mind notes how beautiful, serene, sun-dimpled bird-singing, everything is. But it is far away, the rest of the world, and she is inside an aching haze, a dim grey-lighted head-aching eardrum-banging world.

At first, she doesn't see the black shapes on the side of the next small meadow because her eyes are stupid with no sleep and so much walking and concentrating on not falling down again. Then they take form, heads down grazing, four legs, switching tails nagging at the flies. Colours. Red and bay, pinto and buckskin shining in a mosaic of grass, sun and green-yellow willow.

Carefully, putting one leaden foot in front of the other, she tries to approach them. Before she can even get close, they snort in alarm and thunder in a multicoloured wave out of the meadow. One of them is Duster, holding his head high to keep from tripping over his trailing lead rope.

Nothing to do but follow, on thin rubber legs, threatening to collapse. If she can get close enough to call to Duster, maybe he'll let her come up to him. Or maybe, if she just hangs around for a while, the horses will get used to her and let her approach.

She stumbles on. The whole situation is ridiculous. She can't take it seriously. Why should she? Who is she to take it seriously? Once or twice, she even tries to sing a little. Her voice comes out a sad squawk. She lurches when she walks but the trees catch her and hold her up. She tries to skip a bit but that's ridiculous. Her legs tangle around themselves and she finds herself lying on the ground again. In her head, she's still skipping, walking down a nice soft path, walking, walking, walking. Tears come to her eyes.

"Duster," she calls, her voice rasping. That's silly. He won't come. But she calls again anyway. She wants him to come. He's the only friend she has. If he deserts her again, now, she *will* be all alone. Very all alone.

She's tired. She's so, so tired. She would like to sleep a little, just a little, take a nap here in the sun, and then she'll go on and get her horse. It's almost warm on the matted cedar needles. She would love to be really warm again, back in Lucille's bed. "Lucille," she mutters, and feels Lucille's arms go around her and hold her. She can sleep now for just a little while. Then she'll go get Duster. She'll come to him, and he'll do what he did as a colt, turn to her, put his heavy head down on her shoulder, sigh his long horse sigh, and chew on her hair.

NINETEEN

NOTHING IS VERY REAL ANYMORE. A boy is sitting beside her, a boy with long braids and brown eyes. He's watching her. His face is thin and a bit sad. He looks to be about her age. She opens her eyes, closes them, trying to remember, make sense of what's happening. It comes back like a weight settling, a stone in her stomach. Duster running wild, her pack and saddle lost, somewhere miles behind her. She tries to lift her head and the effort sends blood pounding through her temples. She lies back, dizzy, colours dance around her. She opens her eyes again. The boy is still there.

"My elders sent me to get you," he says in slow, heavily accented English. "They thought you could probably use some help."

Annie is so confused by this that she gets dizzy again. She clutches the ground while the sky and trees swirl around her. Tears come into her eyes. She blinks and wipes them away. Damn. What a weak-kneed fool she's turned out to be. And now she has to be rescued from her own stupidity by some kind of hallucination. She realizes she's shivering and shaking with cold. "Get up," she thinks to herself. "Get up. Get rid of this boy who's not really here at all. Get on your feet."

But the vision of the boy persists. Finally, it dawns on her that he's really sitting there, waiting for her to do something. It's very difficult to think. Her thoughts wind slowly through her mind, like a creek meandering its way through a swamp.

"I'm okay," she says, sitting up, gritting her teeth at the effort it takes. "I'm fine. I…just need a little help catching my horse…I think he's got in with a bunch of wild horses."

The boy laughs. "He's a nice horse," he says. "I rode him up here yesterday."

Annie stares at him. This whole scenario just won't start making sense. She can hear the words but they aren't, somehow, forming into intelligible sentences. She thinks she should say something, ask questions, but nothing comes into her mind.

"C'mon," says the boy cheerfully. "We should get going." He stands up and holds out his hand. Annie ignores it, stands up by herself, though she has to roll over on her knees to do it. Once she's up, she latches both hands onto

a tree trunk to steady herself. The tree feels solid and com-
forting. She holds onto it for a long minute, wishing she
didn't have to go anywhere. The boy is strange, and her
mind won't settle down into coherency. She shivers, suddenly cold. The boy, who may or may not be real, is saying
something to her, he's in front of her with two saddled
horses, one of whom is Duster…only she doesn't remember him going away. She's still holding on to the tree.

Then everything speeds up. Things are happening without her consent or understanding, happening in jerky frozen images. She wants to say wait, stop, but she can't or
doesn't. Somehow she's on Duster, and riding, hanging on
the best she can. They come to an Indian camp with white
tipis and horses, wandering dogs and running kids. Even
when she's helped to lie down by a fire, with warm furs
wrapped around her, she wants to ask questions, try to
understand, but she's too tired to think of anything and
the words don't come. There is no place and no time for
them in this new, fuzzy, speeded-up world.

The tipi is round and white, full of light and warmth. A
woman brings food, a thin broth. Annie drinks. Nothing
has ever tasted so good, nothing ever will, and she smiles
at the woman, who smiles back, takes the bowl and leaves.

Annie curls up inside the furs, watching the fire and
thinking of going out and finding Duster, then saying,
thanks very much but really, I'm fine. But somehow, every
time she thinks about it, her thoughts wander off again.
Gradually, she puts it all together, thinks herself backwards

in time, back to Lucille, back to the trip, back to her parents dying, back to her brothers, the farm, her grandparents' sad faces, back to being a child, running free on the farm, and the strangeness of that now, so distant from here with people she doesn't know, helpless, unable to move. The memory of her parents brings its own familiar rush of piercing pain, just under her heart. It's like remembering a knife wound. She thinks that as soon as she gets her strength, she'll be on her way again, as soon as she can, as soon as she's rested, as soon as she's slept.

When she wakes again, she's better. She's weak, but when she lies still, listening to her body, she can feel thin trickles of energy returning to her muscles. She has to pee very badly. She wonders where to go. Should she just get up and stagger off to the bushes while everyone watches her go. She can't ask the boy because he's a boy. Does anyone else here speak English?

She can't stand it any longer. She gets up, wincing; things in her body twinge, ache and pain, but they work. She makes it to the door of the tipi and out. It's broad daylight, close to noon, and hardly anyone seems to be around. A group of women sit at the edge of the camp, heads tilted over a hide which is supported by everyone's knees. They're scraping it and talking and giggling a lot in the process. They don't look at her. Thankfully, she walks as casually as she can to the edge of the nearest bush and when she thinks she's out of sight, squats in relief, glad that no one has seemed to notice her.

She goes back to the tipi, unsure of what to do next. She's starving. Her body is yelling for food. She wants some tea. Do these people drink tea? She climbs back through the round door of the tipi and sits down uncertainly on the bed. No one comes. She goes back outside and sits down in the sun. She thinks the women working on the hide must have noticed her but every time she looks at them, they look away. She can't catch anyone's eye; no one will look directly at her. The women chatter quietly to each other. The sun is soft hands on her tired face, and she would be feeling fine if she wasn't so hungry. There is a fire, or at least ashes from one, smoldering in front of her. A pot sits in the ashes and emits meat-smelling steam. A chipped tin bowl sits beside it.

She waits, the saliva gathering in her mouth. It's not her food. Surely she should ask someone for permission. She goes on waiting, and waiting, beginning to feel very irritated. What kind of rude people are these? Is she invisible or something? Do they hate her for some reason? After saving her life, you think they'd at least be interested in her well-being, would want to see how she's doing. Has she offended them somehow? Should she just go find Duster and get out of here, quick, before something scary happens?

Finally, slowly, casually, a woman comes over to her, gestures at the bowl, fills it, hands it to Annie and goes away, still without looking at her. Annie eats, then helps herself and eats again, feeling lonely. But there's nothing to do, nowhere to go, and at least she's warm and full. She shrugs, goes back inside, curls up on the furs, dozes, then sleeps the afternoon away, waking every once in a while to moving shadows and patterns of leaves on the thin, stretched hides, to the distant sounds of birds and wind, to the smells of smoke and fur and leather. She can smell the fir resin from the mat of bough tips she's lying on, and the earth beneath them, beaten hard but still moist with the cool essence of spring.

She wakes up because the boy is sitting beside her. Actually, she realizes, he's not a boy. He's probably the same age as her, probably the same age as those stupid cowboys that worked for Joe. But he's slender, with clean, clear features instead of fuzzy, unwashed hair and a straggly mustache and beard; his hair is long blue-black, braided. She didn't hear him come into the tent, which annoys her. She shouldn't sleep so deeply, she thinks. If she's going to stay alive out here, she's got to get smarter, develop better habits, better ways of protecting herself. She's still angry at herself for being such a fool as to lose her pack and saddle.

Only they're not lost. They're sitting on the ground beside her. She looks at them, looks at the boy.

"Thanks," she says. "Thanks for finding my stuff. I didn't know what I was going to do. How did you..."

He shrugs off her thanks. "The elders would like to talk with you," he says. Yesterday, when he found her, he seemed to find the whole situation amusing, from what little she can remember. Her memories of the last few days are un-

clear, cobwebbed in some places and sunlit in others. But
she vividly remembers opening her eyes and seeing his face,
his black-brown eyes and shining braids with tiny strips of
red cloth wrapped and tied around their ends. Right now,
though, he looks serious.

She gets up and follows him outside. It's dusk; the air is
still. The light slants in long dusty arrows towards them.
For the first time, she notices the valley around the camp.
The tipis are in a circle, set in the middle of a broad flat
valley, which is then surrounded by mountains, huge jagged
vertical rocks glowing ochre and rose-grey in the evening
light, their peaks lit by pink light on snow. She stops, held
by it, wanting to take it in, grasp it, hold it, gather it in by
the armful, this silence, this beauty. He waits for her, not
looking at her, just waiting.

"It's…nice here," she says, gesturing. "The mountains
and everything…"

The young man shrugs. "It's our home," he says. "Come
now, please."

A circle of old men and women are sitting on the grass
at the edge of the camp. They are laughing and joking
among themselves. He leads her to the circle, gestures at
her to sit down. There is a long silence which stretches on
until Annie has to hold herself tightly to keep from twitching, scratching…anything.

"Jeezus," Annie thinks. "These people sure never do anything in a hurry." She wonders what they're thinking about,
if they're thinking at all. She can't guess what kind of

thoughts lie behind the strangeness of their faces, different than hers, different than what she's used to; brown, wrinkled skin, deep-set eyes, black hair.

One by one, she examines their faces. They all have long hair, worn braided, in two braids or one, some with ornaments and feathers, some without, some wrapped in leather or cloth.

One says something to the young man, nodding towards Annie, and other people nod and a low laugh goes around the circle. Annie feels her face turn red. Whatever he said, it was directed at her. She feels a sudden flash of anger. She can't help not knowing where she is or what she's doing. She tries to think of what she could say, how she could explain to these people the idea of homesteading and home, and how important it is to her, and that she is simply on her way to somewhere else, she hasn't meant to stumble in here and offend anybody.

One of the oldest people, a tiny woman with deep wrinkled skin like sun-dried leather, and pure white hair, addresses a question directly to Annie. The woman's eyes are almost black, set far back in her face. Annie thinks her eyes look sad and fierce at the same time.

The young man translates. "My grandmother asks, who are your people? Why do you come here, so far, alone and with nothing?"

Annie frowns, puzzled. Who are her people? What does the woman mean? Her family? Does she mean white people?

Carefully, talking slowly and a bit too loudly, she answers, "My mother and father are dead. I come from the East, from a land far away. We came with wagons and horses to find a new home. When my mother and father died, I left my brothers and came to look for land for us to build a home. My horse was frightened by a bear and ran away. I came to look for him. Thank you for finding me and helping me. It was very kind of you."

The young man translates and there are nods around the circle. Then the grandmother speaks again and he says, "She asks again, who are your people?"

Annie panics a bit. What is the old woman asking? What does the question mean? She doesn't know what she should answer. She doesn't know. She looks at the old woman and says, "I don't know. I don't know what you mean. I don't know if I have any people. I don't think so...maybe just white people, is all, I guess..."

The old woman looks at her while the young man translates and this time she nods but says nothing.

One of the other men speaks, and then several others in turn. The young man turns to her. "My grandfathers would like to know more about this bear that visited your camp. Did you see it? What did it look like, black, brown, silver?"

"I didn't actually see it," says Annie, frowning, trying to remember what she had seen. "I mean, it was dark when it came. I was asleep. It came over to me and touched me and sniffed me. It rolled me over. It smelled really strong.

I was too scared to really notice much."

He interprets. There is more discussion, more nodding of heads. They ask for more details, but she shakes her head.

"Why are they so interested?" she says. "What's going on?"

"They say, maybe it was a bear, maybe it wasn't...maybe it was the old man of the mountains," he adds cheerfully.

"It wasn't a man. It was huge."

"Well, who knows?" says the young man, shrugging. "They say a lot of things. Maybe it was a bear. Maybe it wasn't."

He listens again to the grandfathers. "They say to tell you last winter we had a lot of sickness in the camp. It was a new kind of sickness and they don't know where it came from and they didn't have any medicine for it. Many people died. My mother died," he adds, pausing. "They say you are welcome here, you should stay and rest your horse for a while. He's very tired." He laughs. "They say you look like a deer after a bad winter, all bones and hair."

"Oh, thanks," says Annie, surprised. Then she laughs too. She nods and smiles at the elders, who smile back. When they smile, she thinks, they look more like real people, normal people. Then she thinks, no — that's not right. But everything about them is strange, their clothes, the strong stink of leather and smoke that surrounded them, their easy way of folding to the ground when they sit.

"C'mon," the boy says now, getting up and wandering off. "Now you can meet my family," he calls.

Annie hurries after him. "How come you speak English?" she says, "and what's your name? My name is Annie."

"My father used to live as a white man but he is a good hunter. Now he lives with us. He used to take me with him, trading fur. But he doesn't like white people so much anymore. He says they don't know when they are telling the truth and when they are lying...now when he goes to trade fur, he won't take me. But I will go when I am older. I learned some English when I traveled with him. I know lots about white people," he adds, just a little smugly.

"But, your name...?" Annie persists.

"I have an Indian name and a white name from my father. One of my names is Aaron, but sometimes lately the people call me a name which, in your language, means Shadow." For a moment his face is dark and closed. Annie wonders about the name but she doesn't ask anything more.

Shadow continues. "It is because I still weep for my mother and her shadow will not leave me," he adds softly. "Perhaps she is waiting for me to come to her. Or perhaps her spirit won't rest because of the sickness and the people who died. I don't know."

They wander together through the camp; people nod and smile. Everyone seems busy at something. Naked children with tangled hair run past, laughing and screeching and calling out to Shadow. They stop to stare at Annie and then run on, laughing. Annie tries to keep from wrinkling her nose at the smell. The hides stretched over the tipis reek of smoke. There is a pile of strong-smelling green hides at one edge of the camp. Dogs forage among the tipis, wait by the fires, snap at any tidbit of food, gnaw at the bones which litter the ground.

It's evening now and quickly getting dark, but the camp is full of light and flickering shadows from fires inside and outside the tipis. The tipis glow from inside, luminous and huge in the darkness. Silhouettes of people move against them. Good smells of meat cooking surround her. Shadow stops to talk to someone and Annie waits, listening to the strange language. Above the noises of the camp, she can hear the wider noises from outside, the creek chuckling and dancing in its trough of polished stones, the evening down-draft coming off the peaks, soft and lonesome like an old sad song. Her guts turn over and hurt, as if someone was squeezing her from inside. She thinks she has never been so happy, so confused and so lonely all at the same time, here with these unknown people, at home in their own place. Part of her stays on guard, walks stiffly, feels their eyes on her back. For a moment all she wants is Duster and to be alone, far away on the mountains in her own silent camp, even if there are bears that walk like old giant men. But she also wants to walk into one of these tipis and sit down and eat and listen to the wind blow and speak a language that everyone understands. The language blows like a soft breeze around her. She feels shut out by it, disconnected. How can she tell these people who she is?

Outside Shadow's tipi, his family are sitting cross-legged on the ground, with bowls of food and a black kettle steaming on the fire. A white dog slides past her, growling. A young woman silently hands her a bowl of food and Annie sits down beside Shadow. The family converses in their language. Annie sits looking into the fire and listening to the wind. People walk by and call greetings, other people stop, come over, sit, talk, leave again; the dog comes close to smell her. She holds out her hand to it and scratches its head. The dog's teats are heavy with milk; she must be nursing several pups.

There is laughter and joking around the fire. She can't understand any of it. She tries to decide which one is Shadow's father. None of the men look white to her. They all have long braids and lined faces.

She leans over to Shadow. "Which one is your father?"

He points. The man he points to is thin and quiet, with a narrow face and pointed chin. Now that Annie knows, she can see the resemblance in Shadow's face. The man nods at Annie but otherwise ignores her. She remembers Shadow's remark about his father and white people.

"That's my sister," says Shadow. "In English, her name would be…" he knits his brow "…something like 'rain falling on the soft grass'. I guess you can call her Rain." Rain doesn't look at Annie, even though she's sitting right next to them.

"We went to a white school for a while," he continues. "My father wanted us to go. He said it would be good to know about white people, that maybe a time would come when we would want to live with them. I thought it would be exciting. White people have so many good things. So we went for a while and we didn't like it. We had to run away and come home. It was hard. We didn't know where we were, but we found some people who helped us. We got very hungry but we helped each other and then we were okay."

"School..." says Annie, astonished. "A real school, with teachers and books and everything?"

But Shadow doesn't answer. He stares at the fire. After a while he says, very softly, almost to himself, "They cut off my hair as soon as we got there...days and weeks in a wagon and right away, they took me in this small dark room. I didn't know what they wanted. I thought they were going to kill me. I remember seeing these big scissors, like knives flashing in my face...and I don't remember anything more until the day I decided to leave. Then my heart came to life again...and now I am home."

Annie is silent. None of this fits with her pictures of what Indians might be like. She can't picture Shadow in a school, sitting behind a desk. And why is he nice to her, when the rest of his family is treating her like she doesn't exist.

"Where did you come from, Annie?" The question takes her by surprise.

"Oh, back there somewhere," she sighs, "a long ways. There was a settlement, and then we crossed some plains, and then last winter I stayed at this ranch." She stops, wondering if she has said too much.

"But where is your family, the rest of your family. Why did you not go to them when your parents died?"

"I didn't want to go back East. There's only my grandma and grandpa anyway, and they're old. And no one would take us back there."

"But what about your aunties and uncles and your other grandparents, your cousins?" He is plainly puzzled.

She shrugs. "Don't have any."

His eyes widen at this. "You are very alone then," he says, "without a family. And now you have no home." He shakes his head. "Perhaps you could find a family here to adopt you."

Annie shakes her head. "I'm doing this on my own," she says. "I'm going to find my own place, somewhere, somehow, a place of my own." Shadow doesn't say anything more, but she can tell he feels confused and sorry for her.

One of the men takes up a drum, beats it gently, and sings in a high quavering voice. It's completely dark around the camp now. The white dog lies at Annie's side and she scratches its ear. People slip away from the fire, one by one, until only she and Shadow are left. Then Shadow stands up, unfolds and stretches, and Annie is left sitting by the fire. No one has told her where to sleep. No one seems to care much about her, one way or the other. She makes her way back to the tipi where she stayed that afternoon. It's empty but someone has lit a fire and left it burning for her. Tomorrow, she thinks, she'll get directions and get the hell out of here, before something bad happens. She finds her rifle, checks to make sure it's loaded, lays it beside her. She should go check on Duster as well. But right now, she's too tired to even think about moving, let alone travelling.

TWENTY

A WEEK LATER, ANNIE AND SHADOW are riding side by
side through an alpine meadow, towards a lake which he
especially wants her to visit. She hasn't left. Every day she
thinks about it then puts it off for one more day. It's hard
to think about going. It's hard to remember why it's even
so urgent. Nothing seems as real as this valley among the
mountains, as the rank upon tossing rank of wildly coloured
flowers in the meadows, as the sun-streaked flat granite
walls, over which water trickles and spouts and slides and
streaks and collects together into a hundred silver joyful
streams which run through the meadow under the horses'
feet. It's still spring up here. The flowers riot in a joyous
frenzy in front of them as they ride through the meadows,

209

masses of tossing white, red, yellow, blue, purple, pink petals absorbing the sun.

Duster snorts and nuzzles at the other horse, a grey mare, which squeals back at him. They climb steadily together, while Shadow points silently to things he thinks she might miss…an elk crossing a ridge, two whitetail deer standing in the shadow of trees, a small pica rock rabbit whistling and scuttling for its hole.

They climb a final steep rocky trail to the lake, a serene blue eye shielded by hooded granite boulders, fringed with bent and twisted black spruce. A moose calf bleats and scrambles awkwardly across the reedy shallows at one end of the lake, disappearing into the trees.

They tie the horses. Shadow silently leads the way to a flat boulder that forms a platform in the shallow lake. He sits and Annie sits beside him. They are silent for a long time. An eagle slides down a column of air above them. She hears a noise and turns to look. Shadow is crying. Tears slide in shiny flat wet streaks over his whole face.

She doesn't know what to do. Men don't cry and when they do, something is disastrously wrong. She reaches out a hand but he ignores her, snatches his hand away.

"Oh, my mother," he sobs, in a low whisper, "my mother, I miss you, I miss you, why did you die and leave me, oh my brave mother, your child is here, missing you." He continues in his own language. He weeps and weeps.

Annie sits on beside him in embarrassed agonized silence wondering what to do, whether to leave him alone, or try to get him to calm down, or just leave instead of having to witness such a display of weakness.

Crying. She never cries about anything, except for that night with Lucille; even when she was lost in the mountain, trailing Duster, she didn't cry. Too damn scared to cry. And her father never cried, and she made sure she never let him catch her crying over anything. He would think then that she was just a girl, a useless girl. Her thoughts ramble and clog. Not even when she was lost and sick and scared, did she give in. No, she's tough, needs to be, needs to stay tough, out here alone, a girl, not going to let herself get so scared again, let herself panic…

"You sit still long enough up here, and an eagle will come by and something will fall on your head," says Shadow, and falls over backwards laughing, tears still wet on his face. Annie laughs too. The contrast is ridiculous. But she's puzzled. How can he go from crying to laughing so fast?

Then he adds, "This is a very special place. If you want to come here sometime, if something is hurting you, this is a place of healing…" He pauses but she doesn't say anything. He looks at her, puzzled, but she looks away. Forget it, she thinks. I'm not showing what's hurting me, to you or anyone else.

"C'mon then," he says, standing and holding out his hand. "I'll show you a bear den."

For the rest of the afternoon they climb and scramble over boulders and streams among the flowers. The whole place is like a garden made by giants, flat places where the grass is soft and green, clumps of tiny, bent, wind-whipped spruce, and over all, the sun buttering the landscape gold with an edging of silver spray from water running everywhere. She and Shadow laugh and play and explore.

It's like being kids again, she thinks, it's like being at the lake in the mountains.

But as the afternoon wears on she becomes more and more conscious of Shadow, of his hand held out to help her up, of his strong bare shoulders, of his smell, musty but pleasant. She's not sure why. Annie realizes that she feels something the same towards Shadow as she did to Lucille. A friend, she thinks in surprise. We're friends. That's what it is. And the thought fills her, buoyant as a bubble shot through with rainbows on a stream's surface. Shadow smiles at her and she smiles back.

At twilight, they ride home. All the way, Annie is caught between the intense beauty of the day, and wondering why she can't weep for her own mother and father so freely and openly. Missing them suddenly lodges in her heart like a knife, which twists and penetrates until she can hardly breathe for the pain of it. She holds on to Duster's reins for dear life, and breathes and breathes, waiting to get back so she can lie down with the pain and be alone.

TWENTY-ONE

"THERE WILL BE A WOMEN'S SWEAT TODAY," says Shadow the next morning. "You could go if you wanted." He's taken to coming in every morning for a visit to discuss plans for the day. He seems to take it for granted that he will guide her and show her around. She's glad to see him; she wonders how she would have managed if he hadn't been there to show her things. Not that he ever explains much. He seems to expect her to understand just by showing her something. He's like her father in that way. She listens, watches, but still, a lot of things are puzzling. He never suggests that she do things. He simply says what he's doing and she's free to invite herself along if she chooses. He answers questions when she asks them, but often he'll simply tell her a long story instead. And he's moody. Some days he hardly talks at all. She remembers what he said about his mother's shadow. She thinks she knows how that feels. Some days the memory of her parents hangs around her like fog, making it hard to move, hard to breathe. Is that why she and Shadow spend so much time together?

She notices that he usually avoids his family, his sisters, though they call to him from the evening fire.

But he does things for Annie; he brings wood for her fire, brings food when she doesn't show up to eat with his family, tells her things she needs to know like where the women go to pee and do laundry and bathe in the stream, what to use to wash her hair and clothes. He seems to understand what she needs and tells her without embarrassment. He hasn't shown any romantic interest in her at all, and she's relieved. That would complicate everything. She likes having him for a friend. At least, she thinks they're friends. She worries that maybe he's doing all this out of a sense of duty, or because he speaks English and someone has told him to look after her.

No one asks her questions. People generally don't seem to notice her at all. It bothers her. Do they think she's beneath their notice? Or maybe they're like Lucille. What someone's done before doesn't matter, it's what they can do or are doing. Lucille seemed to figure Annie would talk about stuff she needed to talk about and the rest was her business. Maybe it's the same here. Annie would like that.

"When is it, the...sweat?" she asks. Shadow shrugs. That's

another thing. There's no time here that she can discern. It feels disorganized, calm but chaotic. Things happen. Hunters go in and out. Meals get cooked, hides tanned and clothes made, food stored and children looked after, but no one ever says a time. Everyone just seems to know while she's still trying to figure it out.

Shadow pauses. He seems to be struggling to say something. Finally he says, "Annie, I'm sorry. I don't know how to say this, but among our people, it is not done to touch someone unless they ask. If someone is feeling sad about something…it…it interrupts. Not just with the hands but with your eyes too…you can touch someone. It, well, it hurts to have someone look at you without giving permission. At that school, they all stared at me. I felt…it hurt me. I'm sorry. I don't mean to upset you or hurt your feelings." And he ducks suddenly back out of the tipi.

A click goes off rudely in her head. So that's why no one looked at her. She thought they were being rude and they thought they were being polite. And she kept staring at them. She stared at the elders. They must have thought her a fool.

All morning, she sulks forlornly in her tent. She watches, and when she sees movement among the women, one by one heading for the edge of camp, she gets up and sullenly follows. No one says anything. The group subtly reforms to include her and she finds herself walking beside Rain, Shadow's sister, who hasn't yet talked to her. Now, however, Rain gives her a tiny smile. Annie does the same.

Their eyes meet momentarily and they both look away.

The old woman with white hair leads the way, along the winding river bank to the women's bathing place, where the creek has been damned to make a pool. A low round hut covered with hides stands there; Annie has wondered about it. Some of the women start to take off their clothes.

Annie's throat closes and her face stiffens. Now she doesn't want to look at anyone. She shouldn't have come. She realizes suddenly she's in the wrong place. She won't know what to do or how to behave and she'll probably make a fool of herself. She should go back to her tipi. What has she gotten herself into? Is there a polite way to leave? Just walk away? Say, sorry—I got confused, I thought it would be interesting but I was just being stupid again.

She is out of place, disconnected. She can't even look at people to get messages about what to do. At the creek, someone has already built a big fire. Everyone stands around for a while. No one says much. Some of the women are staring into the fire, muttering. Others walk around it, their lips moving. A few women swim in the creek. The old woman sits alone; smoke rises from a small shell in front of her. She fans it and sings a steady rhythmical chant. Then she comes around the circle of women. As she stands in front of them, each woman cups her hands in the smoke, and brushes it over her face and body. When she comes to Annie, Annie awkwardly imitates what she thinks the other women have done, but she's sure she gets it all wrong. Her hands are so white. She is out of place, she thinks, an intruder. The strong smell of sage surrounds her.

The women who haven't been swimming strip the rest of their clothes off and hang them on the trees and bushes. Reluctantly, Annie takes hers off. She's never been naked in a group. Her skin shines ghostly, ghastly white. One by one, the women kneel and enter backwards into the little hut. Annie follows Rain. The hut is almost full when they're all in. The floor is covered with fir tips. The place smells of soil and smoke and fir trees, a clean smell. Annie can feel her body touching the women's bodies on either side of her. She hugs her breasts tight, closes her arms across her chest. She'll survive this; she can survive anything.

Some of the women giggle softly. Someone is singing softly, under her breath. The old woman yells out the door and, one at a time, glowing rocks out of the fire are handed in, deftly handled with sticks and placed in a pit in the centre of the hut. Then the hide door is closed. Annie is in total blackness. Someone, must be the old woman, speaks softly and begins to sing. Water splashes on the rocks. A wave of steam rolls over her. Rain says softly in Annie's ear, "Now is the time to pray and give thanks."

Annie is not sure what she means. The only praying she has ever done that wasn't in church was when her mother was dying. She had promised God she would be good, she would stop swearing, start wearing skirts, start behaving the way her grandmother thought she should, anything at all, anything He wanted, if only her mother would live. She had begged and bargained but her mother died anyway. Her mother died and left her and now she's supposed to give thanks. For what? she thinks bitterly.

Well, she's alive. Unexpectedly, she remembers the smile on Shadow's face when she awoke, weak and dizzy under the cedars and he was there, sitting beside her. She thinks of Duster when he ambles over to her and chews on her hair, looking for treats when the horse herd comes into camp. She remembers the pup she's been playing with, the one belonging to the white dog, the one she's thinking of asking to take with her when she leaves.

She thinks about Lucille and her kids. What a selfish monster she'd been to just up and leave them like that. But Lucille had smiled and hugged her and said it was okay, she understood. She has a friend there, a real true friend. She could go back anytime. Lucille took her in, made her part of her family, just when she needed it most. And then understood when it was time to let her go.

And that bear in the mountains, sniffing her face, turning her over and leaving. She's been lucky, damned lucky. And even farther back, those few sunlit days in the valley she found before Lucille's, playing pirates on a tippy raft with Black Dog, eating berries, sitting naked in the sun. Her throat hurts. Her heart aches like a bruise.

The door is opened. They sit in the steamy gloom; water runs off Annie's nose and drips on her chest. Wet hair sticks to her face. She slicks it back.

More rocks are handed in. The door is closed again. "You can pray for your male relatives if you wish," says Rain.

More praying. Does she want to?

Her father was so angry when her mother died. For three days, she and her brothers had waited outside the house where their mother was lying, trying to give birth. People went in and out and didn't see them at all. Their father went in and out, his face a closed mask, closed to them, closed to everything. Annie kept her arms around her brothers and held on to them. They shook and shivered inside her embrace. None of them said anything. They crouched with her and waited. They were afraid of their father's anger. Their father alone, without their mother to mediate, was a black terrible force they didn't know how to reckon with.

As long as there was activity in the house, people coming and going, they held on, waiting each moment for their mother to return, put her arms around them, laugh, take them back to the wagon, make things all right. On the third day, one by one, instead of going in, people left the house. Only their father stayed inside. They waited through the afternoon while life went on around them; people rode by, horses stood in pens, switching their tails against flies, the sun inched across the sky.

When their father left, he strode by unseeing, his face clenched, a knotted fist. One of the women came and told them their mother was dead, and the baby with her. She was a nice woman. She loomed over them in her skirt and apron, trying to get them to come with her, come inside, eat something. Annie declined stiffly. Instead, they plod-

ded away from the house to the wagon to wait for their
father. Annie fed the boys. While she was cooking, she felt
that at any moment her mother would come bustling up,
take the pan from her awkward hands and laugh, shoo her
away to do some other task. None of them cried. Their
father didn't come.

That night she heard her youngest brother; she crawled
into the wagon and held him while he sobbed against her
chest. "Mooommy, moommmmy," he sobbed and sobbed.
"Like Nat," she thinks. Then her other brother awoke and
being older, only sobbed into his pillow. Annie stared dry-
eyed into the darkness and waited for her father.

But he never came. He left them too, and they were alone.
He hadn't come when they needed him most. She remembers his face when he came outside, the face of a stranger,
distorted with pain. Her father. He taught me everything,
she thinks. Her throat clenches and aches. Her father gave
her Duster and Black Dog and her rifle...she never thanked
him. She was always too afraid.

And then he left them. He left them when they needed
him so terribly. He left her. How could he have done that?
She doesn't, can't, never will understand.

The singing stops and the old woman speaks again in
her soft voice. The door opens. Again, they wait. Outside,
the afternoon light is softening towards late afternoon. She
can see a glimpse of blue sky through the birch and aspen
trees. There are birds singing. Annie is trapped in this dark
cave, alone with the tortured face of her father.

More rocks. When does this end? she thinks to herself. The door closes. They are back in the endless blackness. "Now you may pray for your female relatives," says Rain's polite, small voice.

Her female relatives. That must mean her mother. And she doesn't want to pray for her mother. She doesn't even want to think about her anymore, ever again. How could she be so stupid, getting pregnant. Surely there must have been some way of keeping it from happening. What did she want another baby for, when they were travelling and couldn't even take care of themselves properly, let alone a baby. Stupid, stupid, stupid. Both her parents. Damn them. Goddamn them.

She realizes she's saying the words out loud. But other women are speaking as well, some quietly, some sobbing. Rain, beside her, is speaking. Suddenly, she begins yelling something, screaming and sobbing. Annie hears other women, murmuring. Someone presses in against her. She realizes someone is holding Rain, who is now sobbing and choking and retching. Annie peers through the black. There is the faintest red glow from the stones in the pit and she can see flickers of reflection from the faces around her.

Rain breaks into English. "Why did you hurt me?" she moans. "Why did you look at me like that, why did you want to hurt me? Now my mother is gone, why do you want to hurt our people, oh please, go away, go away, it hurts, it hurts," and she sobs again. Her fists pound the floor. The other women moan and murmur to her. Finally, she quiets. The old woman speaks again. Some of the women are singing, a soft chant. There is a drum or a rattle somewhere. Annie can't tell if it's inside or outside the lodge.

The door is opened. Dim light and cold air rush in. She wraps her arms tight around herself, and puts her face on her knees. If she can just get through this, she'll never, ever do this again, never find herself this defenseless, in this much pain. Black scalding waves fill her like boiling water, like lava. She clenches her nails into her palms.

By the time the fourth set of rocks come in, it's very hot in the sweat lodge. When the old woman sprinkles water on the rocks, steam rushes into Annie's face and she chokes, unable to breath. Rain whispers, "Lie down if it's too hot." Gratefully, Annie stretches out on the floor.

The singing begins again. It seems very loud. So is the drum. Everyone must be singing. Rain hasn't told her what to pray for. She wants to think about what she's doing, this journey she's on. She closes her eyes and the wolf is in front of her.

"Where are you going?" he says.

I don't know, she thinks. I don't know where I'm going or what I'm doing. I thought I was free, but I'm just a kid, I'm not grown up. How am I supposed to know what I'm doing? Another voice says, You have to keep going, you have to keep going, you promised, you said you'd find a place, you'd be responsible, you'd take care of them.

"I can't," she says out loud. "I can't. I can't. I don't know how. I'm too tired, I want my mother, I want my father, I want them back, I want it all back." Strangled, wailing, choking noises come out of her throat. She thinks she might throw up. She feels a hand beside her and grabs it; another hand is offered from her other side and she feels arms reach around, very gently, to hold her and rock her while she lets go, cries and wails like a child, wanting it all back, her home, her family, her mother. And just when she thinks it's done, another rush of agony spews from her mouth. She pounds the floor because the pain is torture, she can't stand it, it's ripping her in half like a rusty saw, and she coughs and chokes and almost throws up. She doesn't try to hold it anymore, can't, has forgotten how, just screams and screams into the memories surrounding her. All the while, soft voices murmur and the singing goes on and on.

Finally, she slows down, can think and breathe again. She pants, chokes and sobs. Rain's hand holds onto hers, and someone strokes her wet hair and face and murmurs soft words and she wishes she could stay here forever.

When the door is opened again, dusk has fallen. Streaks of salmon and rose cross the turquoise sky. The women file out and stand by the fire. Some go swimming; Annie joins them. The water slides like silk over her skin; she splashes and swims and smiles tentatively at the women who smile back. The air glows. They all walk back to the camp together and eat an enormous supper.

Annie goes to bed and sleeps, feeling lost and empty and drained. The black place, the agony of her parents death, is still there but softened, somehow easier to carry. She curls in on herself, loving the feel of the fur robes against her clean skin, the white puppy snuggled beside her, his nose under her chin.

TWENTY-TWO

"I HAVE TO LEAVE, SHADOW," she whispers. "I can't really say why. I just have to." He stares at the ground. She has spent the three weeks since the sweat feeling more and more included in the life of the camp. She and Rain worked at tanning hides together and Rain began teaching her words in their language. One morning as Annie lay in her soft bed, tickling the puppy which was trying to chew her arm off, she tried to calculate how long she had been there. When she arrived it was still spring, with snow on the mountains and wildflowers everywhere. Now the grass is tall, lush and going to seed, the wild strawberries have borne fruit. She spent two days with the women, hunting for the tiny berries, laughing and joking in the sun. Duster is fat and lazy with a slick summer coat.

Goddamnit, Annie, she thinks. You're getting soft. You've let all this comfort go to your head.

But whenever she steps out of the tipi, she steps back into the life of the community; children come running by, tugging at her, wanting her to come and play; people smile greetings, there is always something new to look at, someone to hand her food, the creek to swim in, work to do. She has promised to teach Shadow to use her gun. The people have only a few guns bought from the traders.

This morning, she has gone to find Shadow. She wants to talk to him; she needs someone to talk it over with. But he doesn't want to talk about her leaving. He freezes into politeness and only repeats that she should do whatever she feels she needs to do. If she wants to stay, there is the tipi, and his family. The people will be moving one day soon to look for buffalo. She could bring her gun.

It's no use. She's afraid she'll only hurt him. She leaves him and goes to the creek, wanders through the woods, goes to find Duster. Nothing has any messages for her. She returns to her tipi. If she's planning to leave, she needs food. She goes to find Rain.

That night many people come to Shadow's family's fire. Rain whispers, "These people wish to say good-bye."

They sit in a circle, eating and drinking leaf and berry tea and cracking jokes, most of them at Annie's expense. She laughs with them. Rain or Shadow translates. Then silence falls.

The old woman speaks. Shadow translates, "We are sorry you are leaving. We can see you have far to go, and we are glad you came to stay with us for a while. You have a good heart. Don't worry so much about everything. You are a lost person, with no people and no family, nowhere to belong. Listen to the land. It will tell you everything you need to know. Listen to the rocks and the wind and the little lizards lying in the sun. They will tell you everything that is important. When you get up in the morning, remember to greet the sun and give thanks for your life..." The old woman pauses and Shadow pauses with her.

"There is much that you don't know. You are like a child, still learning all the time. If you stayed here, you could learn a lot more. But if it is time for you to go, then you will find your own way. That is all I have to say."

One by one, other people make brief speeches. A few bring her small gifts, a beaded scabbard for her knife, a pair of moccasins, thongs to tie up her braids. She sits, embarrassed and overwhelmed. She has nothing to give them. Finally, when everyone has finished, she tries to think what to say.

"Thank you," she says, "thank you for everything. My heart is really hurting me right now. I don't really want to go, but I have to. I guess it's true I am a lost person. I don't know where I belong, or how I want to live. But I have learned so much here. I am not as sad as when I came. I won't forget you. I won't forget what I learned. I will remember this place and all of you as my true friends. That is all I have to say." There are nods and murmurs. Gradually, people drift away and Annie goes to her tipi, lies sleepless, staring at the wall.

In the morning, she rises early, before the camp wakes. She saddles Duster and takes the white puppy with her. She rides away without looking back.

TWENTY-THREE

THE MEMORY OF SHADOW AND HIS PEOPLE haunts her. She finds herself thinking too much of Shadow, remembering his laugh and the sadness in his eyes. He touched her hand the night before she rode away, and he wept. She hugged him and wept too, but her mind was already seeking ahead. Now, loneliness grows in her each day as she rides further and further away. Maybe I could have stayed, she thinks. Stayed there, settled down. Plans drift through her mind as she rides, thoughts of her brothers, of the future, airy disjointed ideas about living with Indians. But what stops her is the thought of her mother's disapproval. She has to bring the boys up right, if only she could find the evasive, shadowy thing she's looking for, the crack in the pattern of her life which might tell her when it's time to stop.

She's never really figured how she will know; she thought the journey itself would make things clearer. Instead, she feels confused. There's so much land, so many places, none of them or all of them hers. Shadow's people were so at home where they lived; they knew it so well, had been there, they told her, forever.

Maybe she will just finally have to choose a place and hope it's the right one. Maybe she'll never know.

In the meantime, she's doing what she has to do. The only real choice she has is to keep going, she reminds herself, lecturing herself about moping, forcing herself to go on, instead of turning around like she wants to do. Loneliness is just part of it.

"C'mon, Annie, toughen up," she thinks. Still, she's glad about the puppy, which ranges beside Duster as Black Dog used to. She resolves to do a better job this time, give him a real name, spend some time training him.

She works her way down through the pass, following the trails which Shadow's father told her would be there. He's made her maps and given her information about the country to the west. He's told her where the big bears live, and how to avoid them, and what to watch for when she comes out on to the plains. The women have shown her all kinds of edible plants and where to find them. She has food, new moccasins, and a new country to ride into. She should be glad, but loneliness trails her like a sad old dog.

One night she camps by a creek which rumbles over steep granite boulders. She makes a fire under a pair of giant fir trees leaning out over the water, their heavy branches dipping towards the pool. She catches some fish and then has a swim and washes her hair. She cooks the fish, cleans up and then rolls herself in her blankets.

The eastern sky glows a creamy lemon yellow. She's restless, wide awake. She waits until the moon slides the first crescent of roundness above the peaks, and then she unrolls from the blankets. She starts to put on her clothes, but they're heavy and stiff. She lets them drop. She wades through the freezing water. The white dog splashes in behind, chasing his shadow in the pool, chasing his tail. On the other side, she starts to climb.

The hill opens into smooth granite ledges with tall bunch grass and junipers and thick pale green moss; she climbs and the moon climbs with her. Her body is thin and strong and can climb forever. She scrambles on her hands and knees up narrow clefts in the rock, and dances along thin edges of stone floating above the air.

She stops atop a small round knob of mountain jutting from the steep peak beside it. The place is a garden in the flooding silver light, the junipers and cedar and pines bend towards her, whispering in the night wind off the peaks. Moss covers the hollows between the rocks. She raises her arms to the moon.

"Hello," she whispers. "Hello." She is alone. She is free and light and alive, on her own, standing on a mountain in the middle of nowhere at all. She whirls, dizzy, laughs at the puppy chasing his tail, then falls silent, listening.

She stands looking east over the silent black hills, towards the tents of Shadow and his people. They will be sleeping, or sitting around the fire telling stories or jokes, eating and laughing, together. She can see them all so clearly. Does Shadow miss her? Do any of them think about her?

And somewhere even farther back is Lucille. Maybe she's outside too, looking at the moon and feeling lonesome; or maybe she's inside with the kids, playing games or eating or reading.

She looks outward, turns to each direction, towards the ranges of peaks which surround her, layer on layer, each range hiding valleys and creeks and cliffs and lakes, places she will never walk, trails she will never ride. She thinks of the silent ones, the deer and elk and wolves, the cougars, the smaller creatures, rabbits, grouse, chickadees, mosquitoes, ants, busy living their lives.

"Live well," she says softly. "Live here in peace." She waits, listening. No answering message comes out of the darkness; no voice speaks, nothing moves. The land is still and peaceful, frozen under hard silver light. Her feet are bruised and freezing on the rocks, and she shivers. The old woman had said to listen. But what if there are no voices to hear?

The dog nudges her hand. "You're like my shadow, eh, I'll call you Shadow," she says softly. He's happy, jumps to lick her face, nudges her hand. Slowly, she climbs back down the mountain, rolls herself in her cold blankets and watches the fire for a long time.

She thinks about the sense of belonging, of being included, which she felt with Shadow's people. Once she got used to how things worked it was easy to be there. It was easy to just live, day to day, doing what needed to be done, not torturing herself with what had already happened or what lay in the future. But now that she's here, on her own with only herself and the silence around her, she knows she's relieved, loves the silence, the sense of her own strength, the aloneness. It's hard to be with people, she thinks. Any people. It was even hard to be with Shadow's people. She was always wary, she was too nice all the time. She never felt unwatched. She could get used to being on her own. Maybe too used to it to ever go back to living inside the rules and binding of a settlement, or even of a family. But family is different—in a family you can make your own rules. With a start, she thinks of her brothers. Some days she forgets all about them. But when the time comes, they'll be her family. It's the task she's set for herself. No backing away from her duty now.

"I'm sorry," she says to them. "I'm sorry. I'll do better. I'll find a place. I'll come back for you. I will, I promise." She grimaces, sets her jaw, sighs deeply, turns, and turns again, before drifting off to sleep.

Over the next few days, they work themselves down out of the mountains into a region of hills, and finally, onto rolling grassland, still heading steadily westward. The grass brushes against Duster's belly. Every day they see antelope, prairie chickens, rabbits; the streams are full of trout. Annie begins to wonder if this could be the kind of place her father had talked about so much. There are Indians here too; she sees signs of fires, places where there's been encampments, but she doesn't see any of the people, even though she looks for them. There are new trees and different grass. The light shines on the tall grass which brushes Duster's sides; purple-green iridescent waves move over its dreaming surface. Each grove of trees is an oasis, each small coulee and hidden valley a surprise. This is more like the land she has dreamed of, the land her father talked about. She begins to pay closer attention to landmarks. She wants to be closer to a river, and maybe some kind of settlement. The boys will need schooling, whether they want it or not.

TWENTY-FOUR

A COUPLE OF DAYS LATER, as she is dreaming in the saddle about the farm she will have and the kinds of animals she'll raise, she rides across a series of wagon tracks cutting across her direction, heading north. She stops, dismounts and studies the tracks. Two wagons, three men on horses. Probably a family party heading out looking for land to homestead. It might be good to see some people, she thinks. It's been a long time. And they'll have news, maybe even news of the settlement and her brothers. They'll have maps and she can find out better where she is, get some information on land and homesteading.

"It's time to make this plan a little more realistic," she thinks. "You've just been riding, dreaming your life away," she scolds herself. "It's time you got on with this dream. It's time you made it come true. Riding along, and living with Indians is all very well, but you've got brothers to raise and you need a home. You're just lazy, Annie," she thinks, and she turns Duster to follow the wagon tracks.

But her heart sinks at the thought of encountering more strangers. Her stomach hurts. She'll have to talk to them and answer questions and ask questions. Experimentally, she tries out her tongue, talking out loud to herself and to the grass.

Before she approaches the wagons she circles to where she can look down on them from a bluff. Her figuring from the tracks was about right. She sees three white men, one black man and two women. Two wagons, the woman driving one and the black man the other. The three white men all ride together out front. No kids. It's strange to see white people again. She watches them for a while. She can smell them, their clothes reek sweat and smoke. They don't seem very watchful. She thinks she should be glad to see them but she's not. For a while, she considers simply riding around them, going on her way alone.

"No, you're going to be sensible for a change," she lectures herself. "Not take so many chances…it will be good to have company, people to talk to, get news from…so you're feeling shy, that's natural. You'll get to know them, they're probably good people, like Lucille, like Shadow."

She comes up to them that evening, riding so they can see her from far off. Shadow hides between Duster's legs.

One of the men calls a greeting and then looks Annie over without saying anything more.

Finally, he speaks again, but without smiling. "You are welcome here. If you're hungry, come and share our food." He has a huge bushy grey-black beard which covers most of his face. He wears a black flat-brimmed hat and heavy canvas pants held up with suspenders. His eyes are blue, set far back under heavy, hooded eyebrows.

"This is our family," he says as Annie comes forward, leading Duster, wondering about his strange manner. "My wife, Esther, our daughter, Sara. These are Thomas and Harold, our friends. And I am Joshua Smith." He doesn't introduce the black man who is standing silently in the rear.

"I'm Annie," she says.

Annie unsaddles and hobbles Duster and then comes back to the fire. Esther doesn't look at her, just hands her a plate of beans and biscuits and turns away. Sara, who looks about her own age, smiles shyly, and says hello. Both the women are wearing long dresses and scarves on their heads.

Annie eats with her plate on her lap. No one bothers her. When she finishes, Joshua comes and sits down next to her. The others sit silently on the far side of the fire.

"My child," he says, in a deep serious voice putting his hand on her hand. "It is indeed fortunate that you have come to us safely in this terrible wilderness. God must have led you to us. You are safe now, and with a family who can care for you. If you need to share your past, you can talk to me anytime. In the meantime, Esther and Sara will take care of you, find you something to wear and show you where to sleep."

"I'm okay," says Annie. "I can look after myself all right. I been doing it for a while now." She tries not to sound too annoyed. Who does this guy think she is? Or who does he think he is? Maybe he's a preacher of some kind and that's why he's so serious.

But he doesn't seem to have heard. Instead, he gazes intensely at her and finally smiles. He has a nice smile, Annie thinks, although it's hard to tell behind all the hair.

"I'm sure you'll relax after a day or two. You must have had a difficult time. Whatever calamity or disaster drove you from your friends and family, it's over now. It was very brave of you to make your way this far. If you need comfort or counsel, remember I am always near."

He pats her shoulder and then abruptly rises and leaves. Annie watches him, puzzled. What kind of haywire outfit has she hooked up with now? Oh well, their food is good and she can leave anytime she wants to. But she likes the fact that he said she was brave. And it's nice that someone has offered her comfort. No one has done that for a while. They seem like a nice family. Esther beckons to her from the wagon.

Esther shows her the pallet made up with homemade quilts and a real pillow. Esther still won't meet her eyes. Annie sighs. She was going to sleep out by herself, but the bed looks invitingly comfortable after so many nights sleeping rolled in a horse blanket with a hide that Shadow's family had given her stretched beneath her. At that moment, a spatter of rain hits the stretched canvas over her head.

"Uh, sure, thanks," she says. "I'll just go check on my horse." Duster is with the other horses, all of them squealing, sniffing noses, getting acquainted. She leans her head against him, then the rain comes and she trots towards the wagon full of lamplight, Shadow close at her heels.

When she returns, the two women are stretched out on pallets of their own. Annie climbs into the wagon and Shadow follows. Esther looks at him with disgust.

"Dogs are dirty," she says. "He'll have to stay outside." Annie thinks about arguing but a large splat of rain changes her mind. She takes Shadow outside and makes him a bed under the wagon. He whimpers miserably before settling down. Back inside, a clean nightgown lies on Annie's bed. She puts it on and stretches out comfortably in the warm blankets. She sighs luxuriously, listening to the rain. This is one night she won't have to worry about bears or waking up shivering on the wet ground.

In the morning she wakes to a clean, warm, bird-singing world. She wanders off to the nearby slough for a wash. Maybe she shouldn't be so quick to judge Joshua and his family. Maybe it's her that's been alone too long and forgotten how to behave. Maybe he's not so bad.

Sara smiles at her as she comes up to the fire and hands her a cup of hot strong coffee. They're probably just wondering about her, she thinks. After all, she is out here by herself, where young women aren't normally wandering around and she hasn't tried to explain herself. When she finishes the coffee, Esther hands her a plate of fried potatoes and bacon.

She rides with the wagons that day. She's asked Joshua about the trails and it appears he's following the same trail that Shadow's father described to her. It makes sense, she tells herself, to ride along. Esther drives one wagon, and the black man the second. Thomas, Harold and Joshua ride together up front. Thomas and Harold seem much younger than Joshua. She wonders how they're all related, if they are. She figures she'll find out in a day or two. In the meantime, Annie has never seen a black man up close and she rides up beside his wagon. She tries not to stare, doesn't quite succeed.

"Howdy," she says.

"Howdy," says the man, looking straight ahead, not smiling.

Annie desperately wants to ask him where he's from and what he's doing out here, but by now, she's learned too well that asking questions about someone's past is considered rude. They ride along for a while, Annie embarrassed, but determined to be friendly.

"What's your name?" she says finally. "We didn't get introduced, back there."

"Name's Quick," he says. Then a long, silent pause.

"Your off horse appears a mite lame," she offers.

"Yep, ma'am, that he is, stuck a foot in a hole a while back and ain't had a chance to recover. I told Mr. Joshua we maybe ought to stop for a bit, but he's all hot and bothered about getting on, so we're getting on."

"Getting on to where?"

"Oh, Joshua says he'll know the place when he finds it, says the Lord is leading us, and I got to go where he's going, so guess I'll just get on along." He shifts uneasily on his seat, looking away and plainly not wanting to talk to her.

Annie gives up and rides up beside Sara, who is swinging her legs over the back of a wagon and looking bored.

"You're such a good rider," Sara says shyly. "I wish I could ride horses like you, but Joshua says I ain't allowed to. I used to ride, once in a while, before Ma married Joshua. But now I'm supposed to get married and act like a grown up."

"Married," says Annie. "You're going to get married?"

"Well, I guess I have to," Sara says, and sighs."Ma and me were having a hard time before Joshua came along. We lived in a little town and Ma had to do washing and ironing. I sure would hate to have to do that. Sometimes we were so hungry. Poor Ma, her hands would get sore and bleed. I'd have to help her haul around them huge tubs of water. And people were mean to us. This is better."

"But who are you going to marry?"

"Joshua says I can marry either Harold or Thomas, I don't care which one. They're both okay, I guess. Joshua says our children will live in the promised land. That's where he's taking us…that's what he says, anyway. Hope it's prettier than this when we get there."

"This here is mighty pretty."

"It's horrible," says Sara, and shudders. "It's either freezing cold or boiling hot, and there's bugs and rattlesnakes and wild animals and even Indians, they say. And no people anywhere. I hate it. I wish we could go back."

"Well, I like it. I think it's beautiful. I'd like to live around here somewhere," says Annie, but Sara shakes her head.

"Not me."

That night, after they go to bed, Annie lies thinking. Her skin prickles and she frowns. She's puzzled. This outfit feels strange and somehow off-kilter in a way she can't quite decipher. She's never encountered people like these before. She thinks maybe she'd be better off travelling on her own. She wonders what Sara meant by Joshua leading them to the promised land. It sounds like something out of the Bible, and she doesn't remember much about the Bible.

She'd thought about it a lot at one time. Everyone was supposed to go to Church, her Ma told them, though no one in their family went. Church was too far, almost half-a-day's buggy ride and that meant giving up a whole day at the farm, and there was never time. Some urgent chore needed doing—haying, or butchering, or pruning, or picking rocks off the plowed fields in the spring.

Sometimes their mother would talk to them about the

Bible, and every morning the teacher at school would read to them from it. But she couldn't make sense out of any of it, even when she thought and thought about it, about the mumbled stuff about God, so she gave up thinking about it, deciding it didn't have much to do with her. But she knew it was important to treat preachers with respect; people who knew about the Bible, knew about God, were special, had special powers. The way Joshua talked made him sound like a preacher. She always thought preachers were special—really good, somehow, and set apart from ordinary people. But she doesn't like Joshua, can't bring herself to like him. Perhaps something's missing, something wrong in her. If he's a man of God, then he's bound to be a good man, and she ought to respect that.

Shadow's people prayed, but they never said who they were praying to. They seemed to talk to everything. They got up in the morning and talked to the sun. Shadow cheerfully talked to plants and animals and horses and dogs and people like they were all the same. But Joshua talks like he has personal conversations with the Lord, and everyone else seems to believe him.

She is drifting off to sleep when she hears a footstep next to the wagon, someone whispering Esther's name. Silent, Esther gets up, leaves the wagon. Sometime later, Annie hears her return. She wonders briefly why Esther sleeps in the wagon instead of with her husband, then she forgets about it.

The next day, Joshua rides his horse up next to hers. His

knee rubs against hers as the horses come close together. Annie decides she should try a little harder to listen to what he's saying.

"I would like you to know we're mighty proud to have a strong brave girl like you join up with our little family. Mighty proud. Must have taken great strength for a pretty thing like you to make it through the wilderness by yourself. Like I said, anytime you feel like talking, I'm here, we're all here, Mother Esther, Sara, and the boys."

"Guess I'm doing okay," Annie says shyly, though she kind of likes being called pretty and brave.

"It's not right for a woman to be alone, without protection, without help, without her family, no matter how brave she is," he smiles. "This country can be pretty dangerous, savages, wolves, bears. It's indeed a miracle that God has preserved you and brought you to us." Annie sighs and shrugs.

"My family's dead," she says. "I been doing just fine on my own, thanks." She wishes he wouldn't ride so close. His knee keeps bumping hers. She moves Duster away.

"Then, whenever you need us, we will be your family," he says, and reaches over to pat her back. For the next hour, he rides beside her, persisting with question after question, until gradually, unwillingly, she tells him the whole story, her leaving the settlement, Lucille, the ranch, the search for a home. The only part she leaves out is the part about Shadow and his people.

At night, when they make camp, Esther is always the

first out of the wagon; she finds wood, makes a fire, carries water, makes supper and does the dishes, moving with hurried frantic energy. Annie observes all of this with some astonishment and tries to help as much as she can. The men unharness the stock, leave the rest of the chores to Quick, and then sit around the fire, waiting to be fed. Sara skulks in the wagon, coming out only to get a plate of food.

After supper, Annie offers to fetch more water and wood, and Esther gives her a grateful, if astonished smile. "Why, thank you," she says. "That's mighty kind of you." But she finds other things to do, mending, sewing. In her frantic working, she reminds Annie of Lucille.

Joshua lolls on the ground next to the other two men. After supper, he brings out a flask of whiskey, and Esther heats water to make the men toddies with whiskey and sugar. The women don't drink and neither does Quick, who only comes to the fire to get a bit of food. Annie tries not to stare at him. She's heard about black people being kept as servants and slaves but she's never seen anyone be treated with such total indifference. Quick cringes when he comes near the fire to scoop up some food, and then scuttle away. Joshua yells after him to be sure the stock is properly watered and fed.

The men sit up after the women go to bed, and Annie can hear them through the thin canvas, their loud laughter and sudden bursts of song. She wishes they'd shut up and go to bed. She drifts to sleep, is awakened by the same loud whisper demanding that Esther wake up, which Esther, ever obedient, does. In the dark, Annie shakes her head in disgust, can't imagine it, being at someone's beck and call, wonders how Esther stands it, why she puts up with it, why she doesn't fight back.

She rides with them for the next three days. As long as they're following a direction that suits her, she figures, it's just as well. If she left, she'd just have to keep dodging them. Though she tries to stay out of his way, Joshua comes often to ride beside her, ask her questions, ask her for her comments on the trail, the weather, the condition of the horses. He rides too close and finds excuses to touch her back or her shoulder.

One day it rains, a stinging sleeting rain, then it pours and then one day it hails as well. They are all shivering cold and unhappy; a bitter wind adds to their misery. The wagons get stuck in mud the consistency of glue and Annie and Duster help to pull them out. Joshua is loud in his praise of her but she avoids him as much as she can. That night, though, she's glad for the shelter of canvas over her head.

She tries to find out where they're actually going, but Joshua will only say that he's being led to the promised land, that all they need is to have faith and trust in him. Despite her resolve to be respectful, Annie snarls cynically inside herself. Any promised land that he's going to is one she would want to avoid, man of God or not. She figures she's gone far enough with this outfit. In the next couple of days, she'll make her preparations and go on her own way.

On the evening of the fifth day, they come to a bluff which drops steeply away to a silver twisted braid of river. It stops raining. The men ride off to look for a way to get the wagons down. Esther is busy around the fire, and Sara takes time to heat water and wash her hair. Then she sits by the fire, combing and braiding her hair, which is long and red and silky. Esther, for a change, angrily calls her to help and Sara wanders sulkily over to the fire, complaining.

Annie hears their voices and figures it's no quarrel of hers. She and Shadow slink off to find something else to do. She spends some time wandering along the edge of the bluff, thinking perhaps she'll bring back wood for Esther. She finds a place she figures she and Duster could get down, with some scrambling and sliding, but nowhere that the wagons could go.

She slides down in giant strides, through graveled coulees and long sand slopes, riding a tumbling wave of rocks and gravel, slipping and then planting her feet to ride out the slide. At the bottom, she wanders over to the river, which is wide and shallow and flowing in sullen, muddy swirls and tumbles from the rain. It takes her a long time to climb back out and when she does, it's dark and starting to drizzle again.

When she comes back towards the fire, the men have returned. Quick is not in sight, but the other three are standing by the fire. Something in the tension in their bodies says things are not right. Joshua is sitting on the ground, drawing little circles in the mud. Annie stands out of the light, watching.

Thomas is speaking. He's the youngest, and would be good looking, Annie thinks, if he ever smiled; he always seems to be sulking about something, and his mouth and brown, sandy beard are stained streaky yellow from chewing tobacco.

"Well, we've had our say and that's that. We don't want to quit you, but we've had about enough. We don't know where the hell we're supposed to be heading off to. This is such a haywire and gunny-sack outfit, I'm surprised we've made it this far. We need supplies, I'm so damn sick of fried potatoes and beans...we don't know where we are...you say trust in the Lord, but the best thing you and your womenfolk there could do is turn around and come back with us, find a proper guide that knows what he's doing, and get the hell out of here before we all get scalped."

Joshua doesn't say anything, just keeps drawing circles in the dirt. Finally, he stands up.

"Well, boys," he says. "If you've had your little say, now I think it must be about my turn. What kind of men are you, that you let a little mud and a little rain discourage you...that would leave three helpless women at the mercy of this wilderness and its savage inhabitants? I have shared my vision with you, and you assured me that you respected my words and accepted me as a man of faith and vision, a man who could lead you to a land of freedom. Don't you remember what we talked about—about being free to live off the land, as much land as we want, and have our own kingdom in the protection of these plains and mountains. Thomas, haven't I offered you my own daughter as assurance that we will share this kingdom together? Haven't I offered you riches beyond any man's dreams?"

"I haven't seen none of them yet," Harold mutters.

Joshua says, "You must place your faith in the Lord, for I have seen his glory in the sky. I have seen the writing on the clouds, and in the pages of God's book, and I know He will lead us home. What are a few trials of wind and weather in the face of our strength, our faith in God, our fellowship with each other? Haven't we protected and sheltered each other, been as brothers? Of course, it's never easy. Following God's path is not meant to be easy, but the rewards are immeasurable." He pauses. The other two men look at the ground.

"Now, here, we can all have a small drink to our peace and friendship…take our mind off the rain and the cold and all the rest of this. Esther," he roars, and Esther comes running with the bottle and cups.

Annie circles around so she can climb in the wagon without them seeing her. She figures she can sleep hungry, she's done it before. Tomorrow she's getting out of here.

She gets her wet clothes off and crawls, shivering, into the cold blankets.

"Annie, are you there?" Sara's voice comes from the other

side of the wagon. "Where have you been?"

"Down by the river," says Annie. "Checking things out…looking for a way down, checking for game."

"But it's raining…and you didn't have any supper. Come crawl in with me and warm up."

Annie hesitates, but she really is cold.

"Okay," she says, and crawls over the bundles and boxes to Sara's side. Sara scrunches over to make room.

"There, isn't that better?" she whispers. They lie in companionable silence for a while, and then Sara whispers, "Annie, I'm really worried. What's going on outside?"

"Dunno," says Annie. "They're talking…and drinking."

"Annie," says Sara, in a very strange voice. "Can I tell you something. I've got to tell someone and I don't know what to do." Her voice is shaking.

"Sure, of course…" says Annie. There is a long silence. Sara's body is shaking; Annie realizes she's crying.

"I don't know what to say…" Sara whispers, her body shaking. "I can't, I can't…it's just too hard…" and she cries even harder, trying not to make any noise.

Annie lets her cry for a while, then she remembers the sweat, and how the elders behaved, and she moves over and puts her hand gently on Sara's shoulder.

"Put some words to it, maybe it'll help…you have to tell it, you have to let it out."

Sara's sobbing slows.

Finally, she whispers, "Joshua…"

"What about Joshua…"

"This afternoon, while you were gone…he came back…I was down in a gully, Mom made me go, looking for wood and stuff, he saw me, he came over…he, he said some stuff, he…" She hesitates.

"He says *I* can be his wife too, that I don't have to marry Thomas, that we can be together, and it will be okay, that God wants it that way, that it's the law of Abraham or something…and then he grabbed me, kissed me…Oh God, Annie, what am I going to do? I couldn't stand him touching me, but I knew if I screamed, my Mom would hear. I finally got away before he did anything more, but I don't understand…why would he do such a thing…he said…he said my Mom wasn't enough for him…that she didn't understand what he needed…oh, God, I'm so ashamed. I don't want to be his wife. It's all my fault. I can't let her find out…it would kill her, she'll say it's my fault, that I must have done something to lead him on."

They both freeze when they hear footsteps and voices coming towards the wagon, then it's quiet again.

"Annie, you've got to help me…I've got to get away from him…I'll leave a note for my mother…she'll understand. Please, please help me."

"But you've got to tell her," says Annie. "She's your mother. She'll understand, and then she can leave too. The other men are talking about leaving…you can all go with them. Leave Joshua here to get himself out of this wilderness he goes on about."

"No, you don't understand…I can't tell her, he's all she

has…she's got nothing to go back to, no family, no one to take care of her…"

"But you can't just abandon her, just leave her here with that man…he's no kind of husband…anyone who wanted two wives…that's the craziest thing I ever heard of. Whoever heard of such a thing! I can't believe it."

"She'll be okay…once I'm gone. She'll have Quick to look after everything…and Thomas and Harold won't leave…he's got them too bamboozled with all his stories…they've threatened before but they never leave. Please, Annie, please, I've got to leave, I've got to."

"Yeah, all right, just hang on, let me think." Annie leans back on the rough boards of the wagon. The firelight flickers and dances little witch lights through the canvas over her head.

She doesn't know how far the nearest people might be, and she doubts that Sara would remember much of the country. She could try to take Sara back through the hills to Lucille, but that's a long rough journey and Sara might not be up to it. And then what would Sara do? She doesn't seem much good at looking after herself. She might change her mind, miss her Mom, want to come back. They'll need another horse, food. Sara said she didn't know how to ride very well…maybe they can fake a diversion, get away with a wagon…but then Joshua will come after them. God, what a tangle.

"Sara, we're going to have to watch our chances, steal some food and stuff to be ready. You'll have to stay out of his way until then, stay in the wagon, stay close to me or your mother. I still think she should come with us. Shhh…"

Esther climbs wearily over the front of the wagon, undresses in the dark and crawls into bed. Annie lies still, listening to the loud voices of the men outside, the ragged breath of Sara beside her, still with a catch in it, the tear and munch of the horses grazing, Shadow scuffling in the dirt under the wagon to make a bed, the occasional piece of wood popping and spitting in the fire. Sara's body is warm next to hers. Her rifle is lying in the corner of the wagon with her saddle. She reaches over, pulls it next to her, and falls asleep finally between Sara and the rifle, dozing and waking to each loud noise through the long night.

The next day Joshua and the men sleep in. When Annie gets up, Quick is busy doing the work as usual, catching and harnessing the stock, checking the wagons, tying things down. Esther, Sara and Annie sit, make breakfast, drink too much coffee, while they wait for the men to wake up. Finally Annie goes to help Quick. He gives her a shy, terrified smile, but lets her have one of the teams. She backs them up to the wagon and hitches them, and then saddles Duster.

"Which way is the trail down to the river?" she asks Esther.

"Well, I don't rightly know," says Esther. "I don't know as how they said anything when they came back."

"Well, I'll go look," she says. "Sara, why don't you come with me?"

"I can't ride," says Sara, looking scared.

"Time you learned," Annie grins. She saddles Joshua's big grey horse, boosts the reluctant Sara into the saddle, and sets off north. It can't be this easy, she thinks. It isn't. She tries to persuade Sara that this might be a good time to leave, but Sara insists she's not ready.

"I've got to talk to my Mom," she says. "I don't know if I can just go off and leave her. I've got to think about this." Annie doesn't push it. She needs more time to make her own preparations anyway. She wants to get away clean, with better supplies and another rifle and she wants to have it all figured out where to go.

They find a good way down to the river and leave a marker, a strip of cloth, for the wagons. The wagons catch up to them at noon. Sara and Annie have a fire going and are happily cooking fish from the river and eating wild raspberries from the bushes along the bank.

When the wagons pull up, Joshua climbs down from the seat of the lead wagon, strides up to them, and cracks Sara openhanded across the face. The slap sounds like a pistol shot. Sara crumples to her knees from the force of it.

"No daughter of mine will act like a whore," he says. "Don't you ever run off again without my permission. And riding astride a horse is a whore's activity. You stay in the wagon where you belong and you learn some manners and obedience. And you," he turns to Annie. "You! I accepted you into our family, rescued you when you were lost in the wilderness, fed and kept you, and you repay me by en-

254

couraging my daughter in your own whorish ways. I can't ask you to leave, that would be unfit behaviour, but from now on, you ride in the wagon, you wear a proper dress, and you learn silence and obedience like a normal woman. Esther, take her to the wagon and make sure the next time I see her, she is dressed like a proper woman!"

"No," says Annie, words spilling from her in a fury. "I'm not your daughter, and I'm not a whore. Neither is Sara. You're the one that can't be trusted and you know bloody well what I mean. *We* weren't doing anything wrong."

"A broken heart and a contrite spirit are what pleases the Lord," says Joshua. "You'll learn to obey or I'll beat it into you. Get her."

Annie turns and sprints for Duster but Thomas and Harold are there before her. They grab her arms and twist them behind her back. Joshua walks up to her and slaps her triumphantly across the face.

"Tie her in the wagon," he orders and stalks off. Shadow is barking and growling hysterically, running in circles. One of the men boots him hard in the belly and he falls on the ground, yipping, and crawls off under one of the wagons.

The men hoist her off the ground, carry her under her arms, throw her onto her belly in the wagon and tie her hands and feet together. Frantically, she twists her body round and round, flopping like a fish, until she's bruised and gasping. If she can't get free, she'll go crazy. But she can't get free. When she's exhausted and hurting, and realizes she's not doing herself any good, she stops fighting.

The wagons start off again with a bone-crunching jolt. She never realized how much the wagon lurches and thumps over the ground. They swim the river, and she hears the men yelling and cursing at the teams. She wonders where Shadow and Duster are. The afternoon wears on. Annie starts to tear and work at the ropes again, but they only get tighter. If she ever gets out of here, she's going to shoot Joshua, just like a deer, but this will be a lot more satisfying. She wonders where Sara is…and Esther. What's Esther thinking now? Surely she won't stay with a man who beat her daughter. Her face hurts, her hands and feet are numb, and she has to pee. "Kill," she hisses through her teeth. "I'll kill you. Just wait, just wait until I get free."

When they finally stop, no one comes near her. She waits. Finally, Quick climbs over the wagon with a plate of food, unties her hands and feet and stands back.

She stares at him. "Quick," she hisses, "why do you stay with him? He's a monster. Help me, please, I've got to get out of here." But he only turns his head away. She climbs from the wagon and heads for the nearest bushes. She can hear him behind her. She doesn't look at him. When she goes back to the wagon, past the fire, she doesn't look at anyone. She keeps her body stiff and still. She climbs in the wagon and sits down staring straight ahead.

"I'm supposed to watch you, ma'am," mutters Quick. She looks at him but he looks away. She wonders what hold Joshua has over him. He goes back and sits on the wagon seat.

Annie holds herself with the attentiveness of a wild animal watching for prey. She might find a chance to get away, but what about Sara and Esther? She hears the familiar clink of the bottle on cups as Esther makes drinks for the men. She'd like to put something in those drinks. She'd like them to fall down, holding their bellies in pain and die like the yellow-bellied cowards they are. When Esther and Sara finally come in, they go to bed without looking at her. She doesn't talk to them either, just goes on sitting, her back against the canvas and boards, thinking about ways to cause Joshua pain.

The next morning, Esther beckons her out of the wagon and leads her to Joshua.

"I'm sorry, my child, that I was a bit rough with you yesterday. I felt it was necessary to get you to understand the error of your ways. I have been watching you carefully, and I feel that once you have learned proper humility, once you understand our ways, you will be more willing to listen, and be properly governed and taught. Obviously, whoever your parents were, they neglected some of your training."

Annie stares carefully at the scenery around the camp, listens to what birds there might be, wind sounds, looks for Duster, who is grazing unhobbled near the team horses—his coat is dusty, needs brushing. Shadow comes from under the wagon and runs to her, wagging his tail in glad relief. She kneels, pats him, feels him over for bruises. He licks her face, snuggling in close.

"We will watch you until we are sure that we can trust you again," he announces. "Now go and help Esther with the cooking. She will give you some proper clothing."

Helping Esther cook doesn't seem to mean much more than watching her cook. Esther ignores her and Annie sits on the ground, calculating her chances of running for Duster, and wondering where her rifle is. Sara is not in sight, nor is Joshua. Annie sits.

"Esther," she says, finally, "where's Sara?"

Esther doesn't answer at first. Finally, she straightens, one hand on her back and looks around. "I believe Joshua sent her to get wood, or some such," she says. "She'll be back directly, and then I'll get her to fetch you some clothes. Joshua's watering the stock; he'll be back directly."

Annie looks at Duster and Esther catches the glance. "Look," she says in a low voice. "I don't particularly want the care of you, but Joshua's the man here and he makes the decisions and I got to abide by them. I got no choice, see. Now just sit still and mind. It ain't such a bad thing to wear a dress and learn some manners. Can't understand anyone wanting to ride around the country alone anyhow. He's not really a bad man. He's been kind to me and mine. I need him. You got to understand that. You play along with Joshua, he'll treat you fair. "

"Like he treats Sara so fair?" rasps Annie. "Are you sure you know where they both are right now?"

"What do you mean? What are you talking about?" Esther snaps.

"Nothing," says Annie. "I ain't talking about anything at all. Except there they come together, yonder."

Sara and Joshua come back to the wagons. Sara ignores her mother and hurries into the wagon. Her face is scarlet. It looks like she's been crying. Joshua demands food and Esther hurries to fill him a plate. When Esther throws a dress to Annie, she ignores it.

"Put it on," Joshua says.

She ignores him, stands up, and starts to walk over towards Duster. Joshua runs around, grabs her arm and swings her around to face him.

"Don't touch me," she says, loudly and clearly. "I'm not your daughter, I'm not your wife, I'm not anything to you, you filthy bastard. Get your hands off me. Don't ever touch me again."

For an answer he backhands her across the face and this time she fights back with total fury, booting him hard in the knee, kicking, biting and gouging until Thomas and Harold come to Joshua's aid, pulling her arms behind her and holding her while he slaps her, hard, twice more. Harold watches, snickering.

"Yep, that'll teach her," he says. "Women got to learn to mind." He's a beefy, red-faced man who doesn't say much, just nods assent to whatever Joshua says.

"Throw her in the wagon," Joshua mutters and turns away, limping.

Annie's eyes water from the pain. Her ears are ringing and her whole head aches.

She lies in the wagon, gritting her teeth. That was stupid. She's got to plan, got to get out of this, rescue Sara, and get revenge. Anger won't solve anything. She's got to be smarter. Got to, got to.

When they finally stop for lunch, Esther brings Annie her food and turns away. Joshua rides just behind the wagon. Harold rides in front. Esther, as usual, drives the team. Annie's not ready to risk being beaten again. They're bound to sleep sometime. And Sara, she wonders, what's happening with Sara? Why did she go off with Joshua again? She's not real sure just what it is Joshua is planning on doing to her. But Sara is obviously desperately afraid of him. And what the hell is the matter with Esther, that she can't see what's right under her eyes?

She thinks about Joshua. Nothing in her experience has been like him. Her father was gruff and mean, rarely said anything kind, but she knew he was fair. The mountain men she met in her valley were shy, but they had been kind to her. Joe was a conceited fool, at first, but after she got to know him, even she had to admit he had his good points. He helped Lucille out whenever he could, and he was stern but fair with the boys working for him. But this man…Annie shivers. She remembers his face when he slapped her. She remembers the feel of it. She thinks she'll never forget it. And, she vows, he'll never get a chance to do it again.

TWENTY-FIVE

THE DAY DRAGS ON. She's allowed out of the wagon to pee and eat, but that's it. They're all watching her, even Sara, but no one speaks to her. She and Sara are never alone together, not even at night when they are all sleep in the wagon. Esther lies between them and Annie lies awake, watchful. Several times that night she tries to get up, only to have Esther wake up at her slightest move. Finally, exhausted, she gives up and goes to sleep.

The next day dawns grey and cold with a thin bitter wind searching out the worn places in their clothes, tying shivering knots in their muscles. By the time they set off, the wind is flapping and screeching around the wagons; the canvas cracks and bangs, the horses are nervous and hard to handle. The wind steadily increases and the temperature drops. By evening, there is snow on the wind. When the horses are unharnessed they stand, backs hunched and heads down, in the shelter of the wagons. Esther can't manage a fire and instead they eat a few cold, dry biscuits and try to sleep dressed in as many clothes as they can, rolled up in their blankets to wait it out. By night, the storm has become a fury; snow blows into the wagons. It's impossible to sleep. Finally Annie sits up, pulls her blankets around her. The canvas covering on the wagon strains and cracks; the wind worries and snarls at it. Finally, it rips and shreds completely, and the wind pounces on them. Esther and Sara scream and flounder, trying to hold their blankets around them.

"Get under the wagon," Annie yells in their ears. "There's no shelter here. Get going." She can't believe how cold it's gotten. The snow streams by in thin bitter flakes.

Frantically, she wrestles what boxes and bales she can find in the darkness, hoists them over the tailgate, shoving them in against the wheels. She works until she has made a shelter under the wagon, and finally, mercifully, inside this cave the wind dies to a distant moan although it still blasts through the cracks and holes.

Esther and Sara are shaking and shivering with cold and fear. Annie makes them all huddle together and wraps what blankets she has managed to salvage around all three of them. Shadow has crawled in with them. The dull warmth generated by the four of them together finally begins to seep through her clothes, but her feet are freezing. She pulls off her boots and wet socks and tucks her feet in under Sara's legs.

Annie feels a hand come stealing into hers. "Thanks, Annie," Sara whispers. "I'm sorry. I haven't been ignoring you. Joshua threatened me, if he caught me talking to you, that he'd take a horsewhip to me and my mom."

"Sara," comes Esther's sad weary voice. "Stop saying those things about Joshua. He's your father now, you owe him respect."

"Ma," Sara snaps back. "He's loco and he's been after me and you know it. I know why you married him, but it's not worth it. We've got to get out of here. Annie has said she'll help us. You will take us, won't you, Annie?"

"Sara, please don't say things like that, and don't talk to her. She's a trouble-maker, a little whore. Joshua told me about her, always sneaking around, making up to the men, trying to get him to go with her. Why, she even tried her tricks on poor old Quick. You stay away from her."

"Mother, that's lies, all lies. None of it's true, it's Joshua, he's the one sneaking around," Sara cries, but her mother turns away.

"Don't tell me," she says. "I don't want to hear…if you want to leave me, go ahead. Maybe you *should* go back…maybe that's right, there's not much future for you out here, no men, no parties, no boys, no nothing. But don't tell me about anything else. I don't want to hear. I can't hear. Don't you understand? He's my husband, I got to live with him. I got no future, nowhere to go." Her voice is dreary, beaten flat.

There's silence then except for the distant scream and howl of the wind. After a while, Annie drifts off, shivering and waking and dozing again. The ground is freezing cold, even with a blanket underneath her. Finally she realizes it's growing lighter, but there's no cessation in the wind. It's a little warmer in their wagon cave. Snow has seeped in through the cracks, smudged tiny drifts around them. She wonders how the men are doing; she would have thought they'd have come around by now to check on the women, after all their talk about women being in the care of men, but she's glad they haven't. Shadow shakes himself and paws at the side of the boxes to get out. Finally he squirms through. Annie pokes her head out after him. Snow stings her face and the wind slaps at her cheeks and nose.

She pulls her head back. "It's bad," she says, "real bad. I never knew you could have weather like this, this late in the spring. We're gonna need to figure how to melt snow for water. I'll try and climb up in the wagon and find some food."

"There's some dried meat in the wagon," whispers Esther. "But we can't cook it. Oh, my God, I'm so cold," she moans. "I'm so cold."

"There's dead grass," Annie's thinking out loud, "under the snow, we could twist it up real tight so it would burn slower…if we make a fire under here, we'll suffocate from the smoke. Wait…" She starts digging at the side of the drifted snow with her hand. She moves some boxes, makes a cleared area just under the side of the wagon away from the wind. She's also dug up a lot of long, dry, dead grass in the process. She lights a small fire; it blows out quickly and makes a lot of smoke, but it lets them half-cook the tiny strips of dried meat Annie finds in the wagon. The boxes she brought down are made of thin wood which can be splintered and ripped apart. They burn parts of them as well.

After a while, with the heat from the fire reflecting back from the snow walls and the underside of the wagon, they become almost warm. The food helps, makes them sleepy. They melt snow in a shallow dish and take turns sipping at it. The wind keeps blowing. They wait it out for hours, dozing and shivering. It gets dark again, and they try burning a little more grass and cooking more bits of the meat. Annie cuts off meat for Shadow and feeds him.

Hours pass. Annie dozes, wakes, dozes again, conscious of the ache in her feet and hands. Finally, she thinks it's sounding less furious. She cautiously pokes her nose out. It's still snowing, and although the wind has dropped, it's still a blizzard. A thin edge of grey glimmers behind the blackness surrounding them.

"Esther," she says urgently, pulling her head back in. "You don't want me around and I sure don't want to stay. If I'm gonna go, it's now. Where's my gun and saddle?"

Esther looks at her. Her face is gaunt and hollowed and shadowed. Her eyes are sunken. She looks ancient. "Take

Sara," she whispers. "Take Sara away from here, please. I know what you think but I got to stay. I'm going to have another baby."

"My gun…"

"I don't know…I think it's under the wagon seat, with the rest of your stuff."

Quickly Annie pushes her way out of the snow cave, climbs back in the wrecked, snow-filled wagon, gets the rifle which is under a heap of saddles and harnesses, and climbs back down. In the dark it takes her a while, but she finds Duster, head down and caked with snow, standing patiently with the other horses in the shelter of a small clump of willow.

"Okay, buddy, this is it." She takes his hobbles off, slips a piece of rope around his neck and loops it over his nose. She grabs a second piece of rope and halters the big grey that Joshua rides. She brings them back to the wagon. They don't want to move, don't want to face the snow. Working frantically, she digs out what she thinks are the right saddles and bridles, finds saddlebags, then saddles and bridles the two horses. She goes back in the dark and takes the hobbles off the rest of the horses.

From what she can see, the canvas in the second wagon, though torn, looks intact. They've got it pulled down tight, lashed the openings. Bloody cowards. Wouldn't even come see if the women survived. She watches for any movement. The men must still be in there, drinking or drunk. She wonders where Quick got to. Maybe they all froze to death.

Then she notices a roll of canvas, covered in snow, under the second wagon. Reluctantly, she goes closer, until she can see Quick's curly head. His face seems ancient and sunken from cold. She hesitates. He could come too, if he wanted. It would be a hell of a nuisance, but still…She bends down, beckons, but he says nothing, just closes his eyes and turns his head away. His face is grey, shrunken. Annie stops. He might die here, he needs to get under shelter, probably needs some food, something hot. But if she says anything, tries to persuade him, she'll give herself away.

Finally, she turns away, stops again. He'll have to save himself. Her heart sinks at the idea of leaving him there. But it's time to go, blizzard or no blizzard. Thank God the wind is still making so much noise. No one can hear her moving around. They must be wondering by now, she thinks again, how the women are faring. What the hell is wrong with them…big, strong men. She checks that the rifle is loaded.

Now for Sara. What about Sara? Sara will be a burden and a nuisance. Sara is lazy and scared of everything. Sara could have fought harder against Joshua and her mother. Sara is just a girl, and it's going to be difficult enough to survive once she gets away from here.

"Damn it all, Annie," she thinks, "just get out of here. Leave these people to their own mess."

"Are you coming?" she says ungraciously, stooping down. "If you are, then get a bloody move on."

"But Annie, it's still dark, and snowing and it's so cold…" Sara wails.

"Shut up," Annie hisses. "If we leave now, the snow will fill in our tracks and no one can see us. Now come on… please, before they hear us…"

"Mom…" says Sara starting to weep, clutching at her mother. Esther holds on to her like a drowning person.

"I got you a horse," says Annie. "Get dressed in the warmest clothes you can find. Wrap up your feet. Come on!"

Still sobbing, Sara tears herself away from her mother, gets dressed, and moves out into the cold and dark. She manages to awkwardly scramble up the side of the grey gelding and get herself mounted.

The gelding is strong but hard to manage. He balks but Annie slaps him hard and he comes plunging after Duster through the drifts. Shadow struggles after them. It's hard for him in the deep snow, but he follows the horses' broken trail. Slowly, the other horses wander after them.

Annie leads them, heading away from the wind, with no idea where they're going. It doesn't matter. The horses won't head into the wind, that's for sure. What they'll have to do is find some shelter, a gully, some trees, anything to break the force of the wind and let them build a fire. But they're away. Finally. Her heels drum Duster's sides but he can only move so fast through the snow. She sucks a deep breath through her teeth. She's away, free. The big draft horses drift farther and farther behind them. They'll find their own shelter.

The snow is a hissing white wall around them, an endless room of black and white through which they push on for what seems like hours. She gives Duster his head, hoping he'll find them some place in which to shelter. She wraps the reins around the saddle horns and her arms around herself. They could still freeze to death. Already her feet are numb. She shakes. Her teeth bang together. It's impossible to believe that two days ago, she and Sara were sitting in the sun, broiling fish.

She's stiff with cold, nodding in the saddle, when Duster hesitates and she urges him forward. She feels him start downwards, and she leans back, yells at Sara to watch out. Duster slides, catches himself, slides and plunges, rocks back on his haunches for a breath and slides and heaves himself downward again. Annie hangs on. It's all she can do. She feels like they're falling down a cliff, and only Duster's occasional contact with dirt is keeping them from flying out into white space. She can hear an occasional shriek from Sara, but there's nothing she can do.

Abruptly, Duster stops, and behind her, Sara's grey comes plunging and crashing to a halt beside Duster, both of the horses trembling and snorting. It's quiet. A few bits of snow drift down but they're out of the wind; it feels warmer now they're out of the main blast of the blizzard. Shadow has no trouble with the hill, comes up beside them, still struggling with the snow but keeping up.

"Duster, you angel, you wonderful horse. You did it. Sara, he did it, we're below the blizzard somehow." Annie looks around. She can't really see where they are, although it's near dawn, and the light is growing, but she can hear water. Dry willow cracks under the horses feet. When she gets off, the sandy ground crunches under her. They're in a steep narrow gully. Brush and cottonwoods offer shelter. They head towards the sound of running water, and find a bit of flat by the creek with sand under the snow.

Annie slips off Duster. Far away somewhere, her numb feet ache and burn. Frantically, she scrabbles for dry willow twigs, bits of paper-thin, twisted bark, fumbles a flint and steel from her saddlebags. She strikes spark after spark, blowing patiently. Sara has crumpled to the ground, but Annie doesn't have time to see how she's faring. Finally, a thread of smoke, then a yellow tulip of flame begins to lick at the twigs. Carefully, she lays on one stick at a time, bits of dry grass, larger sticks, until the fire is two feet high and roaring with heat. Then she strips off her boots and socks, prods Sara, makes her do the same. She had managed to put the last of the dried meat and a small tin pot in her saddle bags. She puts some of the meat in water to make broth. Finally she crouches on her haunches, warming her hands, brooding into the fire.

This is what she's used to, she thinks with satisfaction. This is where she belongs, free and on her own, looking after herself. Only Sara's presence, on the other side of the fire, disturbs her.

"We'll stay here, dry out, hunt, and then head southeast, try and pick up your wagon tracks and backtrack," Annie says. "We've got to find a town and some people to take care of you." Sara doesn't say anything but when Annie looks again, she's crying silently to herself.

Annie tries to just let her cry but it's too hard to listen to.

"Sara," she says finally, slowly, not knowing what else to say, "crying don't get you nothing; you're gonna have to learn to toughen up. This is not a country for crying in."

"Sure, be like you," Sara flashes angrily. "Tough as a hammer, never show your feelings, never talk about anything. You don't care if you're freezing to death or falling down a cliff. It's all the same to you. You're worse than a man."

"What?" says Annie, shocked. "I'm not anything like a man."

"Oh yes you are. You think because you're out here and you're such a cowgirl, you have to be tough and strong and never talk or let anyone know who you are. I don't know who you are. I don't know anything about you and here I am, sitting beside a fire in the middle of nowhere, and my Ma is somewhere back there in a blizzard, and you've got the nerve to tell me not to cry. Well, to hell with you, I'll cry if I damn well want to." And she does.

Annie is too astonished to say anything at all. They've just escaped from a terrifying situation; they're still in the middle of a blizzard, probably with the men out hunting them, and they're already fighting.

"I only meant..."

"I don't care what you meant," says Sara, and turns her back. Then she turns again to Annie. "What am I supposed to sleep on?" she says. "I don't suppose you remembered sleeping, you know—blankets? Or maybe you sleep with your horse…"

Now Annie is furious. "Sleep on your saddle blanket," she says through gritted teeth. "Roll yourself up in it. That's it. That's what you get to sleep in. No feather mattresses out here. Just couldn't figure how to fit one on a horse."

"But I'm freezing," says Sara." And it's all sweaty and covered in horse hair."

"That's why I built the fire here," sighs Annie. "Sleep between that big rock and the fire and you'll warm up. The sand is almost dry there. Now, if you don't mind a whole lot, I'd like some quiet so I can try and think my way out of this mess you've gotten us into."

"I got us into? You're the one who had the brilliant idea of running away and getting us lost. You're the one who upset Joshua."

"What? That is such malarkey. You asked me to save you from him. I didn't want to bring you. I was doing just fine on my own. Having you around my neck is the last thing I need."

"Fine," says Sara, bursting into tears again. "I'll find my own way back. I can look after myself. You're not the only one. You think I'm such a weakling, I'll show you."

"Fine," says Annie. "Show me after I've had some rest." She gets out her blanket, pulls it over her shoulder, and squats by the fire, trying, but unable to shut out the sound of Sara's desolate sobbing and long, shuddering sighs. The heat makes her sleepy, and she curls herself deeper in the blanket and lies down. Shadow curls up between her and the fire.

The ground is cold and hard after the nights in the wagon. Her face is still sore where Joshua slapped it. She remembers the feel of his hands on her, the days he spent riding beside her. And she had felt flattered. She thought he meant it when he told her she was brave and pretty. She thought he must be a good man because of all his pious prating about God and the promised land. She wishes she could have hurt him back. She'd like to have him in front of her now, and slap *his* face until it burned and shook and swelled into a pumpkin.

But no, she doesn't want to touch it, dirty and hairy as it is. She'd like to go back, take the wagon, leave him naked and freezing on the prairie, tied to a tree; she'd go back just when he was dying, then cut him loose and watch him crawl. She dozes, dreams that she and Joshua are swimming in a river together. She tries everything she can to kill him, pushing his head under the water, hitting him with a rock and finally pulling him on shore and burying him in the sand. Through it all, he remains smiling, passive, unhurt no matter what she does. In the dream, she screams and screams her frustration, but she can't hurt him.

Annie jerks awake from the dream to a cold rain and grey sky; Sara is sitting hunched on the other side of the fire.

TWENTY-SIX

WITHOUT A WORD, Annie takes the rifle and heads off, drifting quietly through the breaks and tangled willow thickets, the sandy clearings, the muddied gullies, past the quiet rain-pebbled pools of water. She kneels; there is a lot of deer sign, but Annie waits a long time in the peaceful grey rain before she kills one, not wanting to break the silence, not wanting anything except time to wander and feel free. She brings the meat back to the fire. At least Sara has moved enough to gather wood.

"Use dry willow. It doesn't smoke," Annie grunts at Sara.

"There is no dry wood," Sara snaps. Then she hesitates, looking around, plainly nervous. "Do you think Joshua has followed us? Do you think he can find us here?"

"I don't know. He seems pretty crazy to me. Hard to say what he'll do. I bet he's mad though. Ha! I would love to have seen his fool face when he finally crawled out of the wagon. They must have been drinking in there, or they would have come earlier to check on us."

"Annie, tell me what you think of this. I've been thinking a lot about it," Sara says hesitantly. "He said he was only following the law of Abraham, that in the old days men had lots of wives, it was in the Bible and everything, and there wasn't anything wrong with what he was doing. He said that once he explained it to my Mom, she wouldn't mind. He said lots of people lived like that, and he was going to find them and join up. What do you think?"

"I think he has fog in his head," Annie says slowly. "I think there's something very wrong with him. I don't understand it. I don't understand any of it. I just know I was so angry I wanted to kill him. I wish I could talk to Shadow about it."

"Shadow?"

"Oh, a friend."

By midday, they have the meat cut up and drying around the tiny smokeless fire. The sky clears, the sun comes out and it starts to warm up. Annie climbs the sand cliff behind them and stares out over the prairie but there's no sign of anything. The snow has almost all melted. Blue pools of water shimmer in the hollows among the iridescent green mat of grass. Annie picks a grass blade and chews it. The sun warms her back. She watches a tiny, green frog in a puddle of water, and a ladybug climbing a stalk of grass. She turns in all four directions like she remembers Shadow doing.

"Thank you," she says. It feels awkward to say it out loud. "Thank you for...well, for everything. No, wait...thank you for the blizzard, and for the shelter and for Duster and for...well, for all this." She waits on the glistening broad flat earth, while the wind licks her cheeks and the smell of damp ripe soil comes up from beneath her feet. I feel at home here, she thinks. I really do, I could live here. She turns and slides back down the sandy slope, raising dust and rolling stones, and goes back to the camp and an unhappy, sulking Sara.

TWENTY-SEVEN

THEY HAVE BEEN RIDING FOR DAYS, heading south and east, hoping to pick up signs of people. Annie has questioned Sara about the country the wagons came over, but she can't remember much. Sooner or later there's got to be something, a river, tracks, smoke, a pile of ashes, something that will let her know that people are near. She feels lost. She *is* lost. She doesn't tell Sara that.

The country gets rougher as they near the mountains. Sara complains constantly about the travelling, the weather, the lack of food. Annie grits her teeth. Soon, she thinks, soon she'll get rid of her. They can't find much to talk about. Sara's main preoccupation is what she'll do when she gets back to where there are people. She thinks she can get a job looking after kids or as a maid or even doing laundry. She's done that before. She'll buy some new clothes, look for a man, get married. "It should be easy," she says, "there's lots of men out here."

"I'd like to find a rich man," she fantasizes out loud, "someone to take care of me, maybe take me to a big city. I wish Mom had married a rich guy. There was this one guy who used to come sniffing around her. He was okay, I thought. He sold stuff or something, but she couldn't stand him. I don't really care much what kind of guy it is, just so long as he takes care of me. Maybe if I get tired of him, I'll ditch him and find another. I don't know what else to do. I'm not like you, Annie. I hate this rough life, and I don't, don't, don't want to live like this."

Annie thinks that the life Sara is outlining for herself might be rougher, but she doesn't say anything. After all, she doesn't know much about men. Maybe she'll get married herself someday, and maybe she won't. She hums to herself while riding; "maybe I will, maybe I won't," repeats itself in her head like a song.

Sara complains most about not being able to get clean. She washes herself and her dress every night. She frets over her hair. So when they first sight smoke in a distant valley, she says, "Oh, please, maybe they have some soap."

Annie says, "Slow down…we don't even know who they are…or what they are. Could be almost anyone." She's damned if she's going to walk into another situation where she isn't sure what's happening. If she didn't have Sara with her, she wouldn't go near another settlement, not for a long while.

It takes them almost all day, struggling over rough terrain, to get to a place where they can look down on the smoke. Most of it turns out to be dust.

"Well," says Annie. "It's a place…of sorts. Looks like it's all men…can't tell what they're up to, digging or something. Must be mining."

"Gold, maybe," says Sara, "I heard talk of it when we left. God, what a mess. They're digging everything up. It looks so ugly and dirty. C'mon, hurry, let's go down. They'll have somewhere we can stay, they'll have real food. Beds, maybe."

But Annie stays, sitting on Duster, looking down. Dust comes smoking up through the slanting evening sun. There are at least fifty or more men down there, and the beginning of a few rough shacks, a lot of tents sitting on log platforms in the mud, what could almost be a road, teams of mules and horses hitched to wagons standing around among tree stumps. It's noisy; even from up this high, there's a buzz floats up with the smoke, a combined clanging, rattling humming noise that jars her teeth. She doesn't want to go down there. It's a raw scar on the earth, a grey ugly gash in the calm blanket of hills and trees surrounding them. It stinks. She can smell it from here. Mud, manure, smoke.

"Sara," she says, "let's stay here for the night and go down in the morning. Give us a chance to organize ourselves and figure out what we're going to do."

Sara is immediately furious.

"I figure to sleep in a building tonight, safe, with people, instead of out here with who knows what prowling around—wild animals and Indians, horrible bugs and cold."

Annie says, "We haven't seen any wild animals for days. Or bugs either. And it ain't even cold." She hesitates. "I just don't want to go down there right now."

"But those are men, white men," cries Sara. "They'll protect us. They'll help us out. Come on, what are you waiting for?"

Annie shakes her head, but Sara has already started kicking the grey horse into reluctant motion. Duster starts after and Annie lets him, fear braiding her spine into knots. Sara is well ahead of her now and she pulls at Duster, stiffens her back, slowing him. She does not want to go down there, be locked up again, stay in a building, deal with men's voices and men's eyes and men's meanness and her own fear.

But she does. She gets out the rifle and lays it across her legs, holding it with one hand. Duster curls his neck under the restraint from her tight hands and tight legs, tucks his chin and throws out his legs. He skitters sideways, prancing and catches up to the grey and they ride that way into the middle of the miners, who look up and watch them coming, standing still with their shovels and pickaxes, grey clothes and grey, hard, bearded faces.

One building is more finished than the others. A crude sign over the door, lettered in charcoal says "Bar" and underneath, in smaller letters, "Assay office."

They leave the horses standing and go inside. The bar has a dirt floor and a canvas roof and a few dusty bottles of liquor standing on a log table. There are three other tables and a couple of crude benches made from logs. The seats and tabletops have been flattened with an adze, although they're not very flat. No one is around. Annie goes to the back and yells but no one appears.

She goes back and sits at the table with Sara. They look at each other.

"Want a drink?" Sara whispers, giggling. "There's no one around. We could steal a couple."

"No," Annie grits fiercely at her. "I don't want anything. I want out of here."

"Wait," says Sara. "Someone will come. Someone's got to be in charge here."

A short, round man comes through the door, which isn't a door but only an opening covered by a sheet of canvas, and stops abruptly when he sees them.

"Ladies…" he says. "Well, well, well. My goodness. Well, this is a pleasure. And where ever have you come from and whatever can I do for you? My, my, ladies, in these wild parts. Whatever will happen next? My name is Samuel McNeill, and would you be wanting a drink or a bit of gold weighed out, or a meal perhaps? We don't see ladies much here, y'see. In fact…" he hesitates, "we don't see them at all, y' see…" his voice trails off and he mumbles to himself and then stoops to wipe the rough counter with a filthy bit of rag.

Still he's friendly and unthreatening. Annie reserves judgment for now, but refuses to smile back at his effusiveness. Sara expands like a tulip in the sun.

"Oh, please help us," she says. "We've been travelling so long, and we've had to sleep out and we need soap and baths and a place to do our laundry and meals and sleep. We're so tired. We're tired of cold and wild animals and everything."

"Well, my, my, you poor things," he says, astonished. "Yes, indeed, we'll have to see what we can do. My, my," and he rubs his hands together and bustles around, but without much effect that Annie can see. She sits on the bench for a while, watching, while he runs out to get water and then comes back and runs out again for something to light the stove with and forgets to light it and starts to cut up some meat and potatoes for stew and then runs out again to shout at someone on the street to take care of the horses.

Annie looks at Sara and sighs. She gets up, quietly and efficiently lights the stove, finishes making the stew, boils the water and finds a wash pan and some soap. Samuel rushes back in and out several more times, flapping his arms and his mouth and his coattails. When she and Sara have eaten, Annie goes out to find the horses and make sure they've been taken care of. Shadow stalks at her heels.

She finds them tied in a lean-to shed with their saddles still on and no feed in sight. There's not much grass in this narrow valley and what there is has been trampled into mud. There's no place to turn them out to graze. Annie finds some musty last year's hay, and a few dried cobs of corn in a bin in the corner. She brushes the horses down, gives them the hay and leaves them standing. She doesn't intend to stay here past tomorrow anyway.

When she comes back into the bar, Sara is sitting on one of the tables, surrounded by miners, her legs swinging. She's recounting adventures that Annie, even by stretching her imagination to the furthest, can't remember happening. Joshua doesn't figure in any of them and Annie notices that Sara is careful to avoid the whole issue of where they were coming from or why.

"Oh, and here's Annie," cries Sara. "She's so brave. And smart. Just like a man. I mean really. She can hunt and shoot and everything."

The men look at her like she is some kind of new and foreign creature and turn their attention back to Sara. Annie can't figure what it is they find so fascinating. Sara is laughing and tossing her head and waving her arms around. Annie thinks the whole thing is silly. One of the men brings a bottle of whiskey and sets it in the middle of the table.

"Oh, just a tiny one," cries Sara, and has a sip from a glass, chokes, sputters and recovers.

One of the men pours some whiskey in a glass and holds the glass out to Annie. The brown slopped liquid shivers in the glass. She takes it, and holds it to her nose and then takes a mouthful. It burns as she swallows it but she keeps her face expressionless. She keeps swallowing until the glass is empty and one of the men promptly fills it up again.

She manages to pour out the second glass onto the dirt floor. Sara is giggling; her voice and the men's voices get louder and louder. Annie realizes that she doesn't quite know what's going on anymore. She can't understand what anyone is saying, they seem to be talking nonsense. The men's faces, bearded, dirty, their looming teeth and dirty clothes, the stale stink coming from them fills the room. She clutches the rifle and stays absolutely still in the corner, hoping no one will notice her. No one does. After a while, her head clears and she rises and stalks to the door. No one stops her. She steps outside in the clear air and the silence, surprised to find that it's still light. The air is damp; grey thin mist cloaks the trees and hilltops. She shivers. What she needs is a warm corner to curl up in, a place to sit until her head is quiet, but there's no place like that here. She goes to the lean-to and sits down, leaning against Duster's legs. Duster puts his head down and chews on her shirt. Shadow nudges and nudges to be petted. She's freezing cold. She puts her head on her knees and closes her eyes.

When she wakes up, it's dark. Sara. Where has she gotten to? Annie hurries back to the bar. Sara is nowhere in sight, only Samuel, playing cards by himself.

"If you're looking for your friend," he says, "she's cozied

up in the back room, sleeping. Guess I'll have to bunk in here on the floor. Well, won't be the first time. You'll have to crawl in there with her. Hot water's on the stove. You can pay me tomorrow."

Annie doesn't answer. She still has the money from Lucille but she's decided it's going to be her stake when she does find land and settle down. She's not going to pay this inefficient babbler for food she's cooked herself and a chance to sleep on his floor. Maybe she can work something out tomorrow, do some work for him. In the back room, Sara is curled up and snoring with a ratty torn quilt pulled over her. The bunk is made from poles, with hay stuffed in canvas for a mattress. Annie sighs. She could make a lot more comfortable bed outside somewhere, but she doesn't want to leave Sara here on her own.

Sara grunts as Annie shoves in beside her. "Move over," Annie says and shoves her over. Sara obligingly squeezes in closer to the wall. Annie crawls in beside her warm breathing and lies awake. Sara's body fits into the warm spoon shape Annie makes.

Why are she and Sara so different? She doesn't want any of the things that Sara wants. Sara had charmed those men this afternoon. More important than that, she can control them somehow; there is some magic there that she, Annie, doesn't have and can't understand. Grizzlies and dogs and horses and shooting; those she understands. And she learned to understand Shadow and his poeple. But a room full of men, looking at her and expecting something from her which she doesn't care about and isn't interested in, is terrifying.

She wishes she liked Sara better. Maybe they could have been friends, like she and Lucille became friends. She still misses Lucille too much. But she could ride up to Lucille's door anytime and they'd still be friends. And someday she will. But Sara? Well, when Sara finally gets where she's going, Annie figures this whole episode will be just an embarrassment to her. She won't want to remember it or tell it to her grandchildren and what's more, anybody that could ride off and leave her mother with a monster like Joshua, not knowing what was going to happen...But then, what else could she do? And what else could Esther do? Maybe if Annie hadn't been so gutless, if she'd faced Joshua down, pulled a gun on him and made him admit what he'd been up to with Sara, she could have changed the whole situation. So why hadn't she? Because Joshua is a man and she is just a girl, is why. Because facing down Joshua would have been like facing down her father. Not because there were three of them and one of her. It was something different. They were men and all her life, what men said was what happened. Even she and Lucille had paid attention when the men came around. That crazy Joe just naturally felt he could give the orders, and they'd never really questioned it. She's never thought about it before, how different it was to be with women, with Lucille or Sara. Even as silly as Sara is, everything changed when they got here. Now it feels dangerous again, scary and mysterious. She never felt like that with Lucille. Lucille wouldn't hurt her. If and when they fought, they fought on equal ground. She'd liked being able to yell at Lucille and have her yell back.

But Shadow had been her friend as well. As little as she'd known him, she hadn't been afraid of him nor, she thinks with surprise, of the other men in the Indian camp. That's strange because they were supposed to be terrifying "savages," torturing and kidnaping people; but they had shown such kindness to Annie.

So if these men are so terrifying to her, why isn't Sara frightened? Because she has some power, some excitement, some way of controlling them? But if she needs to control them, then there must be something worth fearing. It's a mystery. Annie's thoughts tumble over and over, like worn, polished stones in a stream bed.

Sara turns and her breasts brush against Annie's arm. Annie moves as far away as she can but there's no room and no blankets and she's still freezing cold. She rolls out of the bunk and onto the floor, miserable. Shadow whimpers beside her. Finally, she curls up in a corner on the hard, damp, miserable floor, her head on Shadow's soft belly, and there she finally sleeps uneasily while the faces of strange, bearded men drift in and out of her dreams.

TWENTY-EIGHT

"WE'RE GETTING OUT OF HERE, NOW," says Annie, the next morning. Sara shakes her head, sleepy.

"No," she says. "You go. I'll be fine here."

"I can't leave you here," says Annie impatiently. "Don't be so stupid. Come on. I don't like it here."

"It's warm, there's food, and I happen to like it just fine. Now leave me alone." Sara glares at her.

"It's a damn mining camp full of men drinking and fighting and who knows what. You need to get to a town, where there's other women. I said I'd take you. I said I'd take care of you until we got there."

"Take care of me? You? You don't even *like* me. How can you take care of me? It's not safe out there on the prairies, where we were. And you want to drag me out there again. No. I'm staying here. You go, go chase wild Indians or bears or whatever stupid dream you're after. Just leave me alone. Go away. I'll be just fine here." Sara turns her back and pulls the tattered quilt over her shoulders. She's crying again, Annie notices with impatience.

Outside of the bar, everything is quiet. Very quiet. It's still grey and cold. No one is visible on the churned mass of mud, tree branches, rocks and holes that serves for the road going up the hill towards the various mine workings. The hills are bare of trees, only stumps and branches remain. Pickaxes clink on the rock face; farther up, there's an occasional muffled explosion. Annie looks around. She needs to find some feed for the horses and she still can't decide what to do about Sara. Grey, cold fingers of mist still cling to the trees and the hillside. What stray bits of grass remain are thin and forlorn, fringing the rocks and growing among clumps of moss.

The horses are glad to see her, nosing hungrily at her clothes and hands. She hobbles them and turns them loose on the hillside to browse for what they can find. As she comes back down towards the bar, she hears a shout. A man comes running, stumbling down the hill, sliding and jumping from rock to rock.

"Injuns coming. Injuns!" he yells. He spots Annie and yells, "You women git inside and stay there."

Annie wants to shoot him on the spot, but she restrains herself and instead, turns and climbs and scrambles back up the bare hillside and then the rock face above it, until she can look out over the rumpled fir-clothed hills and valleys. At first she can't see anything; then she spots the file of horses and riders among the trees. The sun is poking thin holes through the cloud cover. One of their horses is white; it seems to catch the light and reflect it back.

A lump rises in her throat. She watches as they ride slowly down the winding path, their horses picking their delicate way over the rounded granite rocks and under pines, over the orange-red needles under the trees, and the purple-shadowed sage. She hears shouts and activity from the camp below her. Jabbered excitement floats up to her, and the Indians keep riding, silent, like people in a dream.

"Take me with you," she thinks. "Take me with you." But someone below is yelling, waving his arms at her. She waves back, dismissing him. The men have formed themselves into a ragged formation. Someone seems to have taken charge. Most of the men have guns. Three of them mount horses and ride out of the camp; she watches their progress. They make their way towards the Indians, who halt under the pines. The sky darkens again. It's hard to see what's going on. The men on horses and the Indians meet. Annie holds her breath.

Then one of the men points his gun at the sky and fires it. The echoes shatter and crash on the hill. The Indians turn and ride back into the darkness under the pines, and the men come back, whooping and racing on their horses. When Annie slips down the hill and into the bar, the men are gathered around a bottle of whiskey, congratulating themselves on their bravery, and making plans for the future defense of the camp. Most of them decide to form themselves into a group and follow the Indians, track them to wherever they're going. They make indignant noises about safety and protection. Annie figures they just want themselves a holiday from the tedious work of mining.

Sara is still in the back room, huddled under the quilt. Annie sits down beside her.

"There's nowhere that's safe, really," she says, after a while. "Not here, not out there. You just have to choose. We'll take another day or so to rest and then we'll go, all right?"

"All right," Sara whispers. "All right, if you say so. I don't know what else to do. I don't feel like going nowhere, just staying in this bed. I just feel like wherever I go, it won't matter much, cause there ain't no place I can find what I want."

Almost no one is left behind in the camp but a few men who seem determined to spend the day in the bar, drinking what supplies of liquor are left. Annie spends the afternoon trying to get some supplies and hay for the horses. But here, she's expected to pay for every little thing. She offers to work for their food, shelter and hay, but the little man behind the bar isn't interested.

"C'ain't you cook?" he asks, narrowing his eyes. "I'm not needing a man to do the sweeping, but a woman's hand to cooking, that would be a nice change."

"I can hunt," says Annie bitterly. "I can scout. I can track.

I can rope. But I don't know much about cooking…except making biscuits over a fire. I can do that."

But the man laughs. "We got scouts," he says. "When them Indians come back here looking for a fight, for sure, they're going to get one. They're in for one big goddamn surprise. Yeah, we got scouts. I noticed you packing that there Henry rifle around. Figured it was for show. Scare these boys off if they get carried away."

"It's not for show," says Annie.

The man sighs. "Well, guess there's some sawlogs out back you can buck up. That'll take the starch out of your apron, I'd be reckoning, and keep you out of my hair. We've got to clear the hatches and buckle down for a raid. Reckon that was a scouting party coming by, just looking for easy pickings. Well, we'll show them. We'll give them a taste of their own medicine. They ain't driving us out, not by a long shot."

Annie sighs. Another pompous fool. Well, it won't make any difference to her and Sara. They'll soon be out of here. In the meantime, it's back to the torture of the cross-cut saw for her. First, she gets what supplies she can out of him, tea, coffee, flour, a couple more pots, bacon, beans, fishing line, and packs them away in her saddlebags.

The afternoon passes. The sun comes out and toasts her back and the woodpile grows. Sara comes out after a while and sits on a stump, watching Annie work.

"Annie, do you think we're really going to be attacked by Indians?"

"No," says Annie, "but it's a good excuse for them lazy fools to sit around drinking and bragging about how brave they are."

"But some of the men said…"

"I heard what they said. I saw the Indians. They looked like they were on their way somewhere and stopped by to have a look. I would too, if someone was tearing up my backyard and making such an ugly mess. Look, I've heard Indian stories ever since my folks and I left back east, and I figure we're in a lot more danger from Joshua if he decides to show up. That's one reason why we've got to keep moving."

"All right," Sara says, tossing back her hair, which is freshly washed. "But I don't see how come you always figure you know everything. You're just a girl like me. These men live here. They should know what they're talking about…"

"They don't live here. They don't know anything about it. Look at how new everything is. They haven't even had time to put up a decent shack or two to sleep in."

"Well, I'm glad we're here anyway, where we're protected." She leaves and wanders back to the bar.

Annie saws on. She could have asked Sara to help but she'd just as soon be out here by herself. There's a lot of laughter and noise from the bar. They'd be fine protection if anyone did attack, a bunch of drunks stumbling around looking for their rifles.

A shrill, screaming, screech claws the air. Sara! Annie

grabs the rifle and runs for the door. She tears aside the canvas blanket opening. Someone yells. She can barely see into the gloom.

"Sara!" she shrieks frantically, above the din.

"Hey, come to join your friend?" someone hollers to a chorus of laughter.

Another series of screams. Where the hell is she? The back room. With several strides, she's across the room and yanks the blanket aside. Sara is struggling on the bed with some man. Her dress is ripped. She's screaming. Annie fires a shot into the wall just over the man's head and he leaps up and backwards, swearing, jerking at his clothes, falls on the floor, and crawls backwards out the door.

"Watch it," someone hollers from outside the room. "She's got a gun." Annie figures she has about one moment before someone takes a shot at her. She aims and fires, and one of bottles on the table explodes. A man's hoarse voice screams, yelling.

"Jeezus, I'm hit, I'm hit."

"Sara, come on," Annie bellows, " get out of there." With one huge stride, she leaps across the room, grabs Sara and drags her off the bed, holds her with one arm and they come back out of the room, move slowly, step by step, back towards the door. The men watch her but don't move.

She looks around. "You filthy bastards," she snarls, then she and Sara are at the door. Just for good measure, as she leaves, she fires at one of the bottles on the bar, and shatters it into glass splinters. Men dive for the floor. Then she

fires at the roof, the floor, the walls, and finally, she's outside still dragging the moaning Sara down the street to the
shed. The horses are still picketed. She dumps Sara uncer-
emoniously on the mud floor and pelts for the horses,
brings them back at a trot. Someone pokes his head out of
the bar, and she fires another quick shot. There's a hoarse
yell of pain from inside. Damn. The slug must have gone
through the boards.

The horses are jumpy and hard to saddle. She gets Duster
saddled, throws the packs on, slings Sara over Duster and
climbs behind her, leading the steel grey. She boots Duster
into a rough gallop, holding Sara with one arm and the
rifle with the other, past the bar, through the mud, down
the long grey valley, up the rock-ridden slope and into the
welcoming shelter of the trees, onto the path the Indians
came down. She jerks Duster's head to follow the trail,
then slows him to a fast trot over the broken granite, rotten logs, jumbled bushes and tree roots.

I knew I hated that goddam camp, she thinks. Last time
I let anyone talk me into something when I know better.
Sara is hard to hold on to. Annie takes a desperate clutch
at her dress but feels her slipping. Annie needs another set
of hands to hold Sara, lead the grey, and control Duster,
who is excited, wanting to run.

"Can you ride?" Annie yells at Sara. She doesn't answer.
Her eyes are rolled back in her head and there's blood on
her dress. Annie hangs on and keeps moving. She watches
Shadow. She watches Duster's ears. If there's someone on

the trail behind them, they'll be the first to hear. Poor Shadow. She's almost forgotten him in all this mess. He trots along beside Duster, head high, sniffing the air.

When they come to a clear, flat place in the trail, Annie stops, lifts Sara down, and then hoists her onto the grey horse. "Hold on," she demands, with desperate urgency. "Just hold on until we're somewhere safe." Sara doesn't answer but her hands clutch the grey's mane. Annie swings back on Duster and leads them both at the fastest pace she can manage, trotting on the brief pieces of flat trail, pushing Duster through brush and over logs and rocks. The trail splits, and one side takes an abrupt turn down a steep bluff, switchbacks through gullied gravel and eroded boulders, down to the side of a green-foamed river rushing black under steep, over-hanging, moss-laden cliffs. She sees no sign anyone else has been this way for a while.

The path continues down and they follow it, Sara bent over and clutching with both hands around the grey's neck. Annie pushes them on, listening for sounds of pursuit, and trying to go slow over the most difficult parts of the trail. They steadily drop down and down. Towards the end of the long afternoon, Annie sees a brightness reflecting off water ahead. By dark, they have made it onto the gravel shoal covered with rounded, water-washed rocks where the river empties into a vast, dark lake. There's still no sign of pursuit. Sara slides off her horse and falls onto the ground. Annie gets a fire going, sets water to boil, makes a bed for Sara and helps her onto it.

Sara looks bad. She shivers and shakes. Her eyes are closed. She doesn't seem to hear anything Annie says to her. Annie makes tea and puts her arm around Sara to help her sit up. Sara's teeth clatter against the tin cup and the hot liquid runs down her dress. She twists away and lies down again, turning her back to Annie.

Annie goes to the edge of the black water. She baits a line and throws it out. Immediately something grabs it and tears furiously away. Slowly, cautiously, she pulls the fish in, onto the bank. It's a big, dark, spotted fish, gleaming in the light from the fire. She kills it with a rock, and then throws the line out again. Another furious vibrating blow at the end of the line. She pulls in another fish and then another, and takes them back to the fire, cleans them, throws the guts in the river and comes back, splits and filets the fish, and sets them on sticks to barbecue close to the fire. When the fish are done, she puts some on a battered tin plate and takes it to Sara. Sara doesn't move. Her eyes are closed. Annie feels her head. It feels much hotter than it should be. She wonders if she should check Sara for injuries but decides not to wake her up.

She leaves again and goes and sits cross-legged by the river. The water plays gurgling tag with the sandy shore. Annie plays a little with the fine dry sand, tossing it into the water just to see it being sucked away by the current. There's enough faint starlight to outline the black silhouette of the hills around them. No noise but the river. Shadow brings her a stick to toss, but she pushes him away.

She sits for a long time, and then checks on Sara again, who seems hotter than ever, though she's still shivering. Annie takes her shirt and puts it over Sara and builds up the fire. She whistles to Shadow and backtracks up the trail, listening carefully, but she hears nothing and Shadow behaves normally. The horses are grazing on the tall grass growing among the boulders. Everything is peaceful.

Except Sara is sick and hurt and she doesn't know where they are, and now they may have two packs of men on their trail. She can't figure out how any of it happened, or why.

She plays with Shadow for awhile, tossing a stick for him, wrestling with him in the smooth fine sand at the edge of the water, and then feeds him the rest of the fish. When she checks on Sara, she seems to be asleep. Annie tears the tail off her shirt, wets it in the river and pats Sara's forehead and cheeks. She wonders if she hurt or killed any of the men. She waits, staring out at the water gleaming under the faint starlight, listening to the lipping and splashing of the lake. Snow gleams from the mountains on the other side. After a while she falls asleep, her head pillowed in the sand and Shadow curled up beside her. She wakes, terrified, thinking that Sara is calling her for help, but it's only coyotes, screaming and yelping. Shadow growls but doesn't move. Annie builds up the fire and sits by it until the first light shimmers in split rays over the plateaued hills behind her, and the water shivers under the dawn wind off the hills.

Sara is lying in bed, her eyes open, looking at the sky. She shudders when Annie goes to touch her forehead but doesn't say anything. She still feels hot.

"We got to keep going," Annie says gently. "I know it's hard but we got to get you to somewhere safe. You got to get up now, get cleaned up, have some food."

Sara doesn't move but when Annie puts her arm around her, she doesn't resist. She lets herself be hoisted to her feet, helped to the river, where Annie washes her face, and then lifts her skirt and gently sponges the dried blood from between her legs. When Annie lets go of her, she simply folds her legs and sits on the sand, head down, unmoving.

"Sara," Annie pleads. "You got to snap out of this. Come on now. I know it was bad, but we got to get moving, in case they come after us. I might have killed one of them." Sara doesn't respond. Annie hoists her to her feet. When she lifts her, she sees the wet place in the sand. Sara has piddled there like a child, unconscious and uncaring.

She won't eat from the dish Annie places in front of her, and when Annie tries to feed her, she turns her head away. Annie fetches the horses, brushes them, saddles and packs their scattered gear. She hoists the limp Sara on to the grey. Sara won't hold the reins, but she seems conscious enough to hold onto the saddle.

She finds a rough trail leading south along the lake's edge. It's more a deer trail than anything, winding through trees and under dead-falls, down steep, jagged slabs of granite, over shale slopes where the rocks slide and crack under their feet, along beaches of sloping yellow sand. The sun is bright and hot. The rocks beside the water are folded, grey loaves of granite, flecked with driftwood. The sun bounces and flickers off the water. Sara slumps on her horse, hands white around the saddle horn, her hair uncombed, draping off the sides of her thin, white neck.

They stop for a break along a stretch of rocky sand, fringed with stunted thick firs. Annie pulls Sara off her horse. Sara's legs fold under her, and she lies on the sand, eyes closed.

"Sara, come on, snap out of this. I can't do this. I can't do this," Annie yells suddenly. "I told you, I told you that place was bad, why did you go in there? Jeezus. Why?" She grabs Sara's hands and drags her, limp and unresisting, to the lake. "Come on, you've got to wake up, you've got to talk to me, you've got to face this. You can't sleep the rest of your life away. You can't pretend you don't know anything. This is stupid. Wake up!" She grabs Sara's shoulders and shakes her, but there is no response.

Annie slips off her boots and her heavy skirt, her shirt and vest. She thinks grimly that if anyone *is* chasing them, this would be a lousy time for a fight. She leaves Sara's clothes on and drags her into the water, which is freezing, bone-biting cold. Annie gasps but drags Sara in deeper, splashes water on her face, yelling, "Wake up, come on, wake up, pay attention. It's me, Annie, you're safe here, you can wake up now." They stand in a frozen tableau, Annie and Sara in the water, Sara's skirt floating around her, Shadow on the shore watching anxiously, the horses, reins dropped and ears pricked forward, watching as well.

Sara stirs under her hands. Annie lets go of her and Sara moves, starts swimming feebly, paddling away from Annie, away from shore. Then Sara ducks her head under the water, trying to dive. Annie lunges, grabs her. "Hey," she says, "hey, what are you doing? Come on, now, this is crazy, come on, wake up, talk to me."

She pulls Sara back and Sara opens watered blue eyes and stares into Annie's face.

"Let me go," she whispers hoarsely. "Just let me go away…Let me go. Let go of me. I want to die. I want to die, I want to die, I want to die." She starts to struggle, twisting and grappling with Annie's restraining hands.

"Let go of me," she yells and her voice rises to a shriek, "let go of me, let go of me, let me go, get away, get away get away…"

Annie holds her and holds her, even though her legs are aching fiercely from the cold water. Sara stops screaming and begins to sob, and Annie drags her backwards, out onto the warm sand, and collapses beside her. Sara lies on the sand, shrieking and screaming and pounding her fists. Once she tries to crawl away, back towards the water, but Annie drags her back and holds her, while Sara struggles and weeps and hits at her.

"Talk to me, Sara, please talk to me," Annie says. Maybe if Sara starts talking, she'll at least stop screaming. Sara mutters something, too low for Annie to hear.

"What? Sara, what is it?"

"I said, don't let go," Sara gasps, very softly, and Annie doesn't. She holds her and rocks her in silence. Sara's wet hair straggles against her cheek. She breathes steadily, softly and deeply. Suddenly, she lifts herself away from Annie. Her eyes open wide.

"My Ma…I want my Ma…I wish I knew how she's doing, if she's okay," she whispers. "It was wrong to leave her there. I shouldn't have left her. We've got to go back. We've got to go back and get her. C'mon." She tries to scramble to her feet, but Annie holds her. Sara shrieks and swings at Annie.

"I'll kill you," she screams. "Let me go, let me go, I've got to find Ma." They topple over, wrestling in the fine sand. Annie gets a lock on Sara's arms and holds her. Sara screams and tries to bash herself on the head with a rock. Grimly, Annie holds on with all her might.

Finally, not knowing what else to do, Annie simply starts talking. "Sara, it's okay, I won't let you hurt yourself, I won't let anyone else hurt you, you're safe now, you're safe, do you hear me, the men are gone, the men are all gone… I'm here, Sara, I'm here."

Gradually, Sara's screaming softens. She cries and cries but this is normal crying, sad crying. Annie holds her and rocks her.

"Yes," says Annie, "You're right, we shouldn't have left your Ma, but we can't go back now…your Ma will be okay with you gone."

"But when will I see her again? How will I find her? Annie, please, let's go back."

"We can't," says Annie flatly. "I think I shot a couple of those miners. I think they're probably after us."

Sara is silent, then she asks, "Where are we now?"

"I'm not sure…but we're still going south. This lake is a long one, and there will be a river at the end of it. Rivers are good places to find people."

"Annie," Sara sobs, "I'm so sorry. I guess I owe you a lot. I was stupid, so stupid. You were right. Annie, I'll try and make it up to you, I will."

Annie doesn't say anything. She still doesn't like Sara, and sure as hell doesn't feel like forgiving her for being so stupid, but they're in this mess together, and now they'll have to get themselves out of it together.

"Let's dry our clothes, eat something, and get going. Things are bound to look brighter once we're moving," she says, finally. She tries to grin but it's a feeble attempt.

Sara tries to smile back but her shoulders are still drooping, and her breath still comes in shuddering sighs. She sits by the fire, playing with a stick, putting it in the fire, taking it out. Annie watches her covertly while she gathers firewood, takes their clothes and hangs them up to dry, mixes a bit of flour and lard into biscuits, and sets them to bake. She makes tea, thinks that the horses are going to need some time to graze. They didn't have much food at the mining camp, and there isn't much for them along this lake shore. They need a rest, but they won't get one until

Annie is sure they're all out of danger.

They eat the dry biscuits, drink tea and go on. The going is rougher now. The lake shore is steep. They finally come to a place where the rocks and stubby trees pitch straight down into the water. They climb, scrambling over downed logs and sliding on the moss-slick granite, leading the horses, which struggle and blow great breaths of air, and then climb after them. They finally make it to a ridge where Annie calls a halt, collapsing onto the ground, wet with sweat. Sara is pale and faint. She spent the last part of the climb on her hands and knees, puffing and pulling herself from tree to tree. Now she lies flat on her back.

"Let's stop," she says, "Please, let's just stop. I can't go much farther. I'm going to be sick if we don't stop."

"There's no food here," says Annie, "not for us, not for the horses. We'll rest, then we'll go on. We've got to find some grass, and a place where there's deer." The horses stand with heads dropping to the ground, sides dark, laced with lines of dried foam.

They go on. Sara doesn't complain anymore. They have to backtrack several times to find a way down. Darkness drifts down the mountainside; Annie leads the way. The grey is tied loosely to Duster's saddle. Sometimes she just lets go of Duster and lets him find his own way down. Sara stumbles behind. Occasionally, she falls, and Annie can hear her breath ragged and rasping in her throat. They go on, still down, blindly, under the black torn roof of fir branches, and when they finally come to a stream with a bit of grass growing beside it, Annie calls a halt. She makes beds for them, unsaddles and hobbles the horses, and they sleep, cold and hungry, but too tired to stay awake. Shadow lies beside Annie, ears perked, staring into the dark.

TWENTY-NINE

THE NEXT DAY IS EASIER. They make it back down to the lake. Towards the south end, the ground is flat, but laced with tangled brush, driftwood, and mudholes. Mosquitoes, a whining monotonous haze of them, mat on the horses' sides and welt Annie's and Sara's faces.

They curse and tear their way through the willow thickets, a nightmare of twisting, low, deer paths, where often they simply have to get down and crawl. Beside the water, the way is clearer, but the mud sucks at the horses' feet. And then, finally, they're through and onto a level benched area, open and covered with huge pine trees, clear spaces, meadows with summer grass, bees and flowers. They stop and let the horses graze. She and Sara lie flat on their backs,

ANNIE

waving away mosquitoes, cushioned by the grass, staring at the sky. Annie drifts with the clouds, rocking and floating, deeper and deeper, letting herself fall upwards into the blackness behind the sky.

She awakens with a sudden start, seemingly hours later. She looks around. No Sara and no horses. She sits up, listening. It's late. The sun is low. Damn, how could she have fallen asleep and left Sara alone? The men could have easily been following them all this time, just waiting for a chance to get at them. Have they snatched Sara away. She holds herself still, trying to figure what to do next, and then from far away, she hears a voice, singing. Sara is singing. She hoists herself up and wanders down the meadow. Sara has made a camp, a fire, gathered wood. The horses graze nearby.

"Look, Annie," says Sara, with delight, when she spots her. "Look what I found. My Mom and I used to go and pick wild food when I was a kid. It was one of the ways we got by. I went and picked us some stuff for tea. There's even a few early mushrooms and raspberries. What a great place this is. It's just beautiful, isn't it?" Annie looks around in wonder.

Sara has made camp in a clearing beside the meadow. She's tied a rope between two trees and hung out their blankets. She's laid everything else out and has arranged a flat rock to serve as a rough table; it holds the food. Sara has even picked flowers and stuck them in a pot.

"I'll get us some more food," Annie says abruptly. She

gets her fishing line and hurries through the trees down to the river. She pulls in several trout, and then shoots two rabbits. When she comes back, they cook the meat together, and then Sara makes up the beds, side by side, and they lie down. Sara sighs and curls up in the curve of Annie's body. Annie puts her arm under Sara's head and they lie there, warmly curled together.

Well, thinks Annie. Well, isn't this something. She smiles to herself, thinking that at last she's made another friend, even if it was a very long time in coming.

"Annie," Sara says sleepily. "What were you like as a kid? Were you always so rough and tough? Tell me a story about yourself...I need a story to put me to sleep."

"Well," Annie says slowly, thinking out loud. "When I was a kid, I wanted a horse. I wanted a horse so bad. I don't know why, really. I just knew that was what I wanted. And then I got Duster. I loved that horse. I still love him. He's getting old now. I forget he's a horse, we've been together for so long. Sometimes I go out in the morning to saddle him, and it surprises me that he's a horse and can't talk. Before I got him, I had pretend horses. I had stick horses, sticks with bits of string tied around them for bridles. I used to dream about them at night. I gave them names, the most beautiful names I could think of, like Princess Beauty and Starlight. I could almost see them. I had one of every colour, a steel grey and a shiny black with a white star and a copper red and a black and white pinto. And I used to ride them everywhere. I think my Dad gave up and decided to get me a real horse when he saw that.

"He didn't believe much in fun and games. Maybe he thought a real horse would cure me of living in my dreams so much. But it didn't work. After I got Duster, I made him play too. We'd play war, and cavalry, and wild Indians, and hunting, sometimes other games. There was a rock in the pasture that I'd pretend was an elephant. One day, I remember going out there, and the rock wouldn't turn into an elephant. I sat there and everything was just the same, the hills were hills and the sky stayed blue, but I couldn't lose myself, my sense of myself. I was terrified. But then it came back and I rode away and me and that elephant waddled all over some foreign country and people cheered and flags flew.

"My brothers and I used to play all sorts of stuff. We had a creek near our house. The sand on the bottom was like gold, and it had quartz crystals in it. The water was so clean, and it had little fish and turtles and frogs and a snake every once in a while. We thought the quartz was diamonds. One side of the creek was all brush and we made hideouts and forts there and the other side had sand and mud and we could make dams and channels in the mud and play with stick boats tied to string. We loved it down there. We spent all our time there, when we could get away from our chores.

"One day my Dad found us. He stood there looking, with a frown on his face. I realized suddenly that my hair was all tangled and my clothes were ripped and dirty and that he'd told me that morning to help my mother make bread.

"He just said, 'Get up to the house, and help your mother, and don't let me catch you down here again.' And I went. I didn't go back there for a long time, and then when I did, it wasn't the same. The cows had come and trampled the creek bank, and the creek was muddy and it looked plain and ordinary, not a magic place anymore. After that, I didn't play much anymore. Life was hard and serious and that's just what it was…"

Annie is silent. Then she adds, "What I've never been able to really figure out, is why my Pa brought me Duster. He complained about him, he threatened to sell him, but he never did. He gave me Duster and my dog, and when I was still a little kid, he gave me this rifle and he showed me how to use it."

"He must have really loved you, Annie," says Sara dreamily. "I wish I had a Pa who cared about me like that."

"Well, he sure never showed it," she retorts.

"He gave you something, didn't he?" flashes Sara back. "He gave you what you wanted, what you needed most. That's more than anyone ever done for me. Annie, he did show it, the only way he knew."

"Do you really think so?" Annie wonders. Inside her, a faint warm light glows where before, there was only a pit of darkness. "You think he…cared about me?"

"Yeah, he did," Sara says with assurance.

Then Sara squeezes Annie's hand and wiggles to get more

comfortable. "Now it's my turn," she announces.

"When I was a little girl," she continues dreamily. "I used to play house. I wanted a house of my very own. I dreamed about what it would look like, the kitchen, the nice shiny pots and pans, and pretty coloured curtains, and the Persian rug I'd have in the living room. I would serve tea to the neighbour ladies when they came over. I'd make little cakes with pink icing and I would have a cat, a big ginger cat who would sleep on a pillow on the couch. Maybe it was silly, but it seemed to me it would be so wonderful, just to have a house of my own. I didn't care, really, if there was anyone else there. I just wanted something that was mine, that I could make beautiful, and private and clean. When I was little, even while my Pa was alive, we didn't have much, just dirty old rented houses, sometimes with a dirt floor, no windows or nothing. I wanted something that I could fix just the way I thought it ought to be. And nobody would come and mess it up. I guess that's still what I want. I want to be all safe and warm in my own little place. I don't know if I ever will."

"Sure, you will," Annie says, but she's not sure. She's still thinking about her father. She wants to go away and think about this new idea, this new thing about her father, that he did care, that he hadn't just left her without anything at all. Her heart twists and clenches; it aches like an old, tough scar. But a light shines on the ache.

"He loved me," she thinks fiercely to herself. "He did. He gave me Duster. He taught me to shoot, he must have.

He did. He really did." She falls asleep hugging that thought to herself like a warm blanket.

When they wake in the morning, the sun is hot on their faces, hot on the grass, hot on the horses' shining coats. Shadow dances and jumps and Annie spends some time throwing a stick and playing with him. They run together and she falls on the grass and wrestles with him while he grabs her shirt sleeve and growls and tugs, and when she gets up, he runs mad circles around, barking, his tail waving frantic circles in the air. She keeps thinking they ought to move on, but she's so tired. Back at the fire, Sara has hung up all the bedding again and built a little fireplace. The horses tear and crunch the long meadow grass.

They make tea from a bunch of different plants that Sara and Annie pick together. Annie shows Sara the plants that the Indians taught her to look for. Then they go down to the riverside, and Annie ties a twig on her line for a bobber and throws out the baited hook, and they lie on the sandy bank, watching the bobber and not saying much.

They catch two trout for dinner; Sara digs some more bulbs and Annie goes wandering through the pines and gets some grouse and another rabbit. After they eat, they lie lazily in the sun. Suddenly Shadow stiffens and his ears shift, swivel. He growls.

Annie doesn't wait. She's off on a dead run to the meadow where the horses are grazing. They jerk their heads up, startled. She grabs Duster, throws a rope halter on him,

ANNIE

undoes the hobbles with desperate fingers, grabs the grey,
who tries to lurch away but can't go far, gets his hobbles
off and heads them both on a fast trot to the fire. Something puffs into the grass beside her, and then she hears
the shot. She yanks on the ropes and tows the horses, running, into camp, yelling at Sara.

"Here, take the horses, get them down behind those trees
and saddle them." She throws Sara their lead ropes, and
dives for her loaded rifle. She fires a quick random shot at
the hillside, just to let them know she's around, and waits
for movement.

Shadow growls again. His delicate nose twitches, tasting
the air and he freezes, pointing the direction. At first she
can't see anything, then she picks out a faint patch of red
that's a horse's hide, a stray patch of white, a flash of silver
from a bit. She looks behind her. Sara has the horses tied
out of sight, and she's doing a good job of getting the saddles
on. She's moving quietly and deliberately. Her face is white
and grim. She looks like she has to think out every move
before she makes it.

They won't circle below her, Annie thinks. The slope is
too steep and brushy to get down to the river. They might
split up if there's enough of them and then try to get around
her. There's no real cover here except the trees. She and
Sara need to get somewhere they can make a stand, get
some rocks behind them or something. Damn, damn.
What the hell does she know about fighting? Annie looks
at the sky. It's only mid-afternoon, hours until dark and

even then it won't get dark enough. There'll be a moon.

She fires another shot, aiming high. She doesn't want to hit the horses. Sara is having trouble with the grey, who's nervous and throwing his head to keep her from putting the bridle on.

"Come on, hurry," Annie snaps, runs, bending low, to help. She figures the men will lay low for a bit and try to circle around instead of coming across the meadow, where they're exposed to her shots. She and Sara get the grey bridled. Annie fires another couple of warning shots across the meadow.

Then she runs back to Sara. They mount and ride down the path towards the river, moving as fast as they can, trying to keep to the trees. Annie hears a shout behind them. She looks back. The men are on the slope above them, and coming fast.

"Move!" she screams at Sara. She slaps the grey with a rein and boots Duster, and both the horses bolt blindly into the brush and trees. Annie grabs the saddle horn and hangs on, trying to see tree branches coming at her; tangles of brush slash and tear her legs and her face. She hears a couple of shots but there's not much chance of getting hit while they're in the trees.

They come out into a clear patch of grass, with a cliff at the other end. The mountain rises sheer above and falls away below. There's a gully with a creek coming down it. The horses crash down the bank and Annie yanks Duster to a stop, yells at Sara.

ANNIE

"Get down, hold onto the horses," and she's off Duster and up the bank, just in time to see the men come charging out of the trees on the other side of the clearing. There's no time to even think. She aims and a hat flies off one of the men's heads. With a startled screech, he pulls back on the reins, the horse rears and twists, then falls over sideways on the uneven slope. The other horses charging behind him try to either jump over or avoid the fallen horse. One goes skittering down the slope, bucking, and his rider flies in a graceful loop over his head into the grass. Then they're all stopped. Two men are still on horseback and they turn and head desperately for the trees. The others are crawling away, backsides in the air, looking for cover. Annie aims again and a bootheel flies away. The man in the boot shouts, grabs his leg, and scrabbles behind a rock that's too small for him. Just for fun, Annie sends a bullet into the rock. The bullet ricochets, screaming; rock dust puffs over the man and echoes ring back from the cliff.

Then the meadow is silent. Annie looks around. They're in a pretty good position. They've got water and wood, and cover. No one can get above or around them. They can wait it out until dark and then try and get away. The risky part will be crawling down over the cliff face in the dark. It might not be passable with the horses.

Sara crawls up beside her. She's tied the horses. There's a bleeding slash across her face where a branch caught her. "Where are they?" she whispers.

"Back in the trees...see that rock there, there's one guy

315

behind there, shakin' in his boots cause his rock's too small."

Abruptly, Sara starts to giggle. Annie stares at her. Sara laughs harder and Annie gets the joke and giggles too, louder and louder, both of them nervous and hysterical with laughter. She wonders if the men can hear them. She doesn't care.

Abruptly, they calm down. "What I'm thinking is, if we wait until dark," Annie explains, "we can try and get away back down to the river. We might have to swim the river a bit, to get past these rocks. It looks steep to me. We can probably get down this creek gully…I hope."

"Well, so much for our nice peaceful day," drawls Sara. "And just when I was starting to relax too."

Annie grins. "Yep," she says, "it never fails. Just when you settle down for a nap, someone starts shooting. Darndest thing."

They lie in the blazing sun. There is nothing to do but wait. After an hour or so, a man comes across the meadow with a strip of white cloth tied to a stick. He stops. Annie stands up, cradling the rifle.

"Well now, girls, seems we got ourselves a bit of a problem here," he says loudly across the space between them. "Whyn't you all come on out and we can try and get this here mess settled somehow and then we can all go on home."

He's a tall man, wearing a vest over his shirt, worn canvas pants, and a crumpled hat. His empty hands are turned out at his sides.

"Why don't you just go away and leave us alone," yells Annie. "We ain't done nothing wrong. What the hell are you chasing us for anyway? We just want to be left alone."

"Well now, there's one man back there with a smashed leg, and another with a bullet in the shoulder, and they figure you got some tall explaining to do," he says.

"Them bastards deserved everything they got. They hurt Sara. You tell them we just want to go on our way."

"Way I heard it, the boys were just having a bit of fun. You girls asked for trouble, and now you got it. Seems like there's another story about a couple of horses missing and a wagon train being robbed up north. I'd say you got a bit to answer for."

"We got nothing to answer for," says Annie. "We're just trying to get by and survive and do the best we can. We weren't trying to cause trouble. Those men did that. Now get out of here, and leave us alone."

"Sorry, girls. Guess we just can't do that. Now we're asking you to surrender and put down that gun and come on over here. No one is going to hurt you. We'll just ask you a few questions about your side of the story, and see if you got some right on your side, and we'll do our best to help you out if we can."

"We got no reason to trust you or anyone else," snarls Annie. "And we ain't going to. So you might as well go on back, cause we're going on our way, by ourselves, and we sure don't need any more of your kind of help…"

"You're being very unreasonable, very unreasonable indeed," says the man. "You girls just don't got any good sense. You're riding around in Indian territory on stolen horses. How far do you think you're going to get?"

"As far as we figure we need to," says Annie. "And I ain't talking to you no more, so go on, get back to whatever hole you crawled out of, and let us be."

The man shrugs and turns and walks back to the trees.

"And we didn't steal any damn horses," she yells after him.

The rest of the afternoon drags by. Sara even dozes a little while Annie watches. She figures the men will try to do something before it gets dark, knowing she and Sara will escape as soon as it's dark enough. She watches the cliff above them and the steep slope on the other side of the gully. Someone could conceivably climb up there and around and down behind her and Sara and cut off their escape. But nothing moves except birds and mosquitoes and squirrels.

When it does start to get dark, Annie goes on alert, watching carefully for any sign, a bird flying up, a squirrel chattering, a branch cracking. There's been no movement at all from the other side of the clearing for a long time, not even a horse switching its tail against flies.

When she figures it's dark enough, she nudges Sara. "Let's go," she says, and they start carefully climbing down the long steep slope to the river. It's not as bad as she figured and they make it with only a few slips and slides. The river is dark and oily and the mud sucks at the horse's feet. The horses plunge and rear until they're out into the current. Annie slides off into the cold water and holds Duster's tail and whispers to Sara to do the same. Shadow swims beside her. The banks are rockier on the other side but the horses lunge and heave their way out of the water. The night air is freezing on their wet clothes, but they hurry on upriver. The travelling on this side of the river is easier, but noisy. Leaves and branches crackle under the horses' feet; brush slaps against their saddles.

Annie comes to something she has been looking for, a place where both sides of the river are solid rock.

"Come on, we're going to swim it again," she says. The current is harder here, sweeping between the two shelves of rock, but they make it and straggle out onto the rocks, the horses panting with effort. They head up the slope from the river, trotting when they can see to trot. The valley flattens out, but there's another mountain range ahead of them.

By dawn light, they're both dozing in the saddle and the horses are exhausted. Annie spots an overhang under a cliff, with a clearing where the horses can graze.

"Sleep," she snaps at Sara, "I'll watch." She leaves the horses saddled but takes the bridles off and so they can graze. She waits, tense, watching their back trail, but there's no movement. After a couple of hours, she wakes Sara.

"Let's go," she says, and Sara staggers sleepily to the grey and hoists herself into the saddle.

Annie leads the way up the mountain. She wants to be

able to see behind them, and she doesn't want to get trapped again. The river swings south and the mountain range with it. They travel all day. Annie is lightheaded and dizzy with lack of sleep. She catches herself swaying in the saddle and gets off to walk.

By night, Duster is limping, the grey is looking gaunt, and Sara is leaning over her saddle horn, eyes closed, hanging on with both hands. Annie keeps watching behind them. There's no sign of movement, but they fooled her once. She won't relax that easily again.

When it's deep dusk, they stop at the edge of a flat meadow under a towering overhang of sheer cliffs. Instead of hobbling the horses, Annie pickets them with short ropes near the edge of the trees. She doesn't make a fire. She makes a bed for herself and tells Sara to watch and wake her when the moon is up. She falls onto her bed and is asleep in seconds. When she wakes up, Sara is asleep beside her. There's no moon. She's muddled, trying to figure the time.

But at least it's really dark. She calls Shadow and backtracks along their trail, stopping often, listening, smelling, watching Shadow. After she's backtracked for about two hours, she sees the reddish glow from the coals in the men's fire.

Wearing the moccasins that she got in the Indian camp, she moves quietly through the trees, stepping flatfooted and feeling for sticks before she puts weight on each foot. When she gets near to the camp, she sees that the men are still awake, despite the lateness. Their horses are hobbled and grazing among the brush some distance away from the fire. The men are drinking whiskey. Her nose wrinkles at the smell of the camp and the smell of the men drinking and smoking.

She sits where she can see and hear them and waits. After a long while, they roll themselves in their blankets. Annie sits on, breathing, sitting still on the ground, Shadow's head in her lap. Her mind drifts and wanders. She feels clearheaded, light enough to float. Maybe I'm invisible, she thinks.

When everything is quiet and she can hear the men's deep breathing, she takes a roundabout route and comes up quietly and gently beside the horses, rubbing them and blowing in their noses to let them know who she is. She cuts their hobbles and leads one away from the camp, back down towards the river. The others dutifully follow. She takes them to the river, and gets them into it and swimming, before slipping off and swimming back to the shore. She watches as the horses cross the river and drift into the trees, heading steadily but purposefully back the way they came.

Then she heads back to her own camp. By the time she gets there, there are very faint streaks of orange and pink in the blue-black sky. She wakes Sara, tells her to watch, rolls in the still warm blankets, and falls asleep.

In an hour, she wakes again and tells Sara about her night's work.

"I don't think they'll keep following us. They'll have to go back and get their horses, so they'll lose at least a day or two. By then we'll be far away, I hope, if the horses hold up. Duster is still limping, and the grey's got a cough."

"Annie, I'm so hungry," Sara says. "Can't we just make a bit of fire? Please, and some tea or something?"

"Later. Come on, we've got to get going, keep moving. We can't take any more chances."

Duster's limp gets worse. The grey coughs. Sara slumps in the saddle and sulks. Shadow's white coat is thin and his ribs show through. Annie keeps them moving all day by force and entreaty. When the day stills and the sun is low, she relents.

This time, they camp beside a small, muddy lake, surrounded by reed beds and low hills, coulees full of brush, poplar trees. All day they've been travelling parallel to a steep cliff-laden mountain range which rises abruptly from the valley floor. All day deer have crashed ahead of them through the brush. Elk and buffalo tracks are everywhere. Somewhere in the back of her mind, Annie notes all this: the tall thick grass, the creeks, the water sources, the stands of pine and larch on the hillsides below the mountain. Be a good place to settle, she thinks idly. Grass for cattle, trees for building, lots of water, game. There's probably Indians too, she thinks, probably closer to the river which she's steered away from.

When everyone is settled and the horses are grazing, she leaves the camp with Shadow and follows their backtrail, slipping from patch of brush to trees to hollow. Then she heads uphill, climbing to where she can see far back over the valley. There is still no movement on their backtrail that she can see, and no sign from Shadow that anything is wrong.

On the way home, she takes a chance and shoots a deer, a young buck that barely looks up when he hears her coming. She butchers it quickly and brings it into camp. They eat the liver, frying it in strips, washing it down with leaf tea, feeding hunks of it to Shadow. By the light of the fire, Annie cuts the rest of the meat into thin strips and hangs it by the fire to dry slowly.

"We should spend a day here," she says to Sara. "The horses need it."

"I need it," retorts Sara, "and you need it. Annie, I can practically see through you, you're so skinny. What would I do if anything happened to you? I'd never get out of this wilderness." She pauses. "Annie, where are we going anyhow? Do you have any idea?"

"No, not really…south, mostly," says Annie. Ducks and geese call and trill out of the night. She can hear one every once in a while, rising to beat its wings and then settling back on the water. A beaver head cuts across the water and the ripples shine in the starlight.

"We could stay here," says Annie, dreamily. The words hang for a long time, shimmering in the air between them. "Think about it. We could stay here together, build a house, settle, make a farm. There's everything here, grass, timber, mountains, game. I've been noticing it, all day. It's...it's sort of what I've been looking for," she says, suddenly feeling shy. She's never really talked about her dream out loud to anyone except maybe Lucille, but even then, she'd never really explained how real it was to her.

"I'd like to build a log house," she continues, "a big log house set on a hill, windows with real glass. And a big porch to set on and watch evening coming after I'd worked all day. I'd like a big garden and fruit trees, and some cows for meat, and horses for riding and a whole pack of dogs, all colours and sizes." She leans over to Shadow. "Eh, Shadow, you'd like that, a whole pack of friends, and you could be boss dog." He thumps his tail, opens one eye to look at her and then goes back to sleep.

"A big kitchen," says Sara excitedly, " with a really good cookstove. And yellow gingham curtains. You'd have to grow wheat, Annie, and grind it so I could make bread. And we'd have to have chickens for eggs. And a team and wagon to go to church."

"Church!" exclaims Annie, giggling. "We ain't even got neighbours yet." She's not so sure she should have included Sara in this private vision.

"But we'll get some. We have to have neighbours. And a church, and a school, and then eventually someone will start a store, and someday there'll be a road, and then we'll know where we are."

"But I like not knowing," Annie frowns. "I don't want neighbours. I don't go to church. Being out here is enough church for me. I been on my own for a while now. I'm getting used to it. And I'd have my brothers. You could find your Mom and move her here, too. We could make our own place, the way we want it to be. We don't need a whole lot of other people messing things up. I want my own place. I want my own family. I want to live my own way. I don't want anyone else around telling me what to do."

"No, Annie," says Sara finally. "No, I couldn't. I'm not like you. I want people, and a community, a family. I want to know where I'm living. I want to get up in the morning with my children and my husband and go to church and come home and make Sunday dinner in my beautiful house which I've fixed up just the way it suits me. I want to know who my neighbours are and I want to say howdy to them and have them say howdy to me, and I want to lie down to sleep at night beside my husband, feeling safe. I want to go home, Annie, please, just find a way to take me home…wherever that might be, please."

"Alright," Annie says. "I will." And then she says, "I'm going to check on the horses, check behind us again. Be gone a while." She slips away from the fire and into the darkness. She climbs a hill and sits there, her arm across Shadow, looking outwards, listening, smelling the soft warm wind that sifts out of the valley beneath, smelling of leaves, water, earth, growing things.

Her heart opens out and yearns toward the land before her. She can see it all so clearly, the red cattle and the glossy shining horses, the fences, the plowed fields, the lake full of fish and the hills full of wild animals.

"I could love this place," she thinks. "This could be home. I want to go home too. I need to go home." She sits for a long time, dreaming and musing, watching the quiet shadows. Then she falls asleep, slumped over, the rifle in her lap, Shadow curled beside her, the valley and the mountains spread in blue dreaming rings around her.

THIRTY

THEY TRAVEL SOUTH FOR ANOTHER WEEK. Annie keeps track of the landmarks. She's going back to that valley, she thinks, someday. She keeps compulsively checking behind her but sees no sign of the men. She doesn't believe they'll give up that easily. Maybe they went back for reinforcements. Maybe they went to find someone who represents the law. She doesn't know anything about law or police or how that's organized, or if there even is such a thing. She's just grateful for the breathing space. But she knows she'll have to deal with them again.

She's starting to feel really hopeless about finding people to help Sara when they ride out on a bluff one day overlooking a vast flat valley. Far below, in the middle of the valley, is a long line of dust, black specks of animals, moving wagons, men on horseback. Annie leaves Sara and the grey on the bluff, and rides down on the plain. As she comes closer to the wagon train, she thinks there's something familiar about it, and she's right. When she gets close enough, she spots a black horse, and then she sees the lead scout, his face, round, covered with black whiskers, his black hair tied back with a buckskin thong. She's too tired to feel surprise.

"Nathan," she says, as he comes up to her.

"Howdy," he says. "Figured that was the same colour buckskin I'd seen somewhere before."

They look at each other for a moment. "Well," he says. "Better fetch whoever you're travelling with and come on in. Seen you and your horses a while back, up on the hill. Some folks you used to know, way up ahead will be mighty glad to hear about you. They made it, most of 'em, found places to settle, busy makin' 'emselves the same kind of place they set out from. Don't know why folk'll do that, but they do." He paused. Annie waited. Nathan always had been a slow talker, and there was no way to hurry him.

"Ain't had no word for a while, since I heard you skedaddled on your own. Sorry about your Ma and Pa. They was mighty fine people. Didn't like to leave them like that. Didn't seem right, but what the hell. Folks wanted to get on." He shrugs. Annie realizes that he's apologizing.

"Yeah, thanks," says Annie.

Nathan nods at Shadow. "Injun dog," he says conversationally. "You been gettin' around."

"Yeah," says Annie, "I been a ways. A long ways." She turns to ride back to Sara. Then she turns back.

"Oh yeah," Nathan says. "I seen your brothers, a while back. They're doing good. Got nice families, people to care for them. Don't need to worry about them. I told 'em I figured you was doing fine on your own. I seen you shoot and ride. But next rider I see headed back that way, we can send word."

"Oh," says Annie. "Oh, yeah, thanks for letting me know." She pauses. "I think maybe I found us a place. Only I ain't sure I'm ready to settle there just yet. I think I might want to do a bit more travelling, a bit more looking around."

"Sure," says Nathan, waving it off. He's heard it before. "Sure, you'll find lots of places. Got a hell of a lot of country to look at. Take your time. Look good and long before you settle. Me, I ain't found it yet. But I might, someday." He laughs, turns the black horse, canters back to the waiting wagons.

THIRTY-ONE

SHE COMES BACK TO SARA. "It's okay," she says. "I know them, or at least I know the scout. Come on."

Sara fusses over her and Annie's dirty hands and torn clothes, makes them take time to comb their hair and try to brush the dust from their clothes. They ride down the bluff and over the flat dusty plain towards the line of wagons. Annie's heart clenches when they come towards the wagons, the sound of people's voices, the smell of livestock, harness, sweat, food, lived-in clothing. People's faces nod and smile. Her parents should be here too, and the boys, but they're not. She holds her head up. When she and Sara dismount, the people make a circle around the grey and Duster, wanting to ask questions, but waiting.

"I'm Annie and this here's Sara," says Annie. "I guess we're a little wore out. We been riding some."

Annie fends off other questions. People press in offering them food, wagons to travel in, to stay in. She looks around the circle. People stare, at her, at her rifle, at the dog, at Duster. She remembers what Shadow said about eyes touching, how rude it felt. She ducks the questions, ignoring them or giving vague answers, claiming exhaustion. She doesn't feel like talking. Every time she sees someone wearing familiar clothes, talking with familiar accents, she sees her father's face, her mother's face behind it.

Finally, she's given a plate of food. She and Sara sit side by side in a circle around a small dung fire. After she's eaten, she goes to turn out Duster and the grey with the other horses. She presses her face into Duster's warm neck. "What the hell are we doing here?" she asks him, but he moves away, impatient to be grazing.

When she comes back to the fire, Nathan is holding the reins of a saddled horse. He looks at her rifle cradled in her arms.

"We're moving on," he says, "too early to stop." He holds out his hand. She hands him the gun.

"Seen some use, this one," he continues. She nods. He lifts and sights the rifle, hands it back.

"Pretty nice country north of here, eh? Nice valleys. Big lakes. Went trapping there once, long time ago," he says abruptly. "Friends of mine up there, Indians...maybe even a kid of mine, who knows. I'll go back there one day. Hey, maybe we'll go back there together, eh?"

She doesn't answer, just stares at the smoking smoulder-ing fire. Nathan yawns, stretches. "Better get moving. You ride point, out front, eh, this afternoon. Hey, you keep care of that good rifle, better sleep with it, keep it warm, better than a man, eh." He laughs and wanders off.

Annie stares after him. A scout. She's a scout again. Well, it's not such a bad idea. She can keep on going, looking at the country, and figuring out what it is she wants, and Sara will be looked after. Who knows. Maybe Sara will even get herself a husband, seeing as how she wants one so damn bad.

Her brothers are okay. She'll write to them, tell them what she's been doing, that she hasn't forgotten them or the dream. When she sees them again, she'll have so many stories to tell them.

She kicks the small dung fire into ashes, goes to mount the new horse, a sad-looking bay, then leans against the saddle. All that way, she thinks, and for what? Just to end up here, in another wagon train, with a bunch of other folks all looking for something. And she's so tired.

Resolve squares her shoulders. She has her own dream, her own destination, hidden behind the mountains, be-hind the blue shadowed haze of the future, and she'll never give up on it.

For now, she's got Duster and Shadow, work to do, a place to sleep, food, company. If things get too closed in, or she doesn't like what's going on, she can always leave again, go north, go back to Lucille or back to Shadow, go where she damn well pleases. She's a free woman, she can survive anything, anywhere. She's learned that much.

She straightens her back and lifts her shoulders. She can find the valley again when she needs to. It will wait for her, all her valleys, all the places she's been, which now hold a part of her. They will wait, quietly, through the seasons, until she returns to them. She looks north, at the shadowed, tree-freckled hills, the sandy ochre bluffs and nods.

"C'mon, Shadow," she says. "Let's get moving. Guess we're a pair of wagon guides for now till we get someplace new."